The Uist Girl Series Book 4

A LOVE WORTH FIGHTING FOR

A heartbreaking but ultimately uplifting family saga novel set during WW2

MARION MACDONALD

Copyright @ A Love Worth Fighting For 2024 Marion Macdonald

All rights reserved.

The characters and events portrayed in this book are fictitious. Any similarity to real persons, living or dead, is coincidental and not intended by the author. Where real persons are mentioned, they are used fictitiously.

No part of this book may be reproduced, or stored in a retrieval system, or transmitted in any form or by any means, electronic, mechanical, photocopying, recording or otherwise, without the express written permission of the publisher. The only exception is by a reviewer, who may quote brief excerpts in a review.

Independently Published.

ISBN – 9798873545001

Photographs for front cover are from Canva

For all the women and children who suffered stigma because of illegitimacy. It's hard for us to understand now, but back then, it was a different story.

God could not be everywhere and therefore he made mothers.

                                              Rudyard Kipling

CHARACTERS

The Macdonald Family

Chrissie Macdonald	Our Heroine
Roderick Macdonald	Her husband (Deceased)
Roddy Macdonald	Son of Chrissie & Roderick
Donald Donaldson	Son of Heather 1 & Colin
Heather Macdonald 1 (deceased)	Daughter of Roderick & Lily (deceased)
Heather Macdonald 2	Daughter of Bunty & Johnny

The MacIntosh Family

Marion MacIntosh	Chrissie's mother
Angus MacIntosh	Chrissie's father
Johnny MacIntosh	Chrissie's brother
Lachlan MacIntosh (deceased)	Chrissie's brother
Morag MacIntosh/Hamilton	Chrissie's sister

The Adams/Hepworth Family

Bunty Adams/Hepworth	Mother of Mary and Heather 2
Mary Hepworth/Donaldson	Bunty's daughter/ Donald's wife
Harry Donaldson	Mary & Donald's son
Charles Adams	Bunty's brother
James Adams (deceased)	Bunty's father
Frederick Adams (deceased)	Bunty's stepfather
Grace Adams	Bunty's mother
Harry Hepworth (deceased)	Bunty's husband

Other Characters

Findlay Simpson	Postmaster and Chrissie's boss
Rosie Simpson	His daughter
Daisy Simpson	His daughter
Lawrence Moorcroft	Heather's Lover
Amelia Moorcroft	His wife
Madeline Moorcroft	His mother
Janet McLeod	Johnny's wife
Donald John McLeod	Janet's nephew
Catherine McLeod	Donald John's grandmother
Aunt Katie	Angus's Sister
Maude	Solicitor/friend of Aunt Katie
Murdo Mackenzie	The Postman
Catriona Mackenzie	Murdo's daughter and Heather's best friend
Theresa Dunlop	Roddy's girlfriend
Morag Campbell	Island Gossip
Archie Campbell	Morag Campbell's son
Mairi Campbell	Morag Campbell's daughter
Shona McIver	Shopkeeper
Dorothy McIver	Her nephew's wife
Michael Hamilton	Morag's husband
Mrs MacGregor	Teacher at Portree High School
Colin Donaldson	Former Factor & Donald's father
Sam Carmichael	Band leader at Benbecula
Mrs Morrison	Crofter's wife on Benbecula
Deiter	Prisoner of War

GAELIC WORDS USED IN THIS BOOK

I'm not a Gaelic speaker but have used some words to indicate when characters are speaking in Gaelic. My apologies if I have used any of them incorrectly.

Athair	Father
Cailleach	Old Woman
Ciamar a tha thu?	How are you?
Dadaidh	Daddy
Leanabh	Baby
Machair	Low-lying coastal grazing land
Mamaidh	Mummy
Mathair	Mother
Mo graidh	My darling
Seanair	Grandfather
Seanmhair	Grandmother

PROLOGUE
North Uist, October 1944

It's a mild autumn day. Perfect weather for travelling. I'm on the pier at Lochmaddy once more saying goodbye to my family and I marvel at the extent of God's goodness. I'm sure you've heard the phrase *Tell the truth and shame the devil,* but when I think back on my life, I didn't work very hard at shaming the devil. Secrets and lies have haunted me since the day Roderick Macdonald came into my life thirty-four years ago. Roderick and I hadn't loved each other when we married in May 1910. We were strangers, and it took a while to grow together and settle into the loving relationship we shared in our married life together. In the years since his death, all I'd ever thought about was my family. I'd never contemplated that I could fall in love again or that someone could fall in love with me. But I did, and I blame King Edward VIII for that.

Well, he's no longer a king as he gave up the throne for the person he loved. I'll never forget the night he made the announcement. Heather was in bed, and I was sitting knitting and listening to the wireless. Father was reading the paper and Mother was ironing. The Scottish Singers programme had just finished, and it was time for the news and weather. After the presenter made the weather report, he then announced the King would make a speech at precisely 10.01 pm. We looked at each other. This was a historic moment, as no other king had ever addressed the nation on the radio before. We all stopped what we were doing.

'Well, well, what now?' said my mother. 'I hope those batteries hold up so we can hear what he has to say.'

'It must be something important,' said my father, 'for them to interrupt The Comic Opera.'

'There's been talk of him and that, Mrs Simpson. I wonder if he's going to announce they're getting married,' I replied, feeling excited.

The King was very dashing, and I loved to read about him in the newspapers. The life he lived was so different from our quiet existence here on North Uist. But it wasn't his marriage he was announcing, it was his abdication. The news shocked me as much as anyone, but afterwards it made me think. What would it be like to love someone so much that you would give up everything for them and what would it be like to be loved by someone that much?

After the king abdicated, I felt a shift within me, like a door opening to let love in. I hadn't been consciously looking for love, but it had found me. It was a slow burn, not a love at first sight kind of love, but oh my, it had set my heart on fire when I realised what was happening to me. But, of course, things didn't go smoothly. Nothing in my life ever does. Consequences from past secrets and lies always seem to rear their ugly heads. And then, of course, there's the war. The uncertainty and fear created by this terrible conflict has left its mark on all our lives and it's not over yet. But I can't wait any longer. As I look at my family, my thoughts drift back to the twists and turns of my life that have led to this. It all started after Donald and Mary's wedding in 1935, when the truth of Heather's birth became common knowledge to everyone in the family except her.

1935 - 1939

FINDING LOVE AND LOSING A DAUGHTER

CHAPTER ONE

After the wedding, when Heather, Mother and I got back to North Uist, we were exhausted, but I was happy. It had been a tense and emotional time leading up to the wedding, with so many things threatening the proceedings. I was terrified Bunty would learn the truth about Heather and would expose my secrets and lies. She might even want to take Heather away from me. There was also something going on between Roddy and Mary that I didn't fully understand, and my fear was that their relationship, whatever it was, would stop Mary's marriage to Donald going ahead. The mere thought of what would happen filled me with dread. However, whatever had gone on between Mary and Roddy, it hadn't stopped her marriage to Donald, and I must say they looked radiantly happy the next morning at breakfast. What a relief. I wasn't sure Donald could have coped if Mary had jilted him. I could see it was hard for Roddy and felt sorry for him. Although he'd had girlfriends over the years, he'd found no one he loved, apart from the Catholic girl, Theresa Dunlop, and that had been a disaster from the start. Hopefully, someone new would come along for him soon.

Although Bunty found out the truth from her brother, Charles, she was very gracious and generous in her reaction. In fact, she gave her blessing and showed no inclination to take Heather away from me. All I needed to do was tell Heather that I was not her birth mother. It was only fair, given that everyone else in the family now knew. She would be so upset if she somehow found out the truth through one of them. But it wasn't straightforward. One night, not long after we got home, she asked me about Bunty. She was due to go to Portree secondary school, just as Roddy had done, and we had spent the last week getting her things ready. She was in good spirits and excited about going. But when bedtime came, she was quiet and asked if I would come up and tuck her in. I smiled at her.

'It's a wee while since you've wanted me to do that.'

'I know, but I'll be going away soon and won't have you to tuck me in,' she said, looking at me with her big brown eyes and I noticed her lips were trembling.

So up I went, feeling extraordinarily pleased. She had become quite independent recently, and I missed our wee chats before she went to sleep.

'*Mamaidh*, can I ask you something?'

'You can ask me anything *mo graidh*.'

'It's about Mrs Hepworth's baby.'

Oh, no. Did she suspect something? Was this the moment I was going to have to tell her the truth? But I was unprepared. I hadn't decided yet how to tell her or what I would say? I felt sick inside but kept calm and let her tell me what it was she wanted to know.

'Yes,' I said. 'What about her?'

'I've been thinking a lot about Mrs Hepworth and the baby. I think it's because I've been reading Anne of Green Gables and wondering what it must be like to be an orphan. Being given away to strangers must be a truly awful experience. I keep thinking that baby would be the same age as me now, wouldn't it? And for all I know, I might meet her at school or something, but would never know?'

I smiled. How I loved Heather and her vivid imagination.

'You should become a writer or go into acting, Heather. You have such a creative way of looking at the world.'

She looked pleased at my words but then frowned as I hadn't answered her question.

'But you're right, that baby would be the same age as you are now. So, what is it you want to ask?'

'Who was the baby's *dadaidh*?'

I was speechless. Her question caught me off guard, and as I thought about revealing the truth of Heather's adoption, I realised I hadn't fully considered the consequences for Johnny.

'*Mamaidh*? Are you alright?'

'Sorry, I'm just surprised by your question. Why do you want to know?'

'I was just thinking that the baby's *dadaidh* could have looked after her until Mrs Hepworth was well again.'

'No-one knew who the father was, and Mrs Hepworth couldn't tell us because she was so ill.'

'But it must have been someone on North Uist. We're a small island, so I don't know how no-one knew.'

This was becoming awkward. What Heather said was true, but somehow no-one knew Bunty had a baby. People may have had their suspicions, but they didn't talk about it. Bunty was an outsider, and she had well and truly discredited her reputation, anyway, by behaving the way she did. But what to tell Heather? The partial truth was what I chose.

'The year that Mrs Hepworth was ill, many people left the island to go to Canada. There was a special ship, the SS Marloch, that came for them. Your Uncle Johnny and his wife Janet were two of the people who travelled on that ship. So, perhaps the father of the baby went to Canada too and didn't know Mrs Hepworth was having a child.'

'I see.'

I knew I should ask her if she wanted to know anything else, but I couldn't wait for the conversation to end. It worried me we would stray into other things, which would mean I would need to tell even more lies. It was important that I decided what I was going to do and how I was going to tell her. The longer I postponed the inevitable, the worse the outcome might be. If I'd known then what I know now, I might have made a different decision.

'Right, my girl, let's say our prayers and get the lights out now.'

We said our standard prayer of A*s I lay me down to sleep*, but I also prayed that God would guide me in what to say to Heather when the time came, as it surely would, for me to tell her the truth.

CHAPTER TWO

Heather waved goodbye to her mother as she made the journey that all the young people on the island had to make when it was time to go to the secondary school. Part of her was looking forward to it as it was a bit of an adventure, but the other part of her was sad and she cried a little into the hanky her mother had given her. She didn't want to leave the croft or her family. To her, life on the croft was perfect. She loved helping her granny with the milking, making the butter and the crowdie from it and baking oatcakes and scones. Not like her best friend Catriona, who moaned all the time about how boring everything was and couldn't wait to get away. She was always complaining about her father, Murdo, the postman.

'Just because he and my mother had to wait a long time to have me, they treat me like I'm a precious doll that will break easily. I can't wait to be old enough to leave home and go to Edinburgh to train as a hairdresser.'

Although Heather had never known her father, her granddad was like a father to her. She felt the exact opposite of Catriona and liked the way he treated her. She never felt stifled in the way Catriona did. But sometimes she looked at the photograph of Roderick that sat on the mantlepiece and wondered what he had been like and whether they would have got on. He looked quite old, older than her mother, anyway. Perhaps he would have been like Murdo, treating her like a precious object. She knew there were secrets about their marriage and that Donald was not her proper brother, like Roddy was. But her mother never seemed to want to talk about it and would get her to move onto other things whenever she brought the subject up. At least she had answered her question about Mrs Hepworth and the father of her baby, although the answer wasn't very satisfactory.

Mrs Hepworth, Mary's mother, had had a baby but gave it away because she was ill. Heather thought that was just wrong. Surely the father could have looked after the baby until Mrs

Hepworth was better. But then again, her mother said no-one knew who the father was. That he might have gone to Canada as so many people did that year and didn't know about the baby. She knew people looked down on girls who had babies and weren't married. Somehow, it was the girls they always looked down on. No-one seemed to bother about the boys who had given them the baby.

She remembered the time in Glasgow when Roddy was horrible to Donald after he told them he and Mary were getting married. It was a mystery to her why he was being so nasty and had called Donald a bad name. Her mammy had explained that Donald's mother, who had the same name as her, hadn't been married to Donald's daddy, so she and Roderick had adopted him, a bit like Anne of Green Gables. As she thought of Donald, her mind switched to the wedding. Her heart swelled with pride as she remembered wearing the bridesmaid's dress that Mary had bought for her. Made from silk and tuille, it was coloured yellow and had little white daisies on it. She had felt like a princess walking down the aisle behind Mary on the day of the wedding. She smiled now at the thought and blew her nose. Then Catriona came over and held her hand. At least they would have each other when they got to Portree.

CHAPTER THREE

Fin and I were chatting while we sorted the mail Murdo had brought from the boat earlier. We chatted more now than we used to when he had first come to the island. I suppose he was sad and didn't feel like talking back then and I hadn't pushed him. We still didn't talk about anything very personal. Just a little about our families, the weather, or what was happening in the world. But somehow today we ventured onto more intimate ground.

'How was the wedding? Did you and Heather have a good time? You seemed a bit tense before you went, but you look much more relaxed now.'

I was tense, but it surprised me that Fin had noticed. He seemed to be in another world most of the time.

'Yes, thanks Fin. I feel much more relaxed now that it's over and Heather loved being a bridesmaid. I can't believe she's away to Portree this year. She still feels like my baby.'

'I know what you mean.'

'What age are your daughters now?'

After his wife died, the Post Office had sent him to North Uist and his wife's mother and father had looked after them. They were teenagers at the time, so I guessed they must be working or married by now. I never understood how he could have left them. Having Heather after Roderick died was the saving of me. But perhaps men are different.

'Daisy, my youngest, is 18 now and Rosie is 20.'

'It's so sad your wife didn't get to see them grow up. I know I feel that about Roderick.'

He remained silent and his eyes took on a distant look. I thought he must be thinking of when his wife was still alive, and they were all living together. He must miss them terribly. I know I still missed Roddy and Donald and was fretting about Heather going to Portree. I changed the subject and asked him what they were doing now.

'Daisy is at college training to be a teacher, while her sister Rosie doesn't seem to know what she wants to do. I despair of her sometimes. They're talking about renting a house of their own, but I'm not keen. I would rather they stayed with Ruth's mother and father until they get married.'

'There's more to life than marriage, Fin,' I said, smiling. 'Girls don't need to settle just for married life anymore. The world's their oyster.'

Things had changed after the Great War when those in government and employers recognised how useful women could be. There were still lots of things that were frowned upon where women were concerned, but not as much as before the war.

'You settled for it.'

'I didn't have any other choice back then. My father and mother promised me to my husband when I was five and my parents made sure I fulfilled their promise.'

He looked shocked.

'At five!'

'It's okay. I was twenty by the time I married Roderick. And despite life's difficulties, it turned out to be a good marriage.'

Difficulties was a bit of an understatement, but at the memory of Roderick, I felt my lip quiver and turned away. It always catches me by surprise when I feel upset about Roderick. *Time is a great healer,* it's said, and I've found the saying to be true. But grief still always creeps up on me when I'm least expecting it. What happened next was something I was even less expecting. Fin patted my shoulder. It was surprisingly comforting, so I turned and smiled. He smiled back and nodded as if he understood. Then we got on with our work once more.

CHAPTER FOUR

Heather asking about the father of Bunty's baby got me thinking about the consequences for Johnny and for us as a family. If I told Heather the truth, what would she do with the information? We had kept it all a secret for a reason. There was still a lot of stigma attached to illegitimacy, and how would the community feel if they found out I'd lied to them all this time, pretending that Heather was Roderick and my daughter? It had taken time for them to get used to the fact that Donald was the Factor's son and not ours. Then there was all the carry on when Bunty let everyone know his mother was half Indian.

And what about Johnny and Janet's relationship? We needed to take that into consideration, too. If Heather was open about her birth, word would get back to Janet's mother and father and then to Janet. Although Janet now knew Bunty had been pregnant by Johnny, she had made him promise not to contact Bunty or try to find out what happened to the child. There would be hell to pay if she discovered Johnny had known all along that I had Heather and had been sending him photos and news on her progress.

If I told Heather the truth, then it had to be her decision about what she did with the information. I couldn't ask her to keep it a secret. She might think I was ashamed of her and besides, I knew how hard it was living with secrets and I didn't want that for my daughter. And what if she felt bad about herself? What if she felt unloved because her parents had given her away to me? I couldn't do that to her. The whole thing made me feel panicky, so I spoke to my mother and father after Heather had gone to Portree.

'I don't know what to do for the best. Whatever I do, I don't think there will be a good outcome.'

'Write to Johnny. Tell him that Bunty knows and see what he says,' said my mother.

'It's not about Johnny,' said my father. 'It's Heather you need to think about. What's best for her? Johnny made a mistake, and he must live with it. But Heather's an innocent in all of this.'

I looked at my father, surprised by his words. His hair was white now and his cheeks wrinkled. His brown eyes looked at me and I knew he had chosen my daughter over his son. He had grown to love Heather like his own daughter, and he wanted what was best for her. Johnny was thousands of miles away, making his own life. But my mother had other ideas.

'Och Angus. Nothing is ever about only one person. We can't tell Heather without it affecting all of us. The shame of it all. And I don't want Johnny taking to the drink again if Janet divorces him.'

She began thumping the dough she'd been kneading. Her brown-eyed boy. She couldn't bear to have things go wrong for him.

'Divorce! Surely to God, it won't come to that, Marion.'

'Well, if I found out you'd had a *leanabh* with another woman and had been keeping up to date with what was happening in her life without telling me, I would be getting a divorce.'

She gave the dough one last punch and stormed out of the room.

My father gave me a wry grin, then got up from his chair.

'Never mind us, Chrissie. You make your own mind up what's best for you and Heather. We'll go with whatever you decide.'

I wrote to Johnny. Not for his consent or anything, just to let him know Bunty knew and was okay with it and that I was intending letting Heather know the truth. But my stomach had those blasted butterflies fluttering about when I posted the letter. I didn't hear from him until about six months after I'd sent the letter. It was only when Murdo delivered Johnny's response that I realised I was dreading hearing from him. While I was waiting for his reply, I had the ideal reason not to speak to Heather. I was a coward. And I continued to be one. Johnny's letter gave me an excuse not to do anything. He made it clear he really didn't want me to tell Heather just now. His marriage would be at stake if I told her. Could I hold off until he had time to tell Janet the truth himself? My letter had made him see that just as I must tell Heather the truth, he must tell Janet the truth, no matter the consequences.

As Heather was now in Portree, the need to tell her didn't seem so urgent. So, I agreed to give him the time he needed. This pleased my mother, but my father was less pleased.

'The longer you put it off, the harder it will be to tell her,' he warned me, 'and the more betrayed she'll feel when you do.'

I pondered my father's words and wondered if what he said was true. When I told her wouldn't change anything, would it? The truth is, she's not my natural daughter and her father and mother live miles away from here, living their own lives, which they don't want her to be a part of. I know that sounds harsh, and I know Johnny would have Heather in his life if he could. But, at the end of the day, he's chosen Janet over his daughter and Bunty has chosen respectability, hasn't she? So, would it make any difference if I told Heather now or when she was sixteen or twenty-one or never? All my resolve to tell her the truth seemed to have left me, and I gladly accepted the excuse Johnny had given me to put off the fateful day. But I was to regret that decision when the truth eventually came out.

CHAPTER FIVE

I still hadn't heard from Johnny a year later. It was 1936 and there were rumours about the king being in love with an American woman who was already married. What a scandal. The newspapers were full of it. But when he announced he was giving up the throne for Mrs Simpson, it shocked everyone. It was the talk of the island.

'Well Chrissie, what do you think of the King giving up the throne?' Shona McIver asked me when I was in buying some herring and oil from the shop. I was in Lochmaddy to meet Roddy and Heather, who were coming in on the ferry. Both home for Christmas and New Year. What a treat.

'It's a shame. I really like the King and enjoy reading about him in the newspapers. His life is just so different from ours, Shona.'

'Well, I feel sorry for that brother of his. He was never meant to inherit the throne but here it is being forced upon him,' said Morag Campbell, who still liked nothing better than a good old gossip.

'He must really love her to give up his throne for her, don't you think?' I said.

'Well, there's talk that he never wanted the responsibility, and he was looking for an excuse and he found one in Mrs Simpson.'

'No! He couldn't be that calculating, Morag. No, I think he really loves her and would do anything for her.'

'You're talking like a teenager, Chrissie,' said Shona. 'We all know love and marriage aren't about kissing and romance. It's about commitment and sacrifice.'

What Shona said was true, but I couldn't help feel a little envious of Mrs Simpson. Imagine having a man love you so much, he would give up his throne for you.

As I walked down to the pier, I reflected on how I never tired of this island ritual of the arrival and departure of the ferry. It was a brisk day; the wind was blowing and there was a threat of snow.

But I was happy Roddy was coming home. His apprenticeship was now finished, and he could legally practise as a solicitor, but I knew he had political ambitions, too. I thought about the young man who had become the first Labour politician to represent the Western Isles in last year's election. He was younger than Roddy, so if he could do it, my son could too. I felt my heart swell with pride. Roddy could be unpredictable, but he was a good boy at heart. He'd arranged to meet Heather when the school term finished and bring her home for the Christmas break.

'Roddy, Heather,' I cried when they came off the ferry. 'It's lovely to see you. Come and give your *mathair* a hug.'

They both obliged and as I felt the physical warmth of their bodies against mine, a spiritual warmth enveloped me. I thanked God for his goodness in giving me both my children home for the holidays. Only Donald was missing, but he was now a father to a one-year-old baby boy, so had more to think about than coming to North Uist for Christmas. Besides, Canada was a long way away. He and Mary had set up home in Yorkton, which wasn't too far from where Bunty now lived. Donald had got a post at the Yorkton Star Newspaper and Mary was a nurse in the hospital there. I felt pleased for Bunty that she had her family living close to her now and could be involved in her grandchild's life. They had called him Harry, after Mary's father.

I was so delighted to see them it took me a minute to notice Heather had something on her lips and her hair was shorter than when I'd last seen her. She was now thirteen going on twenty-one and had a mind of her own. Before I could say anything, another girl approached. It was Catriona, Murdo's daughter, her best friend, from over Carinish way.

'Hello Mrs Macdonald. Do you like Heather's hair? I cut it for her. I'm hoping to become a hairdresser one day and she lets me practise on her.'

'It looks grand, Catriona. I'm sure you'll make a fine hairdresser one day,' I said, not wanting to hurt the girl's feelings.

But I was actually quite annoyed. Heather had lovely hair and although it was wild, I hated the idea of her getting it cut.

'And did you happen to put that lipstick on her lips too, Catriona?'

'No *Mathair*, I can put lipstick on myself,' said Heather with a flounce, missing my attempt at sarcasm.

Just then, Catriona's mother called to her. She and Heather quickly hugged, and she ran off to join her family. It was then I noticed Fin, and he was hugging two young women. His daughters must have come up for the holidays too. I felt slightly disappointed he hadn't said, but then again, why should he? It's just our friendship had grown over the last year or so and we generally shared family news. I waved, and he waved back, then I turned to my two.

'Right, you two, let's get you home.'

'I'll drive *Mathair*,' said Roddy, so I gave him the reins as we jumped up onto the gig and squeezed ourselves onto the seat. I smiled. Both my children were changing. Roddy wanted to show he was the man of the house and Heather was experimenting as teenagers do. It was the natural order of things. But as we rode home, my mind wandered back to Fin, and I wondered what had brought his daughters to Uist. Was he thinking about returning to Glasgow? He hadn't said that he was, and I hoped he wasn't planning on leaving. I had got used to working with him in the post office.

CHAPTER SIX

When I went into work the next day, I asked Fin about the two young women he had met off the boat.

'Was that your two daughters I saw landing yesterday?'

'Yes, it was Rosie and Daisy. I see Roddy and Heather arrived safely then.'

'They did. It's so special having them home for the New Year. Although, I think I'm going to have my hands full with our Heather. Would you believe she let that Catriona Mackenzie cut her hair and had lipstick on, brazen as you like?'

Fin laughed.

'You sound like an old woman. As you said to me, things are changing for women, so you'll need to get used to Heather doing modern things.'

'Findlay Simpson, how dare you call me a *Cailleach?*' I laughed back.

'What's a *Cailleach*?' asked a Glaswegian voice.

I turned and smiled at a young woman with short wavy brown hair, staring at me suspiciously with her matching brown eyes. Fin's face became tense, and he introduced her. I didn't understand why then, but soon found out. She was rather an awkward customer.

'This is my youngest daughter, Daisy.'

She returned my smile, but it didn't meet her eyes.

'And you must be Mrs Macdonald, my father's assistant.'

'Yes, I am. Pleased to meet you Daisy. I hope you enjoy your visit here.'

'I hope so, too, but I hate leaving my grandparents at this time of year.'

'Och, it will be nice for you and your sister to have a bit of time with your father.'

'You're right, it will be, but I'm hoping there's lots of things to do around here. I hate being stuck in all the time,' said another voice.

A young woman with the same brown hair and eyes as Daisy looked at me with a playful smile on her lips. Although similar in looks, she was much prettier and smiley and wore her hair long. This time Fin's face lit up, and I realised he had a favourite. Poor Daisy, perhaps that's why she was a bit dour.

'This is my eldest daughter, Rosie. Rosie, this is Mrs Macdonald. She helps me run the post office and operates the telephone exchange.'

'Hello Mrs Macdonald. I'm pleased to meet you,' she said, taking my hand.

She lit a cigarette, took a draw, then blew the smoke up into the air.

'I wish you wouldn't smoke, Rosie. It's a bad habit.'

'Och Daddy, everyone does it nowadays. You're as bad as Daisy. She's always moaning at me about it.'

She stuck her tongue out at her sister.

'Would you like one, Mrs Macdonald?'

'I don't smoke, thank you Rosie. I never had the courage to do it when I was young and now I don't have the inclination.'

'So, what's there to do around here, Mrs Macdonald?'

It took me a minute to answer. What did we do around here? Very little compared to the big city, but I didn't want to sell our small island short. It was my home and much more beautiful than anywhere I'd seen in Glasgow.

'Well, there are some beautiful beaches if you enjoy walking. The closest one is Clachan Sands, but there are beaches all around the island. I could lend you my bicycle if you want to get out and about.'

'I was thinking more about going out to the dancing or the pictures.'

She looked at me hopefully.

'No picture houses up here, I'm afraid, but there will be plenty of dancing at the ceilidh next week to celebrate the new year.'

'That sounds good. I went to one of those with a highland lad and we had a great time.'

'We're supposed to be spending time with Dad,' said Daisy, 'not cavorting about at some ceilidh dance with teuchters.'

Fin looked a little embarrassed at Daisy's remark and I found myself wanting to make him feel better. So, without taking time to consider, I asked if they wanted to come to us on Hogmanay.

'Christmas is just another day on the islands, but we like to celebrate the coming of the new year. On the last night of the year, we all visit each other and take a dram or two. You would be very welcome. My son, Roddy, is home from Glasgow and I'm sure he would appreciate the company of two young women like yourselves.'

Rosie's face lit up.

'We'd love to come, wouldn't we, Daisy?'

Daisy just glared at Rosie, making it clear she would hate to come.

Fin let out a sigh and I could see he was uncomfortable with the way the conversation was going. So was I. The girl was rather rude.

'Why don't you come for afternoon tea on Saturday instead if you find yourself at a loose end? You'll be most welcome.'

The telephone began ringing, giving me a chance to escape. I went through to the back and dealt with the call, hoping that Rosie and Daisy had gone back through to the house and there would be no more awkward conversations. Poor Fin, he would have his hands full, keeping those two girls entertained. They were so different from each other.

CHAPTER SEVEN

Although Christmas day wasn't an official holiday, because we had family visiting, Fin took the day off while I covered. In return, I got the next day off. Roddy and I went for a walk. We took the buggy up to Balranald and visited Roderick's grave at Kilmuir Cemetery. As always, I felt his loss keenly and wished so much he was still with us. The Christmas that Bunty had organised a school play came into my mind, and I remembered how angry Roderick had been about it and how foolish I had been to be taken in by her friendship. I thought of Fin and his daughters. He had told me they wouldn't come to visit us on Hogmanay but would accept our invitation to tea on Saturday if that suited. I must admit, I was relieved. I'd made the invitation on a whim, but really, the thought of having Fin and two young women I hardly knew was rather scary.

It surprised my mother when I told her Fin, and his daughters were coming to tea.

'But you've known him all these years and from what you say, he hardly says two words to you. Why would you invite him this year?'

'Well, we've begun talking a bit more and his two daughters are up from Glasgow, so I thought it would be a hospitable thing to do. I feel sorry for him.'

'Feel sorry for him?'

'Yes, I think he's lonely. His wife died just before he came here, so he's been on his own a long time.'

'So have you.'

I looked at her. Yes I had, but I'd never felt lonely as I lived with my mother, father and Heather and saw my Roddy regularly. From what I could see, Fin lived on his own and only saw his daughters infrequently. So far as I knew, this was the first time they had been to visit him on the island.

'I know, *Mathair*. But I'm lucky. I've got you and *Athair*, Heather and Roddy. I don't think Fin sees much of his girls.'

The sound of the skylarks and the twites chirping their sweet songs as we walked through the machair to the beach brought me back to my walk with Roddy. It was a beautiful winter day. Cold, but clear and crisp. The snow that was threatening to fall when they arrived on the ferry hadn't come to anything. There was always a breeze on the island, but it was gentle today, so I was cosy enough in my knitted hat, gloves, and scarf. Heather hadn't wanted to come. She preferred to stay and help my mother with the preparations for the food we would have over the holiday. There would be soup made from stock from the chicken that my mother would kill and pluck, a crowdie made from milk from our cow and a dumpling that would be boiled in a muslin cloth and then set to dry in front of the fire. Heather loved cooking and baking, and she was good at it. She wasn't at all squeamish and helped my mother to pluck chickens and gut fish caught by my father. Roddy had brought her the Glasgow Cookery Book as a gift, and I was sure she would be delighted when she saw it.

'So, how are things with you, Roddy? You must be glad your apprenticeship is over, and you can now practise. What's your plans?'

'Truth be told, *Mathair*, I'm a bit fed up and hope coming home might settle me and help me decide what to do.'

'What to do about what, son?'

'Whether to continue to be a member of the Scottish National Party and put myself forward as a candidate at the next election or to find a job as a lawyer. I mean, I'm not too young to stand for parliament. Look at Malcolm Macmillan, who won for Labour in the Western Isles last year. He was only 22.'

'There's not any doubt you could become a politician, Roddy, but you sound as if you're no longer sure that the Scottish Nationalists are the party for you.'

'I'm not. I've become disillusioned. When I went to visit Jimmy Thomson, you know my old landlord, he told me his daughter Rosemary has joined the International Brigade and has gone to fight in Spain. It was her who got Donald his first writing job with the Daily Worker and was the reason that Charles Hepworth tried to recruit him, remember?'

'Yes, I remember,' I said, wondering where this was going.

'I can't help but admire her and feel I should do something like that. She's fighting for the Republicans, but some people in the SNP are saying we should fight on the side of the Nationalists, as Russia is supporting the Republicans.'

'But aren't Hitler and Mussolini nationalists? Surely you wouldn't want to support them. The things I've been reading in the newspapers are really upsetting.'

'No, of course not. That's why I'm in a bit of a quandary.'

'Well, we have two pretty young women coming to tea, so hopefully that will lift your spirits.'

He grinned, but I wondered if he was really pleased at the thought of female company. His mind was on other things. I was terrified at the thought of him going to Spain to fight. It was the last thing I wanted. My dream was for him to come back to North Uist and take over the practice from Mr Abernethy, but it didn't look like my dream would come true. I hoped he would get a break from his worries about his future by entertaining Fin's daughters. But perhaps he wasn't in the mood to entertain two young women who were strangers to him. Daisy would be hard work, I was sure, but if anyone could charm her, it was Roddy. He had a way with women, but maybe that was the problem. Perhaps he was too charming and too self-centred to be committed to anyone. But I was wrong.

CHAPTER EIGHT

Things didn't go smoothly on the day Fin and his daughters visited. In fact, it was a bit of a disaster. The weather was awful. A storm had brewed all morning and by the time Roddy went to pick them up in the buggy, it was spectacular. The rain bounced off the roads and turned the fields into muddy bogs. There was no cover in the buggy, so everyone was soaked when they arrived. We hung their coats in front of the range and within a few minutes, the room was like a Glasgow steamie. Not that I knew what a Glasgow Steamie was like, but Katie had described where she would go to do her washing before she moved in with Maude. My father got the whisky out and my mother made the tea.

'You'll have a wee dram, Mr Simpson,' my father said, pouring a large measure into one of the few glasses we had.

'That's very kind of you, Mr MacIntosh,' said Fin, eyeing up the amber liquid in his glass.

'Can I have some too, Mr MacIntosh,' said Rosie. 'We're all in need of something to heat us up.'

My mother tutted at the forwardness of the girl.

'The tea will be ready soon, and that will heat us all up,' she said, glaring at my father. Mother considered it too early in the day for the hard stuff.

'What about you, Daisy, isn't it?'

'Not for me, Mr MacIntosh. Tea will be fine, thank you.'

My father looked at Roddy and me, lifting the bottle. We both nodded. Things were becoming frosty as well as damp, so I needed something to lend cheer to the occasion.

'What can I have, Mammy?' asked Heather.

'Well, not whisky anyway,' I said with a laugh. 'You're far too young.'

'The girls have brought some ginger wine up from Glasgow,' said Fin, 'and I've brought it along. You could have some of that, Heather, if your mother agrees.'

I, of course, agreed, but poor Heather nearly choked when she took it. Although non-alcoholic, it was as fiery as the whisky, and it spurted from her mouth like a fountain when it caught in her throat, and she began coughing. Unfortunately, poor Daisy got the liquid all over her dress. I could tell she was furious, but she said nothing, just stared at the stains beginning to form on her dress.

'I'm so sorry, Miss Simpson. It was just so burnie in my throat,' said Heather, still coughing and spluttering.

She ran to the sink, wet a cloth, and handed it to Daisy. I thought it was considerate of her to do that and was sure Daisy would at least say thanks. But she just took it and began dabbing at her dress without a word to Heather.

'I've only brought one dress with me. Just as well we're going home soon.'

'Aye well, that will only be if the boat is running. With the weather like it is today, I would say you'll be lucky,' said my father, raising his glass to us all and taking a generous sip of his whisky.

Fin, Rosie, Roddy, and I did likewise. Then my mother announced the tea was ready, and we all sat round the table. There were oatcakes with crowdie, hot buttered scones, and thick slices of cold dumpling left over from the day before.

'What's on the biscuits?' asked Rosie. 'Is it cheese?'

'Yes,' said Heather. 'Granny, and I made it. It comes from the milk from our cow, and the biscuits are called oatcakes.'

'You have a cow?' said Daisy, turning her nose up.

'Yes, and sheep and chickens and a horse.'

'How nice for you.'

I noticed Daisy took a scone, followed by a slice of dumpling. The crowdie coming from a real cow obviously didn't appeal. But, of course, something had to go wrong. She had just bit into the dumpling when she let out a yell.

'Ow! There's something hard in this,' she said, pulling a small circle from her mouth.

'That'll be a silver threepenny,' said my mother. 'I wondered where it had got to.'

Putting silver threepennies into the dumpling was one of our traditions, but it's not the first time somebody has broken a tooth on one. Luckily, Daisy didn't.

'Och, I was hoping to get that,' said Heather.

'Well, have it then. I certainly don't want it.'

'But it will bring you good luck, Miss Simpson. You must keep it.'

'Oh, for goodness' sake Daisy, just keep it and stop being such a grump,' said Rosie. 'Thank you for a delicious tea, Mrs MacIntosh. I really enjoyed the crowdie. Lovely and creamy.'

My mother and Heather beamed at each other. Then my father spoke up, his face as red as a beetroot from the whisky.

'Right, our Heather. Give us a song.'

Heather's face went almost as red as my father's, but she did as she was told. She didn't need to be embarrassed, as she had a beautiful voice and had won a singing competition in school last term. Her teacher had even asked me if she could put her forward for the Mòd this coming year. I can't tell you how proud I was. I sometimes wondered, had Lachlan lived, would he have won a prize for his poetry? Heather sang in Gaelic, and I had tears in my eyes as I listened to her. She had such a sweet voice; I was sure she would win the competition. Daisy and Rosie sat politely during the song, but I could see they weren't that interested in this song that they couldn't understand the words of. But I thought I saw a tear in Fin's eye as he listened to the sweet song.

Roddy then told the story of Giant MacAskill, carrying on the tradition in the family of talking about the man from Berneray who grew so tall, he was called a giant. He'd joined Barnham's Circus and became so famous, he met Queen Victoria. The story did not enthral Heather, as it usually did, but then she was growing up. It made me think of when Johnny had told the story to Bunty and Mary. I think that was the start of the relationship that grew between them. And here was Heather, the result of that relationship, sitting here in my home. It made me think of the outstanding matter of telling her about her birth, and I sighed.

'You must be tired, Mrs Macdonald,' said Daisy. 'I expect you've had a long day getting this meal ready for us. Would you mind taking us home now, Mr Macdonald?'

'Aye, no bother. The rain has cleared, so the journey to the post office shouldn't be as bad as the one coming.'

'And hopefully the boat will be on tomorrow and we'll be able to get home.'

I didn't bother trying to persuade them to stay. It had been a tense couple of hours, mostly because of Daisy, and I would be glad of the chance to relax after they'd gone.

'I don't mind if we don't get home,' said Rosie. 'If we don't, will you take me to the ceilidh, Mr Macdonald?'

'Call me Roddy, please. Both of you. You don't need to be so formal with me and yes, I'll be delighted to take you dancing. And if you don't make the ceilidh, then I can catch up with you in Glasgow and we can go dancing there.'

Rosie's face beamed, and I wondered if something would develop between Roddy and Rosie. I suddenly felt a little sorry for Daisy, who was looking down at her feet. Although he had said both should call him by his first name, it was clearly Rosie he was inviting to the dancing.

'Right, let's get going then,' said Fin, turning to me and shaking my hand. 'Thank you so much for inviting us, Chrissie. It was kind of you.'

He held my hand and looked at me. His brown eyes, normally dull and expressionless, now had a mellow glow. I suspected the whisky my father had given him and the light from the Tilley lamp had contributed to this change, but was there something else? He actually looked happy, and it suited him. As I shook his hand, the soft hand of an administrator, I thought of Roderick. His hands had been the coarse hands of a farmer, but how I had loved the feel of them on my body when we made love. I blushed at the memory and drew my hand away lest Fin should see something in my eyes that would tell him what I was thinking.

CHAPTER NINE

Heather enjoyed school, and she was good at some subjects, but not at others. She loved the practical things like domestic science, which included cooking, knitting, and sewing. She wasn't so keen on English and history, but loved arithmetic, maths, and science. These subjects made sense to her, and she saw them working when she baked. Baking was a science as if you didn't get all the ingredients in the right weight to one another and the oven at the right temperature, then the science part of it didn't work and what that meant was a flat cake or a burnt scone. She was looking forward to the school holidays as Roddy was coming home and she always liked when she saw him. He was great fun and would take her to the beach and they would search for things or fish for flounders in the shallow pools that formed. He would talk to her about politics and what a hard time the people on North Uist and other parts of the Hebrides had in the past. Every time he spoke about the past, she felt annoyed at the unfairness of it all.

Roddy was waiting outside the girls' accommodation block when she and Catriona were set free. He gave her a hug and swung her round the way he had done when she was a wee girl, but now she felt embarrassed. She was thirteen; too old to be swung round like that. Also, Catriona had cut her hair the day before and she didn't want it messed up before her mammy saw it. She felt nervous about what Mammy would say. She liked her to wear her hair long, but Heather was growing up now and it was up to her how long she wanted to wear her hair. Catriona had also bought some lipstick off one of the older girls. It was a pale pink, and she thought it made her look pretty.

Ordinary rather than pretty is how she would have described herself, but she had felt pretty in the dress she had worn to Mary's wedding. Fashion was something she didn't really bother too much about, as it didn't really matter what she wore to milk the cow or feed the chickens. But only recently, Catriona had told her she was a fashion leader because she had made herself a pair of trousers for riding Sandy. She loved riding their horse, when he wasn't on duty, pulling the plough or the gig and had talked her mother into letting her wear trousers for riding. She had made them herself with her mother's sewing machine. The sight of her in trousers had shocked some of their neighbours the first time they saw her wearing them. But then Catriona told her some of the Hollywood stars wore them too, so she didn't feel so bad. She doubted she would ever be a Hollywood star or a fashion leader, but it made her think about how she looked and what she wore and realised that it probably mattered more than she thought.

Her mother didn't give her too much trouble about her hair cut or about wearing lipstick, thank goodness, but no doubt there would be some kind of lecture later when it was just the two of them. She always had to explain things, unless it was about family secrets, of course. Roddy got her the Glasgow Cookery Book for Christmas and she was thrilled. He also told her about the Dough School, as it was called, where girls could go to learn to cook and bake. That was something she thought she would like to do when she grew up. Catriona wanted to be a hairdresser. That's why she had let her cut her hair. She needed to practise. It was unlikely there would be much call for a hairdresser on North Uist as most people just got their mothers or sisters to cut their hair. But Catriona said she didn't intend staying on Uist once she finished school. She couldn't wait to get to the big city. She had an aunt in Edinburgh, the capital, and thought she could make a good living there as a hairdresser. Heather sometimes wondered if she should want to leave the island, too. But the thought of it made her sad. She was sure she could get a job as a cook or a baker on the island. Everyone needed to eat.

They had unexpected guests to tea during the holidays. Mammy had invited her boss, Mr Simpson, to come along with his two daughters, who were called Rosie and Daisy. It was a terrible day, and they were absolutely soaked when they arrived and looked bedraggled and miserable. She bet they wished they'd stayed at the post office house instead of coming to them. But what a stramash. When Mr Simpson gave her some ginger wine to drink as the adults were having whisky, she choked and coughed it all over Daisy's dress. She could see she was angry and ran to get a cloth to wipe it up, but she didn't even say thanks. When Grandad asked her to sing, she sang her favourite *Bheir Mi O,* but although Mr Simpson looked as if he were enjoying it, his two daughters looked bored. Polite but bored. She herself became bored when Roddy told the now too familiar story of Giant MacAskill. She'd heard it so many times, it no longer held the magic it used to. And she was too big now for Roddy to lift her away above his head, the way he used to. If she was being honest, she was glad when they left. It was much nicer to just spend the time with her own family. Heather noticed when Mr Simpson left he held Mammy's hand for quite a long time, and they seemed to look at each other in a funny way. When she asked Mammy about it later, her face went pink, and she said she was imagining things. Mr Simpson was her boss and nothing else. Well, she knew that. What else could he be? She didn't understand why her mammy was getting so hot and bothered about it.

That night, after she'd gone to bed, she could hear the murmur of voices below. Sometimes she sneaked down if she didn't fall asleep so that she could hear what they were talking about. Tonight, she was wide awake, so she made her way downstairs quietly, making sure not to stand on the step that creaked. It sounded like her mother was trying to persuade Roddy not to go to Spain, but to stay in Scotland and practice as a solicitor. She hoped Roddy would do what she wanted. Heather didn't like to think of him being involved in a war. Although, Mr Malcolmson, her history teacher, told them it was possible Britain might be at war again if Mr Hitler kept going the way he was. She didn't like the sound of Mr Hitler. He was just like Maggie, a bully at school, who thought she could do and say anything, and no-one would stand up to her. Suddenly her mammy's voice was rising, a sure sign that she was becoming upset, so she concentrated on what she and Roddy were talking about.

'I'd be helping people, *Mathair*. I could join the International Brigade like Rosemary, but I know that would upset you too much. Going over as part of the Red Cross would make me feel I'm doing my bit in the fight against fascism. It just feels like the right thing to do, just the way you think it's the right thing to do to tell Heather the truth.'

Heather's ears pricked up at the mention of her name. What did Roddy mean?

'Has Johnny got back to you yet?'

'No, not yet. But don't let's talk about it. You know Heather has ears like an elephant. I'm just going to check if she's sleeping yet.'

She jumped up and ran upstairs, not bothering with the creaking stair. Her heart was racing. What was the truth her mother thought she should be told?

CHAPTER TEN

Heather waited for her mother to tell her the truth about whatever it was, but she didn't. She hung about the house, waiting for them to have time on their own so that she could tell her, but she didn't. At tuck-in time, she hoped she would tell her, and she still didn't. Her mammy sent her back to school without telling her what it was she thought she ought to know. Heather wasn't normally one to brood too much on things, but she was worried. What if Mammy was dying? What would happen to her? Would she be put in an orphanage or sent for adoption? She quivered with fear at the thought of it. Look at Anne with an e from Green Gables. She ended up okay, but what if she didn't get someone like Marilla and Matthew? What then? The people who would adopt her might make her steal things like Fagan in Oliver Twist. She could end up in prison or dead.

'What's wrong with you, Heather?' asked Catriona. 'You're shaking like a leaf. Have you got a fever?'

She looked at her best friend and wondered if she should tell her what was going on inside her head. But saying it out loud would make it real and she didn't want it to be real. It was better tucked inside this brain of hers and not let out.

'No, I'm okay, Catriona. I think I'm just sad about going back to school. I miss my family.'

She felt tears nipping her eyes. How she would miss her mammy, granny, and grandad if she had to leave them. Catriona put her arm around her and gave her the new handkerchief she'd got for Christmas, which her mother had embroidered with her initials. At the thought of losing the bestest, kindest friend a girl could have too if she became an orphan, she actually burst into tears. Catriona pressed her closer and patted her back.

'Och, it'll be the Summer holidays before you know it. This is a big year for us. We'll need to get ready for the Mòd in October. I'm looking forward to it, aren't you? And think how proud your family will be when you win a prize.'

She smiled at her friend. Normally, the thought of winning a prize at the Mòd would have cheered her up, but now it didn't seem to matter. Nothing seemed to matter. But she blew her nose on Catriona's new hanky and pulled herself together. It wasn't fair to upset Catriona with her worries. They would both be singing in the school choir, but each of them was in for an individual prize for singing, too. So, she put aside her thoughts, and they chattered and planned out everything they were going to do when they got to Portree.

As it turned out, it was Easter when her mammy got round to telling her the truth. She didn't tell her voluntarily. It was only because Mrs MacGregor, Heather's favourite teacher, was worried about her and wrote to tell her mother that something was bothering her, so she had no option but to ask her what the matter was. Her mother let her see the letter Mrs MacGregor had sent.

Dear Mrs Macdonald

I am writing to you because I am anxious about Heather. She seems a changed girl since she came back to school in January and I'm wondering if something happened during the holidays that the school needs to know about. Heather is normally such a happy, hard-working girl and loves her singing. But she seems to have lost her spark. She's falling behind in her schoolwork and her singing is lacklustre. So much so that I'm afraid I might need to take her out of the Mòd competitions. Perhaps you could bring Heather back to school after the Easter holidays, and we could have a chat to see if there is anything we can do to help.'

Yours sincerely

Mrs M MacGregor

'Is what Mrs MacGregor's saying true, Heather? Did something happen during the Christmas holidays that upset you?'

She looked at her mother and nodded. Her stomach was churning. This was it. She was going to find out that her mammy was dying.

'Well, tell me what it was, Heather. You know you can tell me anything *mo graidh*.'

She smiled that encouraging smile of hers and nodded at Heather as if to say go on. She swallowed and told her.

'I heard you and Roddy talking one night during the holidays, when I should have been in bed.'

Mammy's face grew serious, and she thought she looked afraid. How she wished she'd never crept down the stairs that night. Then none of this would be happening.

'Nothing good comes from listening to conversations you shouldn't, you know, Heather. Anyway, what do you think you heard?'

'I heard Roddy saying you felt you should tell me the truth.'

Her mother's face twisted as she tried to put a smile on her lips, but she didn't speak, so Heather did.

'Are you going to die, *Mamaidh*? Am I going to become an orphan?'

Tears slid down her mother's cheeks and she knew she'd guessed the truth. Jumping quickly out of bed, she clung to her mother.

'I don't want you to die, *Mamaidh*. Who'll look after me when you're gone? Will Granny and Grandad put me in an orphanage or get me adopted?'

She wailed at the thought of it.

'Calm down, Heather, sweetheart. I'm not going to die. Well, not yet anyway. And even if I did, you would have *Seanmhair* and *Seanair* to look after you and even Roddy if worst came to worst. She smiled at her, and she knew she was trying to make her feel better, but she didn't want to live with Roddy in Glasgow. She wanted to stay here in North Uist.

Her mother was cradling her in her arms when granny walked in.

'What's going on? What's the matter? Have you hurt yourself, Heather?'

All she could do was hiccup as she tried to answer granny.

'No, she's alright. She's just got the wrong end of the stick. I'll explain when I come down. Thank you *Mathair*.'

'Hush, Hush. It's alright Heather. Everything's alright. There's nothing for you to worry about.'

'But what is it you need to tell me?'

She watched as her mother prepared herself for whatever she was going to say. She felt relieved her mother wasn't dying, but she was still anxious about what she had to tell her.

CHAPTER ELEVEN

When the letter arrived from Heather's school, saying they were worried about her, I was concerned. It was difficult to know what was going on with your child when they were away at school. Although we wrote a monthly letter to each other, I hadn't picked up any signs that something was bothering her. I thought back to the Christmas holidays, but couldn't think of anything that might have upset her, apart from coughing her drink all over Daisy. But I couldn't see how that would make her change as much as the teacher was saying. Something must have happened at school. But what? Was she being bullied? Was she struggling with some of her subjects? Or had she somehow found out the truth about her birth? Was that the problem? But how could she have found out? No-one knew apart from our family.

Unless Bunty had changed her mind and wrote to Heather telling her she was her natural mother. No, it couldn't be that. It was just my guilty conscience. But what if it was? What would I tell her? Johnny had written, but asked me to hold off telling Heather until he had told Janet. But why was I protecting Johnny and Janet? My little girl was more important. However, when the moment arrived, I decided against revealing the complete truth to her. I now realise I didn't want her to know I wasn't her mother. It was me who wasn't ready, not Heather. I wonder if I'd told her the whole truth then, would it have saved a lot of heartache? I still don't know.

It turned out she had been eavesdropping on the conversation that Roddy and I were having about him going to Spain. When she heard him telling me he felt it was the right thing to do, just as me telling Heather the truth was the right thing to do, she had put two and two together and come up with over four. Poor baby. She thought I was dying, and that I hadn't told her. She was worried about what would happen to her if I died. It was a relief when I realised she didn't know the truth. I had a reprieve. Because she had asked me who the father of Bunty's baby was, I told her that part of the truth, not the whole truth about me adopting her. To set the scene properly, I shared with her everything about Roderick's time in Canada, including how James Adams died and what Roderick had done with his body. I left out Lily and Heather and how Donald was conceived as I didn't want to complicate matters too much. I told myself that telling her the background to her mother and father's relationship would make it easier when it came time for me to tell her she was the baby they had created.

'So, this James Adams was Mrs Hepworth's father?'

'Yes. Her stepfather was cruel to her, and she used to dream that her real father would one day come and save her.'

'Poor Mrs Hepworth. Although she wasn't an orphan, she had a terrible life by the sound of it.'

'I think she did, and that made her ill in her head. I think that's why she wanted to hurt Roderick. She believed he was the one who had stopped her father from coming back to save her.'

'But what has this to do with her having a baby? I don't understand.'

'We didn't know she was the person spreading gossip about Roderick and sending poison pen letters to the Laird, so she became a friend of the family. Johnny and she grew close and for a time, we thought they might get married.'

Heather didn't speak. She looked at me, perplexed by my revelation.

'Uncle Johnny was the father of Mrs Hepworth's baby?'

'Yes.'

'Why didn't they get married?'

'Johnny and Janet got back together.'

'And he married another woman even although he knew Mrs Hepworth was having his baby?'

'No. He didn't know about the baby. Not until after he had married Janet. Mrs Hepworth only told him on the day he and Janet were leaving for Canada. By that time, he could do nothing about it.

'So, *Mamaidh*, are you saying it was Mrs Hepworth's fault?'

'Well, not her fault that she got pregnant. Uncle Johnny had a part to play in it, of course. What I'm saying is that she chose not to tell him until it was too late for him to do anything about it.'

'But I don't understand why they made a baby together but didn't stay together. I thought people who made babies together loved each other.'

'Mostly, they do, but not always. You'll understand better when you grow up.'

I used the adult way of avoiding giving an answer and felt ashamed of myself. Heather puffed her cheeks up in annoyance. I understood exactly how she was feeling. I used to hate it when my mother said the same to me as a way out of not explaining things I asked her about when I was a girl. But it was just so complicated. How could I explain Bunty had seduced Johnny? Explain that he had been weak because Janet had turned her back on him. I knew I would only be excusing the inexcusable.

'Stop treating me like a child, *Mamaidh*. Why didn't you tell me all this when I asked you after we came back from Donald and Mary's wedding?'

''Because it's not my secret to share, Heather, and you mustn't tell anyone about this. No-one on the island knows Mrs Hepworth was pregnant, let alone that Uncle Johnny was the father of her child. Janet and her family don't know, and it wouldn't be fair for them to hear it through gossip. It could break up their marriage.'

'Oh, so you think I would gossip about Uncle Johnny?'

'No, of course not, Heather. I know you wouldn't do that. But it's a big secret to carry. I thought it better if you didn't know.'

Tears formed in Heather's eyes, and my heart broke for her.

'I can see you're upset, Heather. Tell me what's troubling you.'

'I feel sorry for Mrs Hepworth *Mamaidh*. It must have been hard for her, being sick and expecting a baby and having no-one to support her.'

'Yes, it must have been. But she had her brother and her mother to help her.'

'I suppose so. But she didn't get to keep her baby, did she?'

'No. She didn't,' I whispered.

I couldn't go on. My voice broke, and I wept. What was I doing? My tears would frighten Heather. She'd never seen me cry before. But I couldn't help but smile at her next words.

'Don't cry *Mamaidh*. Everything will be okay.'

'Och Heather. Come here, sweetheart. You know I love you so much,' I said, tucking her hair behind her ears.

'And I promise I won't tell anyone about Uncle Johnny.'

'Thank you. And you'll be okay when you go back to school?' She nodded.

I was relieved, but I shouldn't have been. Heather kept the secret for a while, but then she didn't, and everything fell apart again.

CHAPTER TWELVE

It was a fine June evening in 1937 when I went for a stroll to Clachan Sands. Whenever I wanted to be on my own and have time to think, I still went there. Although, I never failed to remember my walk after Roderick died and how near I'd come to walking into the sea, it didn't put me off. How glad I am that something stopped me. At the time, I thought I heard Roderick's voice, but now that seems fanciful. If I'd ended my life, I would never have had Heather. I love her with all my heart and wouldn't have missed the chance to be her mother for anything. I was really looking forward to having her home for the summer holidays. The school had written to say she was back to her old self when she went back to school after the Easter holidays and had been selected to take part in a solo singing competition in this year's Mòd. I was naturally pleased and proud about that, but I was relieved too, as I didn't like to think of her being upset. I had a reprieve, but I knew it was temporary and I must tell her the whole truth soon.

My mind drifted, and I thought about the new King's Coronation, which had taken place last month. The authorities decided that since his brother's coronation had been planned for 12 May, they should just go ahead on the same date. Mother and I had listened to all the proceedings on the wireless, but father said he couldn't be bothered with all the pomp and went about his normal crofting duties. It was on the television too. I thought it must be amazing to have a television. It would be like having your own picture house at home. But since we had no electricity on the island, there were no televisions. If we wanted to hear the news or catch a radio programme, we had to rely on our tube battery-operated radio, which often had a weak signal. We had to go to the Lochmaddy Hotel to get the batteries re-powered, as they didn't last long. I had pored over the papers, looking at all the photos. The King, who was now George V1, and Queen Elizabeth had looked beautiful in all the coronation regalia. The government had issued the post office with special stamps to mark the coronation, so there had been an upsurge in people buying stamps recently.

I loved the isolation of the beach, and it was very rare I met anyone there, but today I could see a figure in the distance that looked familiar. Was it Fin? I didn't realise he went walking. He'd never said. Butterflies fluttered in my tummy as I saw him turn and walk towards me. There was nothing else for it but to wave to him, although I felt a little funny about seeing him out of the post office. I don't think I ever had before. How strange. It felt a bit like the first time I saw Murdo without his postman's uniform on and had to look at him twice before recognising it was him.

'Hello Fin,' I called, waving again as he drew closer. He wore wide casual trousers, a pale blue checked shirt, a sleeveless jumper that looked much smarter than the ones I knitted for my father, and a cap. I'd never seen him out of the dark blue suit he habitually wore in the post office and when he went to the bank or on other business, he always wore a hat. This was a new Fin to me, but I liked it. The clothes made him look more approachable.

'I hardly recognised you out of your suit.'

'I hardly recognise myself. My daughters gave me these clothes at Christmas. They decided I needed modernising, but I've been too self-conscious to wear them. That's why I thought a walk on the sands where I was unlikely to meet anyone would be a good idea. But here you are.'

I laughed.

'Well, I think you look very smart. The modern look suits you. How are Daisy and Rosie?'

'Okay, so far as I know. They don't write to me very often, but when they do, they always say they want me to move back to Glasgow. And perhaps it's time I did.'

'We would miss you,' I said, not wanting him to think no one would care if he left. But I realised I would care, even if no-one else would. I would miss him. We were just beginning to get to know each other.

40

'You don't need to make me think people here would miss me, Chrissie. I know I've not mixed much with the locals during the, what is it, seven years that I've been here?'

'Well, it's time you did. You should join the men for a drink in the Lochmaddy Hotel and come along to a ceilidh. You would enjoy it, I'm sure.'

'Perhaps.'

He was being non-committal.

'But the Post Office will decide when I leave North Uist. It's they who choose where I go. As things are looking unsettled in Europe and there's the possibility of war, who knows where they'll want me to go next?'

'That was how Roderick got the job of postmaster when we came back from Canada. The other postmaster had been called upon to help the war effort.'

We walked along for a while without speaking.

'Talking of war. My Roddy has gone to Spain to help in the civil war over there.'

'He's joined one of the International Brigades?'

'No. Thank God. Not that. No. He's helping the Red Cross. The government class them as neutrals as they help the injured on both sides.'

'Still, you must be worried.'

'Och, I am Fin. You don't know how much I worry about that boy. He's just finished his law apprenticeship, and I was hoping he would either become a Member of Parliament or a practising lawyer. But here he is, neither. I think a girl has turned his head.'

He laughed.

'What are you laughing at?' I asked playfully.

'You,' he said. 'Mothers always blame girls when their boys don't do what they want them to.'

'How come you know so much?'

'Well, my mother blamed Ruth when we got married after only knowing each other for three months. But it was the war, you know. It made us all feel that we had to make the most of every precious moment of our lives as we didn't know when it might end.'

His face softened as he spoke his wife's name. This was a special moment. He had never mentioned her name before nor told me anything about how they had got together. I felt privileged.

'I expect you're right, Fin,' I said, laying my hand on his arm. 'Thanks for telling me about Ruth. You must have loved one another very much.'

We looked at each other, not smiling or talking. Just sharing a special moment.

CHAPTER THIRTEEN

Heather found it hard to keep what she knew about her Uncle Johnny to herself, but she had promised her mother that she would, and she didn't want to let her down. But Catriona was her best friend, and they told each other all their secrets and worries, so it made her feel bad keeping something back from her. This year, they were most worried about whether Mrs MacGregor would nominate them for the Mòd. Although Heather hadn't done so well in her practice before Easter and the teacher thought she wouldn't be up to scratch to perform, since her mother had told her the truth about Mrs Hepworth, she felt better and was working hard to get her spark back. She did tell Catriona what she had been worried about and how relieved she was that her mother wasn't dying, but she didn't tell her anything about Uncle Johnny. At least not then.

'Och, Heather. Why didn't you tell me what was worrying you? You know you can tell me anything. That was a terrible thing to keep to yourself. No wonder you lost your spark when you were singing.'

'Well, you know I'm working hard to get it back. I want us to go to Dundee together, Catriona. It's what we've dreamed of all this year.'

She and Catriona wanted to perform in the junior solo championships and Mrs MacGregor was encouraging them in their ambitions. It was coming up to the summer holidays, and it was time to perform in front of the school. Mrs MacGregor would carefully observe how they performed on stage in front of an audience before selecting who she would enter for the competitions. Singing was only part of it. There were lots of other competitions, like poetry reading, playing musical instruments, dancing, among others. On the day of the performance, she was nervous, of course, but she was determined to get her place. As she stood in the assembly hall in front of the entire school, she felt her legs tremble, but then she spotted Catriona in the crowd, giving her an encouraging wave. Mrs MacGregor struck the piano keys, introducing the song she was going to sing. It was *Mo Dhomhnullan fhein,* a slow love song that suited her voice. This was it. Her time to shine and show she had her spark back. When she finished, there was enthusiastic applause from the audience, but the most enthusiastic was Catriona, who continued to clap after everyone else had finished. Heather looked over at Mrs MacGregor and knew from the beam on her face that she had passed muster.

When it came time for the Mòd, she and Catriona were beside themselves with excitement and could talk of nothing else. They were not only going to a place they'd never been before with a chance of winning a prize, but they were getting three whole days off from school. They were the envy of those from the school who had insufficient talent to compete in the Mòd. It was being held in Dundee this year. Heather's only association with Dundee was the comics her classmates read, which were printed there. Neither of them had ever been to Dundee and wondered what it would be like.

'I think it might be like Glasgow, Catriona. What do you think?'

'Probably. But I don't care what it looks like. I just want to go somewhere different. Is your mother coming to see you?'

'Yes. Is yours?'

'Yes. She's booked a bed-and-breakfast place for Monday night so that she'll be here to see me, but she's going home immediately after the performance.'

'My mother's doing the same. It's great that we'll be here unchaperoned by our mothers.'

'True. But Mrs MacGregor will keep her beady eyes on us, I'm sure.'

Heather imagined Dundee might be like Glasgow, dirty and sooty. She much preferred the fresh island air of Uist, but she was happy to leave the island for a chance to perform at the Mòd. There were several people from the Western Isles going along. It was a highlight of the year for some families who had talented people in their family and there was fierce competition among the different areas of Scotland for the prizes. The school had hired a bus to take the competitors to Dundee, and they had to be up early the next morning. When they arrived late on Monday, Heather was tired. She and Catriona had sat up late on Sunday night, too excited to sleep. She thought Dundee looked different from Glasgow. Although it had tenements, rather than the front doors being in a close, they were on the outside on a platform. Also, they had jute mills, which Glasgow didn't have. They drove past The Caird Hall, where the competitions were being held over the next four days. It was one of several beautiful buildings in the city square. Heather had never seen anything so grand and wondered what the inside would be like.

There was an air of excitement the next day when they arrived in the Caird Hall. Smartly dressed stewards directed competitors and guests where to go, and there were stalls selling programmes. Mrs MacGregor bought one and said she would keep it as a souvenir. Heather wished she had enough money to buy one too. She felt part of history as she looked at the programme, with its picture of the Caird Hall on the cover declaring this was the Forty-first Mòd. People were milling about, some dressed in highland dress and others in their best finery. There was the hum of animated conversation interspersed with the sounds of singing and musical instruments. She and Catriona clasped hands and smiled widely at each other as they followed behind Mrs MacGregor to where they were to perform.

At last, it was time for Heather to go on stage. As she looked out onto the lavish auditorium with its plush seats and ornate decoration, she spotted her mother sitting behind the judges. Although she was glad her mother had told her the truth about Uncle Johnny, she still felt sad for Mrs Hepworth and her baby. So much so that as she sang the song, her thoughts turned to Mrs Hepworth and how bad she must have felt when Uncle Johnny left her behind. It was just like the girl in the song who was abandoned by a sailor named Donald. As she sang the last verse, she felt tears stinging her eyes and hoped the judges wouldn't mark her down because of it. But it was the opposite. She received a standing ovation from the audience and the judges awarded her first prize for her performance. And that was how she came to tell Catriona about Johnny.

'Heather, you were absolutely smashing. You looked so sad. I thought you were going to cry at one point. How did you manage to give such an emotional performance?'

'It was because I was thinking about Mrs Hepworth, who is my brother Donald's mother-in-law.'

'Oh. I've never heard you talking about her before. Why does thinking about her make you feel so sad?'

'Because my Uncle Johnny abandoned her and left her with an illegitimate baby.'

Catriona's eyes were wide with curiosity.

'And what happened to the baby?'

'No-one knows. It was adopted. I just think it's so sad. I would hate to be adopted, wouldn't you?'

Catriona thought about it.

'Well, it would depend on who adopted me. I wouldn't mind if they were rich and had a big house and everything. Think what a cushy life I could have.'

'Och Catriona, there's more to life than money.'

But Catriona's frivolous remark made her laugh, and she forgot about Uncle Johnny, Mrs Hepworth, and the baby. But Catriona didn't.

CHAPTER FOURTEEN

I couldn't believe another year had passed. My thoughts went back to last year when Fin's daughters had come up to Uist. What a disaster their visit to the croft had been. I don't think they've been up to see him since, although I know he visited them in the summer. It was also when Heather heard Roddy saying something about me telling her the truth. She had waited for me to tell her the truth, but of course I hadn't, and it had affected her schoolwork. In the end, I'd only told her part of the truth. I don't know why. I suppose I'm just a coward. She now knows Johnny is the father of Bunty's baby, but she doesn't know yet that she's the baby. But, telling her about Johnny made her settle back into school again and my darling girl won a first prize at the Mòd in Dundee. She got a standing ovation from the audience, and everyone remarked how they had never seen a young girl put such emotion into singing a love song.

I wrote to Johnny telling him I had told Heather part of the truth, so he said he would tell Janet soon as it would be awful if the story got out and she heard it from her mother. But he still hadn't written to say he'd told Janet, and I suppose I used that as an excuse not to tell Heather the complete story. Roddy was coming up for Christmas and New Year and I couldn't wait to see him and hear all about his time in Spain. Rosemary was still there, and I hoped she would come home safely. So many young people were being killed over there. Germany and Italy supported the Fascists while Russia was supporting the Communists. But Britain continued to sit on the fence, an unpopular policy in some quarters. I could understand why Mr Chamberlain had a policy of appeasement after all that happened in the last war, which was supposed to be the war to end all wars and yet here we were again.

After our walk on Clachan Sands, a Sunday walk became a weekly ritual for Fin and me. The more I got to know him, the more I grew to like him. We both talked mostly about our families, but sometimes I spoke about Roderick and sometimes he spoke about Ruth. It was nice talking to someone about Roderick.

People rarely talked about him to me in case they upset me. And I felt by encouraging Fin to talk about Ruth, I would find out more about him. It was when we were talking about Roddy coming home from Spain and the involvement of Germany, Italy, and Russia that I found out Ruth was a Jew.

'Ruth's family are Jews, you know. Her mother and father still have relatives in Poland and the letters they send tell them how difficult things are for Jews now. It's possible some of them may try to make their way to Scotland if they can get through the red tape.'

'And you. Are you a Jew as well, or are you Protestant or Catholic?'

'I'm neither. My parents brought me up a Catholic, but I no longer believe in God or practice the Catholic faith.'

'I'm Church of Scotland. I can't imagine not believing in God and not going to church. It's just such a huge part of my life.'

'I can understand that. But I'm afraid my experience in the war made me sceptical. I saw more humanity and goodness in the trenches from my brothers in arms than from any supernatural being. God left us to get on with it, and we did. He became irrelevant.'

It made me sad Fin was so disillusioned, but I remembered the effect of the war on Lachlan and kind of understood.

'What about your girls?'

'I'm afraid they're neither one thing nor the other. Although Ruth's parents have brought them up and they do the Friday night Shabbat, that's where they light candles and say prayers over wine and bread, they haven't tried to make the girls practise their religion. Ruth wasn't a practising Jew, and she wouldn't have wanted them to be.'

'But I imagine they'll still have a lot more understanding and sympathy for the plight of the Jews in Europe than people in Scotland, like me, who know very little about the Jewish religion.'

'Yes, they probably do.'

'So are the girls coming up this year for Christmas and New Year, or are you planning to go to Glasgow?'

'No, they want to stay at home. I'm going down for Christmas, but only for a couple of days.'

'So, you'll be back for the New Year Ceilidh?'

'Yes, but I don't know why you think that's of interest to me.'

'It's of interest to you Findlay Simpson, as I'm inviting you to come to the ceilidh along with me and my family.'

'Oh, I don't think so. It's been years since I danced. Ruth and I used to go dancing whenever we got the chance, but after she died, well, you know, all that stopped.'

'Try it then and see how you get on. If you feel uncomfortable or aren't enjoying yourself, you can leave early, and I'll take you home.'

'Oh, I couldn't ask you to cut short your night for me, Chrissie.'

'I know. You're too much of a gentleman,' I said, smiling and attempted to wink, which made him burst out laughing.

CHAPTER FIFTEEN

The night of the ceilidh arrived. It was a bright night, no rain or wind, and everyone was in good spirits, apart from Roddy. There was a noticeable change in him after his experience in Spain. I tried to talk to him, but he said he didn't want to talk about it. So, I thought it best to leave it alone until he was ready. He was much thinner than the last time I had seen him and the jumper I'd knitted him hung loose on his skinny body. His eyes were dull, and he only spoke when someone spoke to him. Even Heather couldn't bring him out of the doldrums. She was excited to be going to the ceilidh as she was meeting her friend Catriona. The two of them were close, and it reminded me of how Janet and I used to be. But look at us now. We never wrote to each other anymore. I'd betrayed my friend in favour of my brother and so I'd stopped writing. It just didn't sit well with me to keep writing when I was hiding from her that Heather was Johnny's daughter.

When we arrived, the hall at Carinish was jammed with people and the smells of those people. There was a mix of pipe and cigarette smoke, peat smoke, sweat, alcohol and, when passing in the wake of some young men and women, the sweet smell of hair oil or perfume. I loved it. The smell was associated with fun in my mind. I loved to dance. The strathspeys and barn dances of the highlands allowed us to let our hair down and express ourselves with wild exuberance, with no one blinking an eye at such behaviour. The band was tuning up, and we found a table. We all chatted over one another, and I had to wait till later to ask Fin how his visit at Christmas had gone. He, Roddy, and I were sitting while everyone else was up dancing.

'We had a lovely time, thank you. My parents-in-law don't celebrate Christmas, of course, but my family still does, so we visited my mother. She lives with my sister and her family in Govan.'

'In Govan,' said Roddy, speaking for the first time. 'Do you know a family called Dunlop?'

I looked at Roddy. Wasn't that the name of the Catholic girl he had been in love with? Was he still holding a torch for her? I wondered if I'd got it wrong about him having feelings for Mary. Either that or his feelings had been a kind of rebound from the breakup of his relationship with Theresa.

'I'm afraid I don't, but my mother or sister might. Why do you ask?'

'Och, I used to go with a girl from Govan. I just wondered if you might know her, if that's where you come from.'

'I've not lived there for years. Sorry. Do you want me to write and ask my mother?'

'No, it's alright. Theresa's in America now, anyway.'

He looked glum. I silently asked God to help him get over whatever was getting him down and prayed that the dance would cheer him up.

I'm not sure about Roddy, but I had a wonderful time. While I danced with lots of people, I made sure Fin joined me on the dance floor whenever it was appropriate. My mission for the evening was to help him enjoy himself so that he would feel part of the community. From the way he joined in the dancing and the smiles on his face, I think I succeeded. There was only one point when I was unsure of what I was doing. It was when we went outside to cool down. We pulled our coats on and stood outside, our breath blowing out in little white clouds.

'I'm having a great time, Chrissie. Thanks for inviting me. I can't remember the last time I danced like this or felt so happy.'

Unexpectedly, he went to kiss my cheek just as I turned my face to smile at him and our lips touched. There was a faint smell of whisky from his breath, and it brought back, as if it were yesterday, the memory of the dance in Canada when Colin had tried to kiss me. Did I want Fin to kiss me? We stared at each other, neither knowing what to say. The moment was lost when Heather came running out, grabbed my hand and told me she needed me for the eightsome reel.

I couldn't sleep. It was always the same, I told myself. The excitement of it all made it hard to settle. But it wasn't only that. That brush of Fin's lips against mine was making my tummy flutter like a teenager's. I wondered if Fin was thinking about that kiss, too. Then the pleasure I was feeling at the thought of kissing Fin turned to guilt. I was being disloyal to Roderick, just as I'd been back in Canada when Colin had tried to kiss me at the dance in Saltcoats. I had wanted him to kiss me, and it was only the first Heather being sick that stopped me. Shameful. What was I thinking? An almost 50-year-old woman lying in bed dreaming of kissing a man like a silly girl. What an idiot. Fin was probably embarrassed at what happened. But then I remembered how he had held me when we were dancing the St Bernard's Waltz at the end of the ceilidh and a sensation I hardly recognised overwhelmed me. How I longed to feel his arms around my waist again, to feel the heat of his hand through my dress, to feel the whisper of his breath on my ear. Rising from bed, I went over to the window, leaning my feverish brow against the cold glass. I couldn't bear it, this longing, this restlessness. It was almost like being in love.

CHAPTER SIXTEEN

Feeling like a washed-out dishrag the next morning, I rose reluctantly and made my way to the kitchen for breakfast. It didn't matter that we'd had a late night at the dancing, and in my case hadn't slept, we still had to get up to do the morning chores. A croft didn't work itself. My father was sitting at the table with a steaming bowl of porridge in front of him, looking as bright as a button. Despite being sixty-seven, he looked like a man my age.

'Good morning, Chrissie, how are you feeling this morning? I expect you'll have sore legs with all that dancing you were doing last night.'

I smiled wanly at him and nodded. Despite my reluctance to talk, my mother insisted on speaking about last night.

'You and that Mr Simpson were dancing a lot. I heard people remarking on it. You better watch or you'll set the tongues wagging.'

My face grew pink. I hadn't realised it was so noticeable.

'I was only trying to get him to enjoy himself, *Mathair*. If he enjoyed the ceilidh, then he would be likely to socialise more. He must be lonely in that big house all by himself.'

'Don't embarrass the girl, Marion. She and Mr Simpson are two single people. If they want to enjoy each other's company, they're not harming anyone.'

'Chrissie's hardly a girl, Angus. She'll be forty-eight on her next birthday, but she's acting like a young thing looking for a husband.'

'Our daughter's been a widow for nearly fourteen years now. I think it would be a wonderful thing if Chrissie could find someone to love. Heather's growing up and will be off her hands in the next few years. So, it's time for her to think about herself.'

My mother frowned.

'We need her on the croft, Angus. Neither of us is getting any younger.'

'I am here, you know. Stop talking about me like I'm not. And you don't need to worry. Fin and I are just friends.'

But I knew from my feverish night and my excited anticipation of seeing Fin again that I wanted us to be more than just friends.

'Whose just friends?' asked Roddy, strolling into the kitchen. He looked the way I felt.

'Your mother and Mr Simpson.'

'Well,' he said, frowning in my direction. 'I think you looked like more than just friends. I hope you're not thinking of marrying again *Mathair*. My father would turn in his grave.'

Without warning, I burst into tears and ran from the room. I felt so bad at the thought of Roderick and these new feelings I was having. How could I betray Roderick like that? He had always been the kindest of husbands. He didn't deserve it.

There was a quiet knock on my door and Roddy walked in.

'Sorry *Mathair*. I was only joking. I didn't mean to upset you. It would please *Athair,* I'm sure, if you met someone who would make you happy.'

'Och Roddy, I don't know why everyone thinks there's something going on between Fin and me. There honestly isn't. We're work colleagues and friends only.'

I knew I was lying, but I couldn't let my son know I was falling in love. Nothing could come of it.

'Remember how you could tell there was something going on for Donald and Mary before they even knew? Well, that's how I feel about you and Mr Simpson. I could see the spark. It reminded me of when I used to go dancing with Theresa.'

'That's the second time you've mentioned Theresa, son. Are you still thinking about her? I thought you had got over her a long time ago.'

'I thought so, too. But being over in Spain and seeing so much loss of life has made me think. Life's too short not to grab what you want while you can. It's made me wonder if I should have married Theresa despite the differences between us. There's been no one else like her.'

'Not even Mary?'

'I think perhaps I fell for Mary as a way of getting over Theresa. I feel so ashamed when I think about how I treated Mary and Donald.'

I didn't like the sound of that. Had something happened between him and Mary?

'What do you mean, Roddy?'

He looked at me as if he was about to tell me something, but then thought better of it and turned towards the door.

'Och nothing, *Mathair*. Nothing for you to worry about. I just meant it was rather mean of me falling for my brother's fiancé. But you don't need to worry about that with Mr Simpson. The two of you are free agents and can do whatever you like.'

Was what Roddy said true? Could we just do what we liked? If Fin felt like me, he would feel he was betraying Ruth. And what about his girls? They might object to their father marrying again. Although Roddy had said he was joking about saying his father would turn in his grave, he wouldn't have said it unless he had thought about it. And then there were my mother and father. They weren't getting any younger. I couldn't just up and leave them to fend on their own. To complicate matters, I was kind of in the same position as Roddy had been with Theresa. Would it be alright for me to marry someone who didn't even believe in God, let alone come from a different religion?

My thoughts went back to what he had said about feeling guilty about Mary, and it made me wonder if they had become intimate. Mary had a baby almost exactly nine months after she married Donald. What if she and Roddy had been involved with each other intimately? The baby might be his. It made me think back to Roderick and how he never knew if the first Heather was his daughter or if James Adams was her father. If Fin and I began a relationship, I would need to tell him all our family secrets. I shivered at the thought. I couldn't tell Fin the truth without telling Heather.

CHAPTER SEVENTEEN

My heart was in my mouth when I walked to work after the new year holiday. It was only a day since I'd seen Fin, but it felt longer. I wondered how he would be when I got in. Would he acknowledge what had happened between us, or would he just get on with work as usual? As things turned out, we didn't have any time to talk as people were queuing up outside and they kept us busy right until closing time. Everyone who came in talked about the ceilidh and what a good time they'd had. I chatted to the customers as I served them and agreed what a great time I'd had too. But not Fin. He seemed distracted, and I noticed he made several mistakes when giving out money or stamps. Perhaps it was because Morag and some of the other women from the Rural teased me about how much Fin and I had danced together. I joked back, trying to make light of it. But it seemed the tongues were already wagging, and it obviously made Fin uncomfortable.

At last, it was time to shut up the shop. We put everything away without a word spoken between us, and then it was time for me to go home. Was he going to let me go without saying anything? Was he waiting for me to speak? My eyes nipped with tears and my fingers fumbled as I tried to button up my coat. I was so busy concentrating on what I was doing; it was only when I felt his hands on mine that I realised he was standing in front of me. My knees trembled, and I had to swallow the lump that had formed in my throat.

'Chrissie.'

'Fin.'

'We need to talk. Why don't you take your coat off and we'll have a cup of tea?'

I nodded and fumbled with my buttons again.

'Here, let me do it.'

His eyes were tender as he looked into mine and a smile played on his lips as he slowly undid my buttons. The action was incredibly arousing, and I grew lightheaded as I thought about what it would be like to be undressed by him.

'Are you alright, Chrissie? You look as if you're going to pass out. Here, let me help you into the kitchen and I'll get the tea on. It's been a long day.'

I gratefully leaned on his arm and was relieved when he placed a cup of hot, sweet tea in front of me. It tasted wonderful, and I drank it all up almost in one go.

'I can see you enjoyed that. Would you like another?'

'No, Fin. Thank you. You said we needed to talk.'

'Yes.'

He stood up and walked over to pour another cup of tea for himself, not looking at me and not saying anything. I watched as he ran his fingers through his hair and was at once reminded of Roderick. He used to do the same when he felt agitated about something. What would he be thinking just now if he was looking down on me? Would he be happy for me, or would he be jealous that I was becoming attracted to another man? My thoughts then moved on to what would happen if Fin and I got married. What would happen in Heaven? Would Fin spend eternity with Ruth, and would I spend eternity with Roderick? It all felt suddenly wrong, and I jumped up, knocking my cup off my saucer. The noise startled us both, but it didn't stop me from making my escape.

'I need to get home, Fin. That cup of tea has worked its magic. Let's have that talk tomorrow, shall we?'

'No. Let's have it now, Chrissie. Please.'

I sat down again, and he sat opposite me.

'I have feelings for you Chrissie and I think you have feelings for me too.'

He took my hands in his, and I loved the feeling of his skin on mine.

'Oh Fin, I do have feelings for you. But it's impossible.'

'Why?'

'I don't know, it just is. I feel like I'm betraying Roderick. And I have my family to consider. Heather is still young, and my mother and father aren't getting any younger. They need me.'

'I need you,' he said, his voice filled with longing. 'You have no idea how much I loved the other night when we danced. I haven't felt this alive and happy since ... I was going to say I don't know when, but of course I do.'

'Since Ruth was alive?'

'Yes.'

His fingers traced my cheek, then my lips. I trembled. Fourteen years had passed since Roderick's death, and he was the only man I'd ever known intimately. I was transported back to my teenage years, feeling the same mix of excitement and uncertainty that accompanies a first kiss. What was I doing? I was a forty-seven-year-old woman with responsibilities.

'I can't Fin. I need to go now before things get out of hand.'

He looked at me as I jumped up from the table and pulled my coat on, disappointment and surprise written plainly on his face. But he let me go. However, when I was lying in bed that night, how I wished he hadn't. Another restless night followed as I imagined his lips on mine and when I eventually fell asleep, I dreamed of him doing more than kissing.

CHAPTER EIGHTEEN

When I went into work the next day, I half hoped Fin would try to kiss me again, but he didn't, despite my apologising for leaving so suddenly. He was distant and hardly said two words. We were back to where we had been when he first arrived in North Uist. When Sunday came, he didn't meet me for a walk as he usually did. Something inside me died a little, but then I went on the defensive. Well, if that was how he wanted to play it. He was being childish, but then most men were when they didn't get their own way. It was all for the best. It wouldn't have worked out, anyway. But the next few months were torture. I was restless and short-tempered all the time. Not in work. I didn't let Fin see how I was feeling, but at home, it was a different story. It was so bad my mother took me aside one day.

'What's wrong Chrissie? You're not yourself these days.'

'What do you mean? I'm just the way I've always been. Being the dutiful daughter, doing what I can to help around the croft.'

'That's what I mean. The way you say that is as if you resent being here on the croft with us. You never used to feel like that.'

'How do you know how I used to feel? I don't tell you everything, *Mathair*.'

'No, you clearly don't,' said my mother, matching my tone. 'There's something bothering you, my girl, and I'm going to get to the bottom of it.'

'I'm going out for a walk. I can't be doing with this.'

I pulled on my coat and ran out the door. I almost bumped into my father, who was just coming back from preparing the ground for the planting season.

'Hey, where are you off to in such a hurry?'

'Can't I go for a walk without everyone questioning me all the time?'

He looked hurt and puzzled, and I felt bad as I noticed as if for the first time, how wrinkled and weatherworn his face was, how bent over his body was from the outdoor work. He wasn't getting any younger and here I was shouting at him. What on earth was I doing, letting my feelings for a man get the better of me? I decided there and then I was going to hand in my notice. Seeing Fin almost every day was unhealthy. I would get over him quicker if I didn't see him and I could do more to help round the croft.

I apologised to my mother and father when I arrived back from my walk and told them I had decided to give up my job and help more on the croft.

'But you love your job. You'll be bored if you're here with us all the time. That's why you got a job in the first place,' said my mother.

'Well, maybe I'll get another job. But I can't work with that man any longer.'

'I thought you and him were getting on like a house on fire. Sure, a few months ago, your mother was worried you were getting serious about each other. What's happened?' said my father, winking at my mother. She shook her head at him as if to say, *don't get her hackles up.*

Instead of my hackles going up, all my defences left me, and I burst into tears.

'See what you've done, Angus,' said my mother, coming over and giving me a hug. 'There, there *mo graidh.* Tell your *mamaidh* what's wrong.'

I realised then no matter how old we are, there's nothing more comforting than a mother's hug.

'Och *Mamaidh.* I've made such a mess of everything. Fin told me he had feelings for me, but I said we couldn't be together, and he didn't even try to change my mind. The last few months have been so hard trying to pretend I don't care. But I do care. I love him.'

'Then you must tell him how you feel. Give him a chance to make things right with you,' she said, wiping my tears away with her apron. It smelled of mint imperials, the sweets she kept in her apron pocket.

'But I thought you didn't want me to marry again. It would mean me leaving the croft and you said you couldn't manage without me.'

'I know, but I was just being selfish. You deserve some happiness, Chrissie. You've not had an easy life and if this Findlay Simpson is the one who can give you some happiness, then you have my blessing.'

My heart swelled with love for my parents. They had always stood by me despite all the troubles I'd brought to their door.

'Thanks, *Mamaidh*. Thanks, *Dadaidh*.'

'You better tell him how you feel before it's too late. For all you know, he might feel the same as you and ask the post office for a move away from the island.'

Fright gripped me when my father said these words. Now that I'd admitted to them how I felt, it had become real. I couldn't live without Fin in my life.

As I made my way to work the next day, I felt lighter. I was going to make things right with Fin. My heart fluttered with anticipation, but when I got in, he was waiting for me, his face dour and serious, and asked me to come through to the back.

'I've something to tell you, Chrissie.'

'And I've got something to tell you too, Fin. I want to…'

'I've asked for a transfer. I can't go on like this any longer,' he said, cutting me off.

'But…'

'You must have noticed these past few months have been difficult for me.'

'And…'

'Did you think I didn't have the same doubts as you? We could have worked through them. But no, you just gave up without trying.'

He looked at me, his brows drawn down and his lips pursed.

'Well, aren't you going to say anything?'

'I can't get a word in edgeways. But really, I don't want to talk.'

I moved towards him, and he took me in his arms and kissed me. It was a life-changing kiss. So gentle to begin with, then so urgent. Our lips and bodies pressed into one another, and I could feel his desire. I wanted to remove his clothes and feel his skin against mine. But was that the right thing to do? I didn't know. These were unchartered waters for me. Was Fin feeling the same, or had he been with a lot of girls before he met Ruth? Was he an experienced lover? His next words told me as he drew back and gazed at me with sparkling eyes.

'I'm not sure what to do, Chrissie. The only woman I've ever been with is Ruth. All I know is I've got an overwhelming need to undress you and make love to you.'

Just then, there was a banging on the door. It was opening time for the post office. He kissed me again, and I felt my knees go weak. Then he laughed.

'I hope it's a busy morning. I can't wait till we close at lunchtime,' he said, straightening his tie.

'Neither can I,' I said, tingling with anticipation.

As soon as we closed the doors at lunchtime, he took my hand and led me upstairs to his bed. As we undressed each other, I didn't think about the lumps and bumps of my forty-something body. I felt like a twenty-year-old again. He made me feel so alive, so desired. Eventually, exhausted, we lay back in his bed, gazing in wonder at one another. There was no need for words. Our bodies had said it all. I wanted us to stay like this forever, but duty called. Someone was already knocking on the door. It was Morag Campbell.

'Is everything alright, Mr Simpson? I thought I could hear someone crying.'

I felt my face go crimson but luckily I was still in the back shop, or I would have given the game away to Morag.

'Everything is fine, Mrs Campbell. Perhaps it was a cat you heard. What can I get you this fine afternoon?'

It was a fine afternoon indeed.

CHAPTER NINETEEN

The next few months went by in a blur. I felt I was floating on air, as they say. But it's the only way to describe how I felt. Nothing else but Fin mattered. I even forgot about the outstanding business of telling Heather the truth. People remarked on how well I looked, and my mother said I had a definite bloom in my cheeks. I was a much happier person than I had been and went about doing my chores on the croft with a cheerful smile on my face and a spring in my step.

'What will happen now, Chrissie? I can see how happy the man is making you. Will he marry you?'

'Och *Mathair*. We've only just got together. Can't we have a little longer before we must think of practical things like marriage?'

'Practical is it? I thought with you being so in love, you would want to have a hasty marriage so that you and he could become close.'

I blushed, and her eyes narrowed.

'Unless, of course, you're giving him what he wants without having a ring on your finger.'

'It's what we both want, *Mathair*. Desire isn't one-sided. Women have needs too.'

She harrumphed.

'Well, at least we don't need to worry about you having a child out of wedlock anymore.'

I just smiled. It was one benefit of falling in love at my age.

Fin and I got to know each other in depth, not only physically, but we also shared our life stories. I realised I wasn't the only one with complicated family relationships. When I asked him how Ruth had died, I realised it was complicated from the way he looked away from me and wrung his hands.

'You don't need to tell me, Fin. I can see it's difficult for you.'

'But I want to tell you, Chrissie. I want you to know everything about me and I want to know everything about you. That's the way it should be in a marriage. No secrets.'

My mother would be pleased that he was talking about marriage, but I was apprehensive. If he was sharing his secrets, I would need to share mine. Trying to put off the moment, I smiled coyly and said, 'Marriage?'

'Well, don't you want to marry me? Do you only want to have your wicked way with me?'

'At this moment, yes.'

He pulled me into his arms, and for the moment, we shared no more secrets. But I couldn't put it off forever.

Not long after when it was coming up to the summer holidays and Heather was due home, we spoke again.

'I would like to tell Heather about us, Fin. Is that okay with you?'

'Yes, of course. I want to tell Rosie and Daisy too. In fact, I would like us to go down to Glasgow during the holidays so that you can meet my mother and we can tell my family. After that, maybe we could set a date for the wedding.'

'Then there are things I need to tell you, Fin. You said there should be no secrets in a marriage.'

He took me in his arms and looked at me with a light-hearted smile. He clearly thought I had no deep, dark secrets to share. Little did he know. I started off by telling him about Roderick's past and the experiences he had during his early years in Canada. How James Adams had been about to shoot him in the back when the bartender shot him instead. I then talked about Lily and Heather and how he was never sure if Heather was his daughter or James Adams' daughter.

'It must have been a terrible shock for you to find all this out when you went to Canada, Chrissie. How on earth did you cope?'

'Not well. I think I had a kind of breakdown, but I recovered and made the best of it. And Roderick and I grew to love each other. It was when he caught tuberculosis that things went wrong.'

I then explained about Colin Donaldson and how he had taken advantage of Heather and how she had died having his baby.

'We thought it was best to pretend that Donald was our son when we came home so that he wouldn't need to live with the stigma of illegitimacy.'

'I can see why you would do that.'

'But when Colin was injured in the war and realised he could have no children, he claimed Donald as his son. It was such a scandal, and we were terrified he would take Donald from us, and we would have no part to play in his life.'

Tears were pricking my eyes as I talked about these terrible memories.

'Roderick and I thought our troubles were over when Colin died of the influenza and set up a trust with us as guardians to look after Donald.'

'But it sounds as if your troubles weren't over. What happened then?

'Bunty Hepworth came into our lives.'

His face was incredulous as I told him all that she had done. Then I stalled. It was coming to where I would need to tell him about Heather. But how could I? I hadn't told my wee girl the truth. How could I tell Fin? So, I told him only what I'd told Heather. It was a huge mistake, and it came back to haunt me.

'Your turn now.'

We sat side-by-side on the couch, he with his arm around me and me with my head resting on his shoulder. His voice took on a distant tone as he recalled the terrible memory of what had happened to Ruth.

'The post office had sent me to a lovely wee town in the Borders. We were happy there until disaster struck.'

I could feel his body tensing as he spoke.

'Take your time, darling.'

'It was a boiling summer day. I was working and Ruth took the girls down to the river, hoping to cool off. She came in to tell me where they were going. It was the last time I saw her.'

He shuddered, and his voice broke. It took him a minute or two before he could continue. My heart ached for him. She must have drowned in the river.

'There are places on the riverbank that are shallow, and you can go in for a paddle and that's where they went. I'm not exactly sure what happened as I got the story from Rosie, but it sounds like Ruth must have fallen asleep and Daisy went further into the river than she should have. She slipped on a stone and fell into the water. It was deep in that spot and she went under. Rosie screamed and ran in after her. The next thing Rosie remembers is her mother pulling her from the water and setting her on the bank, then going back for Daisy. But it was a man who pulled Daisy from the water. Her mother had disappeared.'

His shoulders were shaking, and tears were streaming from his eyes.

'Oh Fin.'

I reached my fingers up to his cheeks and brushed his tears away. There was nothing I could say that would make him feel better.

'But that's not the worst of it, Chrissie,' he sobbed. 'I blame Daisy for her mother's death. That's why I asked the Post Office for a move and why the girls stayed with their grandparents. I couldn't bear to be near her.'

He put his head in his hands, and I held him close as his body shook with grief. No wonder Daisy was the way she was. She must blame herself for her mother's death, too. Poor girl. I had misjudged her.

CHAPTER TWENTY

It didn't surprise Heather when her mother told her she was going to marry Mr Simpson. Whenever her mother wrote to her at school, she would always mention something about her boss. She wondered what it would be like to have a father. Her grandfather was the only father she'd ever known, and she was happy with that. She didn't really want another father. Would she have to move into the post office when her mother married Mr Simpson? She didn't want that either. Her life was on the croft. She had never envisaged her life being anywhere else, unlike Catriona, who was always going on about moving to Edinburgh when she left school. They only had another year to do before they could leave and Heather intended applying for a place at the Glasgow and West of Scotland College of Domestic Science, or the Dough School as it was called. She had no wish to go to university like Donald and Roddy. She preferred practical learning. Things that were useful. Books and reading were just for fun. When she had finished her course, she would come back and find work as a cook or a baker.

Heather cycled over to visit Catriona at Carinish one day. She couldn't wait to tell her the news about her mother. But when she did, Catriona was shocked and let out a squeal.

'But your mother's a *Cailleach*. Why would she want to get married again?'

Heather hadn't thought about that, but she had turned forty-eight on her last birthday, so Catriona was right.

'Can you imagine them kissing and doing other things?'

'No Catriona. And I don't want to.'

The thought of what men and women did together made her squeamish. Their biology teacher had explained all about the reproductive system and how babies were made. When she took her monthlies, her mother had tried to explain to her what it all meant, but she had been embarrassed and only half listened. However, she knew enough to know she didn't want to think about her mother and Mr Simpson doing that.

'So, I hope that doesn't mean you'll be leaving North Uist and moving to Glasgow. That's where Mr Simpson comes from, isn't it?'

Heather hadn't thought of that either. It had been bad enough thinking she might have to move into the post office. Her stomach clenched. This marriage business might have a lot of repercussions she hadn't thought about. She would need to speak to her mother urgently.

'Whose getting married?' said a boy's voice. It was Donald John McLeod, a boy who went to Portree High School with them. Heather didn't like him.

'Heather's mother,' said Catriona, smiling at Donald John. A reason Heather didn't like him was because she thought Catriona liked him too much. She was always making excuses to talk to him and when it was the ladies' choice at the school dance, she chose him this year. She and Catriona had always danced the ladies' choice together at the end of the term dance.

'Wait till my granny hears. It'll be the talk of the island,' said Donald John, leaning his bike against the wall and taking out a cigarette.

Heather looked at him with disgust. She hated people who smoked cigarettes. He lit the cigarette and blew the smoke out the side of his mouth.

'Do you two want to come down to Clachan Stores with me?'

'No,' said Heather. 'Yes,' said Catriona.

They looked at each other.

'Come on Heather. It'll give us something to do,' said Catriona.

'I've got some pocket money, so I'll buy you a sweetie,' said Donald John.

'No thanks, Donald John. I think I'll just go home. It was Catriona I came to see, not you.'

'Och well. Your loss,' he said. 'Come on, Catriona.'

Catriona had the good grace to look embarrassed, but it didn't stop her mounting her bike and cycling away with him.

CHAPTER TWENTY-ONE

It surprised me when Heather arrived home early. She told me she was spending the day with Catriona, but it was only just after lunch when she came into the post office. She had a grumpy look on her face, and I wondered what had happened.

'Hello Heather. What are you doing here? I thought you were spending the day with Catriona.'

'I was, but that Donald John McLeod turned up and asked us to go to Clachan Stores with him.'

'And you didn't want to go?'

'No. I don't like him. He smokes, you know. I've a good mind to tell his *mamaidh*.'

'Is that the only reason you don't like him? Smoking's not so bad. Your grandad smokes.'

'He smokes a pipe, and I don't mind that. In fact, I like the smell of *Seanair's* pipe.'

She made a face and then continued.

'I think Catriona's becoming too pally with him. You know she asked him to dance at the end of term dance this year.'

I kept my face straight but smiled inwardly. My little girl was jealous. But she and Catriona would soon be fifteen, so it didn't surprise me that Catriona was friendly with a boy. She was more worldly than Heather, who was immature for her age. Long may it continue. The thought of her having a boyfriend and, heaven forbid, doing what Fin and I were doing was not a comforting thought. But it was a difficult time. Best friends were so important in a young girl's life, and if Heather felt Catriona was putting Donald John before their friendship, it must be upsetting for her. I would keep her busy and hopefully take her mind off it.

'Could you help me in the post office today? I could do with someone to tidy up the paperwork.'

Fin was away to the bank and then would catch up with the accounts when he came back, so I was in the post office on my own.

'Yes, okay.'

While we were working, we chatted away amiably and then suddenly she got back to the subject of Catriona.

'Do you know what Catriona said when I told her you and Mr Simpson were getting married?'

'No. What did she say?'

'She said you were too old to get married.'

I laughed.

'Well, I am older than most brides, but I don't think you're ever too old to get married if you love someone.'

'She also said you might move to Glasgow with Mr Simpson.'

'It's possible. But really, it will be up to the Post Office where they send Fin.'

'And you don't mind?'

As I looked at her worried little face, I realised she was anxious about the whole marriage thing and what would happen to her. When I remembered how upset she'd been when she thought I was dying, I knew I had to reassure her. I didn't want her going off the rails again like she had done last year.

'You know you would come with us. We wouldn't leave you behind if that's what's worrying you?'

'No, it didn't enter my mind that you would leave me behind. I am your daughter, after all.'

She put her hand on her hip and made a face at me when she said this. I was glad she felt like that. That she felt secure. Would she lose all that when I told her I wasn't her mother? I dreaded telling her the truth, but I would need to.

'I mean, I wouldn't mind moving to Glasgow as I want to go to the Dough School when I finish school next year, so that would be okay. But what would I do if they move you to Manchester or London or some other place miles and miles away from Scotland?'

'I'm sure there are cookery schools in other parts of the country you could apply to.'

She considered that, then said.

'What about the croft and *Seanmhair* and *Seanair?* How will they manage without us?'

I worried about that too, but they had told me I must do what made me happy. And who knows, maybe the post office would keep Fin on the island.

'They've given their blessing to me marrying Fin and have said they'll get someone in to lend a hand. You know Archie Campbell comes into help sometimes already, so we would just increase the amount of hours he does.'

'And then once I finish college, I'll come back and live with them.'

I laughed.

'What? You don't want to stay with me and Fin. Shameful.'

'Och *Mamaidh*, don't pretend you want your daughter, who will be fit enough to look after herself, hanging about with you and your new husband.'

'You're a good girl, Heather. But seriously, is that what you want to do? You're not just doing it out of duty?'

'Don't be silly *Mamaidh*. I love living on the croft and on this small island. I never want to leave but am happy to do so to learn my trade.'

My little Uist girl. I was glad she felt that way and it comforted me to know she would come back and live on the croft. Johnny would have been next in line to inherit it when my father died, but as he wasn't here, it was only fitting that his daughter should be the one to take on the croft when my father passed. It made me sad when I thought about leaving my home, but there was an entire world out there I knew nothing about, and it would be good to explore it with my new husband.

CHAPTER TWENTY-TWO

Once Fin and I decided we would marry, he wanted to go to Glasgow and tell his family so that we could set a date. He didn't want to make them think it was all settled before he'd even told them about us. We went in August, just before Heather was due to go back to Portree. Fin had written to his mother and the girls to tell them he had news, but didn't say what it was. We went to see his mother and sister first, and they seemed genuinely happy for us. But I got the opposite impression when his mother had a quiet word with me when Fin went out to get a newspaper.

'Has Findlay told you what happened to Ruth?'

'Yes, such a terrible thing to happen.'

'He's never been the same since and it has affected his relationship with his daughters. I was hoping as time passed he could reconcile with them, but he's met you and I think you will take all his attention now.'

Did she mean she would prefer that he hadn't met me? I wasn't sure, but sought to reassure her.

'I think I know how difficult it's been for Fin, Mrs Simpson. But I will do my best to help him. Family is the most important thing to me and now that we are to be married, Fin's family will be just as important as my own.'

'I hope what you say is true. My son deserves some happiness, Chrissie. Please don't let him down.'

I had no intention of letting him down, but I did.

When we went to Ruth's parents to tell them and the girls our news, they were waiting for him. My heart sank as I noticed the dismay on their faces when they saw I was with him. All had gone well with my family, so there was no reason to think there would be any objections on his side. But, of course, I was wrong. The family dynamics between Fin and his daughters was complicated.

'But you can't marry, Chrissie. She's got a young daughter to look after,' said Rosie.

'Well, that's alright. I'll look after her too.'

'But you haven't looked after us, Daddy,' said Daisy. 'You left us here in Glasgow and went off to that godforsaken island.'

'We might come to live in Glasgow, and I can see more of you then.'

'Has meeting Mrs Macdonald changed how you feel about me then?' she asked quietly. 'Do you no longer blame me for Mummy's death?'

There was a hush as the elephant in the room was spoken, probably for the first time. Poor Daisy. I felt so sorry for her. What a burden to carry. And the thing is, what she said was true, but Fin denied it, of course.

'That's not true Daisy.'

'It is true, Daddy. I know you couldn't stand the sight of me. I know you blamed me and that's why you left us.'

'I was just overwhelmed with grief, and I thought you and Rosie would be better off with your grandparents.'

'We were overwhelmed with grief too, Daddy,' said Rosie. 'Our Mummy had just died in a terrible accident. We needed you.'

The girls were in tears, and Fin wasn't far behind them. Ruth's parents looked as uncomfortable as I felt. I didn't want to say anything in case I made matters worse, so just sat mute.

'Girls, girls,' said Mrs Jacobs. 'This is a discussion you need to have with your father alone. Mrs Macdonald, your grandfather, and I can't be part of it. And it has no bearing on your father's news that he and Mrs Macdonald are to be married. Your father has been on his own for a long time now and your mummy would be happy that he has found someone to love and care for him.'

'And besides,' continued Mr Jacobs, 'you girls are all grown up now and will make your own way in the world. No doubt you will meet someone you want to marry so it's unfair of you not to support your father. I think we should raise a toast to their happiness.'

I was relieved they had intervened, but the next hour was distinctly uncomfortable. Mr Jacobs poured us all a glass of sherry and proposed a toast to Fin and my happiness. The girls didn't join in, but like the rest of us, they downed their sherry quickly, obviously in need of the soothing effect that some alcohol would bring. Fin arranged to meet the girls the next day and he and I made our way to Katie and Maude's house, where we were going to spend a couple of days before returning home. We were both upset at how the girls had reacted and Fin kept apologising.

'There's no need to apologise, Fin. We should have expected this reaction. You told me yourself how you feel about Daisy, and she's obviously sensed your resentment since the accident happened. You need to sort this out with her. It's not fair to her and it's not fair to you or me. I don't want to go into our marriage unless everyone gives their blessing.'

I thought matters couldn't get any worse, but when we arrived, Katie handed me a telegram. My heart rose to my mouth. Had something happened to my mother or father? I ripped the telegram open and read:

RETURN HOME IMMEDIATELY – STOP – JOHNNY IS HERE – STOP.

'What is it, Chrissie,' asked Fin. 'Has something happened back home?'

'My brother Johnny has arrived home from Canada. Something must be wrong. I'm sorry, Fin, but I'm going to have to go home right away.'

'What's the hurry? We're due back at the end of the week, anyway.'

My mind was racing. If Johnny told Heather he was her father, she'd be so distressed. I had to get back before he said anything. But how could I explain that to Fin? How I wished I'd told him about Heather when I had the chance. What an idiot I was.

'I know. But you need to meet up with your girls without me being there and obviously there's some crisis or my mother wouldn't have sent me a telegram.'

'Okay. But I was looking forward to having some relaxing time with you now that we've told everyone our news.'

'I don't think you'll be very relaxed, Fin, until you sort things out with your girls. Give them the time you would have spent with me. They'll appreciate it.'

'You're a wise woman, Chrissie Macdonald. I can't wait to make you my wife.'

I hoped he would still feel the same when I told him the real reason I needed to get home.

CHAPTER TWENTY-THREE

Heather was looking forward to going back to school. She and Catriona had drifted apart a bit because of her friendship with Donald John McLeod, so she'd made friends with some other girls during the holidays who were in her dorm. Having several girlfriends wasn't the same as having one special friend like Catriona, but they would do. So, it surprised her when Catriona turned up unexpectedly at the croft one day. She was helping her granny churn butter when she heard Catriona's voice calling her name.

'That sounds like Catriona, *Seanmhair*. Is it alright if I see what she wants?'

'Aye, on you go.'

Catriona was standing in the yard and her bike was lying on the ground as if she had just jumped off it and left it where it fell. Her chest was moving up and down as if she had been pedalling really fast.

'Why are you so out of breath, Catriona? Has someone been chasing you?'

'No. But I've got something to tell you and I had to come right away.'

Heather felt a flutter of fear. What was it? Was she going to say she didn't want to be her friend at all now? Och, I'm just being daft. She wouldn't ride all this way just to tell me that.

'What is it? Don't keep me in suspense.'

Catriona looked round, then said, 'Do you remember you told me your Uncle Johnny was the father of Mrs Hepworth's baby?'

Her voice had dropped to a whisper, and Heather had to strain to catch what she was saying.

'Yes. What about it?'

'I told Donald John.'

Heather couldn't speak. It was as if Catriona had punched her in the stomach. To betray her confidence to *him,* of all people. Catriona's eyes filled up, and she looked as if she were going to cry. Well, let her. Imagine betraying her like that.

'And he told his family.'

Heather gawped at Catriona. Oh, no. Mammy would kill her.

'He said he couldn't help it. Apparently, his mother is first cousin to Janet, and they talk about her and Johnny quite a lot. One day his mother said how sad it was that she and Johnny had had no children, and Janet's mother said it was probably his fault because their family was very fertile.'

'And he defended Johnny by telling them he had fathered a child by another woman? I always thought he was an idiot. I don't know what you see in him.'

Catriona's eyes were brimming with tears now and she was wiping them and the snot coming from her nose away with the back of her hand.

'But why have you rushed all this way to tell me? You could have told me when we were going back to school.'

'Janet's mother is on her way over here to see your mother. She wants an explanation.'

'She's on her way here? Now?'

'Yes,' she wailed. 'I'm so sorry Heather. I better go before she comes.'

And with that, she rode away in a cloud of dust, leaving Heather to deal with whatever was going to happen next.

Heather felt relieved that her mother was away to Glasgow to meet Mr Simpson's family when Mrs McLeod turned up. Her poor granny had to deal with her, though, which was unfair. After Mrs McLeod left, her granny sent her to fetch her grandad. He came right away, and she wondered why. Why was Mrs McLeod coming to see her granny so important that she had to send for Grandad? What difference was it going to make to leave it until he came home for his tea? She was miffed when Granny sent her to her room while she talked to Grandad. She was almost fifteen, not a wee lassie. Eventually, they called her down and gave her an explanation, which was really just what her mother had told her. Janet and her family didn't know what had happened between Uncle Johnny and Mrs Hepworth and if Janet found out, she might break up with Johnny. Heather wasn't really that bothered. He deserved all that was coming to him, as far as she was concerned. The gossip would be difficult for Granny, Grandad, and Mammy to deal with, but it was only gossip. It couldn't hurt them. They'd done nothing wrong. It was Uncle Johnny.

But then someone else turned up. It was a couple of days later when he arrived. Heather saw the Lochmaddy Hotel's taxi approaching the croft and wondered who was in it. Maybe her mammy had come back early. She was helping Granny hang out the washing, and they both stopped and watched as the taxi approached. Granny and Heather exchanged puzzled glances as a tall man, wearing a heavy black coat and hat, emerged from the taxi. He leaned in to pay the driver and then went to the boot and took out a suitcase. The man took his hat off and Heather noticed his hair was black and curly like hers. There was something familiar about him, but she couldn't put her finger on what it was. She looked at her granny to see if she knew him, but she was looking as puzzled as Heather felt.

'Aren't you gonna give your son a hug, Mom?' the man said in an accent that sounded like the actors in a film Katie and Maude had taken her to see in Glasgow. He was American.

'Johnny,' Granny cried joyfully, rushing over and taking him in her arms. 'Why didn't you tell us you were coming home?'

Then she turned to me.

'Heather, run and get Grandad. Tell him Johnny has come home.'

She was so full of joy; it was pitiful to see. Imagine being happy to see a man who had got a woman pregnant, then left her to fend for herself.

'Where's Janet?' Heather heard Granny asking as she ushered him into the house.

'She won't be coming, Mom. Our marriage is over.'

She didn't hear the rest of what he said, as she ran to get her grandad, but she felt a little bad that breaking her promise to her mother not to tell anyone about Uncle Johnny had ended up in him and Auntie Janet splitting up. But then she remembered Mrs McLeod had only found out a few days ago, so Uncle Johnny and Auntie Janet must have agreed to split up a few months ago. It was nothing to do with her, so that made her feel better.

Uncle Johnny coming home was like the return of the prodigal son, the way Granny and Grandad fussed over him, killing a chicken, and getting out the whisky as if it were a special occasion.

'Oh, I don't drink anymore,' said Uncle Johnny when Grandad offered him a drink. 'Had a problem with it and promised Janet I would give it up.'

'That's good, son, but why have you and Janet split up then?'

He looked over at Heather and said, 'I'll tell you later.'

She knew that meant she would get sent to bed early so that she couldn't hear what the reason was. When he turned his attention to her, it surprised her to see how his face lit up. He gazed at her in wonder, as if she were the most beautiful girl in the world. It made her uncomfortable.

'And you must be Heather. My you are a beauty. Chrissie sent me your photo, but it doesn't do you justice. So, tell me all about yourself. You must be nearly fifteen now. What are you going to do when you leave school?'

'I'm planning to go to the Glasgow and West of Scotland College of Domestic Science. I want to be a cook or a baker.'

'Great choice. Everyone's gotta eat. I hope you don't plan to live in Glasgow forever. I was hoping we could get to know each other.'

'No, it won't be forever. I'll be coming back to live on the croft. Mammy is marrying Mr Simpson, so Granny and Grandad will need someone to look after them.'

'Your mom's getting married? She never wrote to tell me.'

'Well, you never wrote to tell her you and Auntie Janet had split up and you were coming home.'

'Don't be cheeky, Heather,' said Granny.

'Fair play,' said Uncle Johnny.

They spent the rest of the evening catching up on all Uncle Johnny's news. He told them the Depression hadn't affected Janet as society always needs nurses, but it had been rough for him for a few years. Many of the motor factories had closed, and he had ended up doing odd jobs wherever he could find them.

'Janet was getting fed up with me, but when I told her about you know who, it was the last straw.'

Heather wondered who 'you know who' was, but suspected it was Mrs Hepworth and her baby.

'I already know about you and Mrs Hepworth,' she said. 'You can speak about her in front of me. I don't mind.'

Uncle Johnny's mouth fell open.

'You know?'

'Yes. Mammy told me you were the father of Mrs Hepworth's baby. And if you must know, I think it was a terrible thing you did to that lady.'

'Right Heather, time for bed,' intervened Granny.

'But …'

'NOW.'

When she got a certain look in her eyes, Heather knew there was no arguing with her, so she went. She fully intended earwigging to see what else she could find out, but fell asleep and didn't get the chance.

CHAPTER TWENTY-FOUR

Johnny was waiting at Lochmaddy pier for me when I arrived back in Uist. When I saw him, I had mixed emotions. It was so lovely to see my brother again after all these years, but there was only one reason he was home. He had told Janet, and it was now time to tell Heather. But this was not the way I'd envisioned telling Heather about her parentage. I never dreamed Johnny would come home. I knew telling Heather I had adopted her would upset her, but in my mind she would get over it more easily as her mother and father were out of the picture. But Johnny being here changed all that. Was he intending to take her back to Canada with him? Could he? My mind raced with all the possibilities of how I could stop him from taking my daughter.

'Chrissie,' he said, tears glistening in his eyes. 'Give me a hug.'

As he grabbed me in a bear hug, for a moment I relished the smell and the feel of him. It had been so long. I loved my brother, but I loved my daughter more. I would do anything to protect her from the shock she was about to receive. The only way to help her would be to maintain as much stability in her life as I could. When we had driven out of Lochmaddy, I asked Johnny to stop the buggy. We needed to talk about this before we got home. Heather would go back to school next week, and I needed to sort things out with her before she went.

'Johnny, what the hell are you playing at? Why didn't you write and tell me you were coming? I've been waiting for ages for you to tell me when I could tell Heather the truth and then you just turn up on our doorstep like this.'

'Hey, sis. Calm down. Let's try to talk about this reasonably. We don't matter. It's Heather we need to think about now.'

My blood boiled. How dare he speak to me as if I didn't know we needed to think about Heather? Where had he been all these years? He certainly hadn't been thinking about Heather then.

'You've got a cheek, Johnny MacIntosh. You chose Janet over Heather, so don't come back here all these years later telling me we need to think about Heather. I hope you don't think you're taking her back to Canada with you. I'll fight you all the way.'

'You won't need to fight me, Chrissie. I've no intention of going back to Canada. I'm where I've always wanted to be.'

I suddenly felt sorry for him. All these years living in another country to please someone else. Where was Janet? Why wasn't she with him?

'And what about Janet? Is she coming to join you or is your marriage over?'

'Yes. Things haven't been good between us for a while and when I told her you had Heather, it was the last straw. It also looks as if the news is out that I fathered Bunty's baby. Heather told her friend Catriona, who let the cat out of the bag. Mrs McLeod read the riot act to *Mathair* the other day.'

'Have you told Heather you're her father?'

'No, of course not. What do you take me for? You're her mother. It must be you who tells her.'

'Oh Johnny. This is such a mess. I'm dreading how Heather will react. When she asked me who the father of Bunty's baby was all those months ago, I should have told her the truth then.'

'I know you were protecting me and I'm sorry I didn't come clean with Janet right away. It's my fault it's such a mess. Everything is my fault. I should never have gone with Bunty in the first place.'

'But if you hadn't, we wouldn't have our Heather. She saved me, you know, after Roderick died. She gave me something to live for.'

Tears were pouring down both our cheeks and suddenly I was glad my brother was back, and that Heather was going to find out the truth at last.

But telling her and her reaction was much worse than I think I had ever expected. When I got home and told her I needed to speak to her straight away, she looked fearful. Her next words told me why.

'I'm sorry, *Mamaidh*. I shouldn't have told Catriona. I'm sorry Mrs McLeod found out about Uncle Johnny.'

How I wished that was all I needed to talk to her about. I reassured her I didn't want to talk to her about that and she wasn't in trouble.

We went up to her bedroom, and I asked her to sit on the bed. I kneeled in front of her and took her hands. Her eyes were like saucers as she waited for me to speak. She was clearly terrified, wondering what I was going to say.

'You know I told you about Uncle Johnny being the father of Mrs Hepworth's baby.'

She nodded.

'Well, I should have told you something else then, but I was waiting for Uncle Johnny to let me know he had told Janet, so I didn't. And if I'm being honest, Heather, I was afraid of how you would react.'

She looked at me with a puzzled look on her face.

'What I didn't tell you is that you are that baby. You are Johnny and Mrs Hepworth's baby. I adopted you when you were born.'

The relief I felt at finally telling her the truth erupted and I burst into tears. She sat and looked at me as if she hadn't heard what I'd said. As if there was nothing to say and I begged her to speak, to say something.

'Don't cry Mammy. Everything will be okay. At least you're not dying,' she said.

CHAPTER TWENTY-FIVE

Her mother came home two days after Uncle Johnny arrived at the croft and had hardly got her coat off when she said they needed to have a talk. Heather knew she was in for it. Her mother had obviously heard that Catriona had told Mrs McLeod about Uncle Johnny fathering a child with Mrs Hepworth. Granny, Grandad, and Uncle Johnny were all staring at her, and she was relieved her mother didn't believe in physical punishment as she was sure she would have got a leathering otherwise. Why had she said anything to Catriona? She wasn't even her best friend anymore because of that Donald John McLeod. She decided it would be best to say she was sorry before her mother talked to her. That might calm her down.

'Och Heather. Don't worry about that now. Let's go up to your bedroom so that we can talk. I've got something to tell you.'

That worried her. What was so serious that she couldn't speak to her in front of Granny and Grandad? Butterflies fluttered in her stomach. Perhaps her mother had lied when she said she wasn't ill. Maybe it was as she thought at Easter. Her mother was dying, and she was going to tell her now. But it was worse than that, much, much worse.

'You know I told you about Uncle Johnny being the father of Mrs Hepworth's baby.'

She nodded.

'Well, I should have told you something else then, but I was waiting for Uncle Johnny to let me know he had told Janet, so I didn't. And if I'm being honest, Heather, I was afraid of how you would react.'

Heather didn't understand. Why was her mother scared of how she would react? It was nothing to do with her. But her next words told her it was everything to do with her.

'What I didn't tell you is that you are that baby. You are Johnny and Mrs Hepworth's baby. I adopted you when you were born.'

Heather couldn't speak. Not because she didn't want to, but because she didn't know what to say. Her thoughts were running wild. *I'm illegitimate. I'm adopted. Mammy's not my mammy. I suppose it could be worse. I could have ended up in an orphanage or adopted by some total stranger.* Chrissie's face was streaming with tears, which made her uneasy. It was an unfamiliar experience to see her crying. What was happening? Nothing was the same anymore. Chrissie was the one who was supposed to make her feel better when she cried, not the other way around. So, when her mother asked her to say something, she tried to make light of what she had told her.

'Don't cry mammy. Everything will be okay. At least you're not dying,' she said, trying to make a joke, but the words stuck in her throat as just for a minute, she wished her mother was dying. Then she would still be her mammy, Roderick would be her daddy and Roddy would be her brother. Instead, she was the bastard child of Mrs Hepworth and Uncle Johnny.

'Why didn't you tell me? Why did you keep it a secret? You've always told me to tell the truth and shame the devil. But you've not done that Mammy.'

'I know Heather and I'm so, so sorry. I thought I was protecting you. I didn't want anyone to look down on you. It can be difficult for children who are illegitimate.'

'I don't care if people know I'm illegitimate. I've nothing to be ashamed of. It's Uncle Johnny's fault, as far as I can see. He married someone else and ran off and left my mother on her own.'

Her mother's face crumpled when she said, 'my mother'. But that's what's Mrs Hepworth was, so she didn't see why she couldn't say it.

'Why isn't *he* telling me? He's such a coward. I hate him.'

It was Heather's turn to burst into tears.

'Come here, *mo graidh*. Come here,' her mammy said, taking her in her arms. 'I know this is a terrible shock and it will take time for you to get used to the idea. But it changes nothing. You are my daughter. I love you very much and will always look after you.'

As much as Heather longed to stay in her mother's arms and be comforted, she couldn't. Although Chrissie said nothing had changed, as far as Heather was concerned, it had. This news had turned her world upside down. She wasn't who she thought she was.

'What if I don't want you to look after me? You're about to get married to that Mr Simpson anyway, so you'll be too busy with him to care about me. I'm going downstairs to speak to my father. I want to hear what he has to say.'

She flounced out of the room, slamming the door behind her. When she went into the sitting room, Johnny was standing with her granny and grandad as if they had been waiting for her.

'So, your mother has told you the truth, Heather, has she?' said her father.

'She has, Father, but I'm wondering why you didn't tell me.'

'I thought it would be better coming from your mother. I hardly know you, honey.'

'And whose fault is that?'

The door opened and her mother walked in.

'It certainly isn't my fault. You kept me a secret because you were worried about your marriage. And look at you now. She's left you, anyway. I hate you for what you did to my mother.'

'It wasn't all my fault, Heather.'

'You're as bad as her,' she said, pointing to Chrissie. 'She told me my mother was to blame, too.'

Heather couldn't believe the way she was talking to her mammy. She knew she was being cheeky and unkind, but as far as she was concerned, Chrissie had been unkind to her by not telling her the truth all these years.

'That's enough, Heather,' said her grandad in his sternest voice. 'Don't you dare talk to your mammy like that! She doesn't deserve it. She's looked after you since you were a two-week-old baby, and you should be grateful.'

It was her turn to burst into tears. Her grandad never shouted at her. Granny did sometimes, so she would have accepted a telling off from her better.

'I'm sorry, Grandad. I'm sorry. Please don't shout at me.'

'Come here, ma wee hen. Come here,' he said, taking her in his arms. And suddenly everything felt safe again as she buried her face in his shirt that smelled of him, a mix of pipe smoke, sweat and the fresh outdoor smell of Uist, her home.

CHAPTER TWENTY-SIX

I could hear shouting downstairs and knew Heather was having a go at Johnny. As much as I didn't want to, I had to go down and face the music. I couldn't leave Johnny to deal with her on his own. They barely knew each other. When I went into the room, everyone was standing up and Heather was ranting at Johnny. At that moment, she hated him, and she hated me. And who could blame her? I'd lied to her and when I had the chance to tell her the truth; I'd continued to lie. What kind of mother was I? There was a terrible argument and Heather said some very cruel things to Johnny and to me. Luckily, my father took control. He scolded her for speaking to me with such disrespect, and the anger in his voice was clear. This deeply upset her. He never gave her into trouble. When she burst into tears, he comforted her, and she seemed to settle a little.

It was late when we all went to bed and I thought she wouldn't sleep a wink, but she was out like a light after we said our prayers. I asked God to forgive me for not telling her the truth sooner and asked Him to bring her peace and the strength to cope with this news that was such a shock to her. I thought he had answered my prayers, as she seemed much calmer the next morning, but then she dropped a bombshell when I asked her if she wanted to delay going back to school for a couple of weeks.

'I'm not going back to school, Auntie Chrissie. I'm going to get a job so that I can earn enough money to go to Canada and see my birth mother. Also, I'm not planning to keep this a secret, so you better get ready for the gossips.'

Her words cut through me like a knife. She wasn't my Heather any longer, so I hadn't a clue what to do. How I wished Fin was here. I longed to talk to him about everything, to tell him the truth, to feel the comfort of his arms around me. I never for one minute thought it would annoy him that I hadn't told him the whole truth, as I was too busy thinking how I would tell him we would need to put off the wedding. Heather was in crisis, and I needed to be here for her.

When he came back and I told him everything, he was quiet.

'I can see it's not the right time, Chrissie. You need to be here for Heather. Of course, you do.'

'And it will give you time to build bridges with your girls, too,' I said, trying to show him there were advantages to putting our marriage off. 'How did things go between you after I left?'

'We have a long way to go,' he said, obviously not wanting to talk to me about it. 'But Chrissie, I don't understand why you didn't tell me about Heather when you told me everything else. You told me all about Johnny and Bunty, so it would have been logical for you to tell me about Heather. Why didn't you?'

His voice sounded stiff, like the old Fin, and I looked at him, searching for that loving spark that lit his eyes when he spoke to me. But it wasn't there.

'You lied to me.'

'I didn't lie Fin. I just didn't tell you the whole truth.'

'But we said we wouldn't keep any secrets from each other. I told you about Ruth and how I blamed Daisy. Did you think it was easy for me to tell you that?'

'No, of course, it wasn't. I don't know why I didn't tell you or, more importantly, Heather, the whole truth.'

He flinched when I said that, and I knew I'd made a mistake. I hadn't meant it like that, but it was true. Just now, Heather was my priority, just as his girls were his.

'I was protecting Johnny and Janet, but I can see now that I was wrong.'

'I think you were protecting yourself, as you didn't really want Heather to know the truth in case she rejected you. And I think you didn't tell me because you didn't trust me enough.'

"Oh Fin. Please don't say that. I trust you absolutely. I can't bear that you think that.'

I was in tears again. It felt that crying was all I'd done this last couple of days.

'Look Chrissie. Things are difficult for the both of us just now, so I agree it would be best if we put our marriage on hold. You know I'd asked the post office for a transfer, well I've asked if they could deal with my request sooner rather than later. I've also asked if they could move me to Glasgow, or an area close to it so that I can spend time with my daughters. I'm sure you understand.'

I shivered, painfully aware that I was alone again. No Heather to console me, and no second chance at love. And I had no-one to blame but myself. I should have told Heather I had adopted her right from when she could understand what it meant, and I should have told Fin the whole truth instead of just part of it.

"Yes, I understand. But I don't want you to leave me like this, Fin," I said, my voice filled with desperation. 'You don't know how much I need you, how much I love you.'

My fingers anxiously clutched at the lapels of his jacket, silently pleading for his understanding. But he moved back from me.

'Chrissie, I love you too. But I just don't understand why you didn't tell me. I feel I can't trust you anymore and it breaks my heart.'

His eyes had the old, sad, numb look, and my body slumped with disappointment. I almost stumbled as I turned away from him and he caught me in his arms. Just for a moment, we stood in that embrace, and I prayed to God that we could find our way back to each other. But there was a part of me that was relieved. The mother in me wanted to concentrate on Heather, and I couldn't do that if I was worrying all the time about my relationship with Fin. Things happened for a reason and I believed God would show me that reason at the right time. I obviously had lessons to learn before that time would come.

CHAPTER TWENTY-SEVEN

I've always said God works in mysterious ways, but I never thought Charles Hepworth would be in God's plan for me and Heather. It was a few days after Fin and I had agreed to put our marriage on hold and rethink our relationship. We were both working quietly in the post office: me serving the customers and Fin doing the paperwork. It was like old times. No chat and certainly no anticipation of us getting together in his bed at lunchtime. When the bell tinkled signalling another customer, I was in the back making a cup of tea. I heard a voice I didn't immediately recognise asking Fin for me.

'Hello, is Mrs Macdonald working here today?'

'Yes, she's in the back. I'll just get her. Who shall I say is looking for her?'

'My name's Charles Adams.'

Charles! What was he doing here? I didn't know whether to be pleased or annoyed. He was another player in Heather's story, and I wasn't sure how she would be with him. At home, she was quiet. There had been no more outbursts against Johnny and me, and I was grateful for that. But would seeing Charles Hepworth set her off again? It was he, after all, who had taken her from Bunty and given her to me. It was he who had schemed with me to cover up the truth of her birth.

Fin came through and picked up his tea.

'There's a Charles Adams asking for you. Shall I bring him through here and let you two talk?'

His eyes were softer as he said this. He had obviously worked out he was Bunty's brother, despite his different surname.

'Thanks Fin.'

Charles looked well. The last time I'd seen him was at Donald and Mary's wedding, which was three years ago. He had been quite unpopular with my two boys because he had tried to recruit Donald to spy on his friends, so we had avoided one another. I had never noticed before, but he was quite handsome in a tidy, civil servant kind of way. You would never dream he was a member of MI5. I realised I was pleased to see him. He was part of Heather's story, and I could talk to him freely about her.

'Charles,' I said, giving him a peck on the cheek. 'What brings you to North Uist?'

'Work. The government has assigned me to the Ministry of Defence. With things as they are in Europe, it's only a matter of time before Hitler tries to invade Great Britain.'

'But I can't believe our wee island could play any part in defending the country against Mr Hitler.'

'Well, maybe and maybe not. That's why I'm here. We need to set up airbases to protect the Atlantic and the Hebrides is the ideal spot. We're looking to set up several air bases on these islands.'

'Where are you looking?'

'Sollas, at the north of the island. I understand there's already an airstrip there. My colleagues and I are planning to visit today. But I haven't come here to talk about my work. I've come to ask you and Heather out to dinner tonight. I'm staying at the Lochmaddy Hotel so they will provide a meal in their restaurant.'

'That sounds like a real treat, but there's something I need to tell you, as I'm not sure how Heather will react when she sees you.'

He raised his eyebrows.

'Heather now knows everything about her birth and is really upset, especially with Johnny and me.'

'I see.'

'Johnny's back home as he and his wife Janet are getting a divorce. When she found out he hadn't told her I had adopted Heather, it was the last straw. From what he says, they haven't been getting on for a while, so it's probably for the best.'

'And how do you feel about this? Does he want to get involved in Heather's life after all this time?'

'I wasn't sure how to react when I found out he was back, but to tell you the truth, Charles, I'm glad he's here.'

And what about Heather? How does she feel about her father

coming back into her life?'

'Johnny would love to make up for lost time, but she's so angry at him, partly because he stayed with Janet instead of coming back for her and partly because he left Bunty to fend for herself.'

'I'm quite angry with him myself. I'll have something to say when I see him.'

My heart sank. This was all we needed, a fight between Charles and Johnny.

'Oh Charles. Please don't cause any trouble. Things are so difficult, I couldn't bear it.'

Yet again, I was in tears. Charles put his arms round me and patted me on the back. I leaned into him, finding comfort in his embrace. I hoped he would understand my distress and not get into a fight with Johnny.

'Is everything okay, Chrissie?'

Fin's voice startled me, and I pulled away from Charles. When his gaze met mine, I detected a hint of jealousy simmering in his eyes, which made me feel guilty, and I stammered my reply.

'Yes. I was telling Charles about Heather and how difficult things have been.'

He nodded.

'I'm sorry Chrissie, but the post office is becoming busy, and I wonder if you could come back through once you and Mr Adams have finished speaking.'

'Yes, of course. I'll be right through.'

Turning to Charles, I shook his hand and told him I'd see him that night.

'We can talk more then. Perhaps it's best if you come on your own. It will give us a chance to talk more about Heather and decide what to do for the best.'

I washed my face and went back through to the post office, where there was only one customer waiting. I looked over at Fin, but he was busy shuffling through his paperwork. Despite myself, I felt a brief glow of pleasure that Fin still cared enough for me to feel jealous.

CHAPTER TWENTY-EIGHT

When Auntie Chrissie told her she had met Charles Hepworth, it annoyed Heather he hadn't invited her to dinner too.

'Why wasn't I invited? He is my uncle, after all.'

'I know *mo graidh*, but you've been so up and down recently, I wasn't sure you would be up to it.'

'You mean because it was him who gave me away?'

'Yes.'

'So, he's scared to meet me then?'

'No, of course not. He would love to see you, Heather. But it's your decision.'

Heather thought about it. Did she really want to see the man who'd callously taken her from her mother and given her to another woman to look after? He was as bad as her father in her eyes, so she had no intention of letting him off lightly.

'I'll see him.'

'Okay. I'll invite him round tomorrow night after work. What about school? Are you sure you don't want to go back? I can write to the school and tell them you need some time off.'

'I'll think about it and let you know.'

When she heard Chrissie telling the family Charles Adams was coming for tea, she lingered outside the open door to see their reaction. Her Grandad and Granny just nodded, but her father looked uncomfortable.

'I think I'll make myself scarce. I don't want any unpleasantness.'

Just like him. What a coward, wanting to run away. He was good at that.

'There won't be. Charles has agreed not to cause any trouble. You should stay and face the music.'

'But Heather is so volatile just now. If he says anything about Bunty, it could set her off again.'

'It's only natural, Johnny. Did you think she would welcome you with open arms when she found out you were her father?

She's fifteen. As far as she can see, you chose your life with Janet over her.'

Heather was pleased to see he looked shamefaced.

'I know. You don't know how much I wish I could find a way to make things right with her.'

'Me too. If I'd told her the truth way back when she was a child, she would have grown up knowing I had adopted her. Not had it sprung on her at this late stage.'

Heather's heart was hard as she listened to Chrissie and Johnny discussing her. Too little, too late, in her opinion.

Charles picked Chrissie up from work the following evening in the Lochmaddy Hotel taxi, and they both looked nervous when they came in. There was an awkward moment when Chrissie introduced him to Uncle Johnny, but he recovered quickly and shook his hand. Part of her wished they had been less civilised and had a fight. After they had tea, he asked Heather if he could speak to her on her own.

'I feel I owe you an explanation and I'm sure you must have lots of questions.'

'I do, Uncle Charles.'

She was trying to be composed, but inside she was a bag of nerves as they went through to the front room, normally only used on special occasions. Although she was angry with her uncle for giving her away to Chrissie, she wanted to hear about her birth, about her mother, and about the family she was part of. To her surprise and relief, he was very open and told her all about her mother's family.

'I think you already know about your grandfather's connection with Roderick and my sister's obsession with taking revenge.'

She nodded.

'Do you understand about mental ill-health, Heather?'

'Not really.'

'Then you won't understand how ill your mother was when she gave birth to you. She would never have been able to look after you.'

'Not then, maybe. But once she got better, she could have. Why didn't you and my grandmother look after me until she was okay again?'

'Because of the stigma. Having an illegitimate child would have meant the end of any chance my sister would have had to marry. And, it would have affected your life. Being illegitimate is a heavy burden to carry.'

'But I'll have to carry it now.'

'Only if you tell people. My understanding is that no-one knows, not even Janet's mother.'

She nodded again, but part of her wanted everything out in the open.

'Your mother...'

'You mean Chrissie.'

'Yes, Chrissie. She tells me you don't want to go back to school, and I wonder why that is.'

'I want to save up and go to Canada to see my mother, so I'm going to get a job.'

'You don't need to save up. Your mother would gladly pay for you to go to Canada if that's what you want. Why don't you write to her and ask her?'

Heather wondered why she hadn't thought about that.

'But can she afford to send me the money? I think the fare is very expensive.'

'Your mother is a wealthy woman. She inherited money from my father. But I think as she's a schoolteacher, she would want you to finish your education first, don't you?'

For the first time since she'd found out the truth about her birth, she felt a glimmer of hope. It was going to be possible for her to meet her birth mother without too much difficulty. She thought about Mrs Hepworth and felt a warmth glowing in her tummy. It was she who had helped her win the Mòd prize for singing last year. Perhaps she had known all along Mrs Hepworth was her birth mother.

'If you think my mother would like me to finish my education, then that's what I'll do. I want her to be proud of me.'

'She's already proud of you, Heather. Chrissie has done a good job bringing you up, and I know my sister is grateful to her for looking after you all this time.'

That put her in a mood again. She wasn't about to forgive Chrissie for lying to her all these years.

'I don't care how good a job you think she's done. She's a liar and I'll never forgive her.'

She burst into tears and ran from the room. But later, when she was lying in bed, she decided she would go back to school and she would write to her mother the very next day, asking her if she could visit her in Canada when she had finished school. She also decided she would tell no-one her secret. It was nobody's business but hers.

CHAPTER TWENTY-NINE

My mother, father, and Johnny looked at me with worried faces when we heard Heather barging out the door and running up the stairs to her room. Clearly, things hadn't gone well with Charles. However, when he came through to the kitchen, he was smiling.

'Why are you smiling? It sounds as if things didn't go well,' I said.

'It went fine until I tried to smooth the waters and said what a good job you had done bringing her up.'

He smiled at me sympathetically.

'I think it's going to take a bit of time until she forgives you, but I'm sure she'll come round. You *have* done a good job, Chrissie. She's a lovely young woman.'

My lip trembled. Had I done a good job? If I had, I wouldn't be in the position I'm in now.

'May I ask what you spoke about?'

'Obviously, she knows her father's family through being brought up here,' he said, nodding over at Johnny, who just looked at his feet, 'but she wanted to know about her mother's family, which is only natural. So that was something I could help her with. She wants to visit her mother and I've told her to write to Bunty about that.'

Of course, she would want to visit Bunty, but what if she went to Canada and never came back? Charles must have recognised my distress as he spoke again with an encouraging smile on his face.

'The good news is she's agreed to go back to school. She'd only wanted to get a job so that she could save up and visit Bunty. So, I told her Bunty could easily afford to pay her fare to Canada and wouldn't be happy if she didn't finish school.'

'That's wonderful. Thank you, Charles.'

'And she's considering whether she's going to tell people she's illegitimate. I think that's a good thing, as it may help her understand why you didn't tell her the truth.'

My poor wee girl. What a burden to carry. Although I was pleased Charles seemed to have talked some sense into Heather, every time he said, 'her mother', it was like someone punching me in the stomach and I felt at the end of my tether. I think my father noticed I was becoming distressed and attempted to change the conversation by offering Charles a whisky.

'No, thank you, Mr MacIntosh. I must get back to the hotel. We are moving onto Benbecula tomorrow to look at the airfield there. You realise this is hush, hush, don't you? I would ask you not to tell your neighbours why I'm here.'

He would be lucky. Nothing gets past us islanders and the visiting delegation from the Ministry of Defence staying in the Lochmaddy Hotel was the talk of the place.

'Is there definitely going to be a war then, Mr Adams?' asked my mother. 'I thought Mr Chamberlain was trying to work with Herr Hitler so that he would leave us alone.'

'It is my opinion, Hitler will never stop until he conquers the whole of Europe, including Britain.'

'If you ask me, this policy of appeasement only makes us weaker. We should stand up to Herr Hitler. He's nothing but a bullyboy,' said my father, becoming red in the face.

'If it works, it will prevent war. But I believe Mr Chamberlain knows we don't have the military capability of defending our country just now, so his appeasement policy also buys us time to sort that. That is one reason I'm touring the Hebrides looking for suitable sites to build an airbase.'

'Well, good luck, Mr Adams, and thank you for talking to our Heather,' said Johnny, speaking for the first time. 'She's had a terrible shock, and she needs all the support she can get from her family.'

'Good Luck to you too, Mr MacIntosh.'

They shook hands. I was relieved he and Johnny had been civil to one another. Although Heather was clearly still furious with Johnny and me, at least she had agreed to go back to school, so that was something.

Fin gave me the morning off to see Heather off to school. Charles had said Heather was considering whether to let people know the truth about her birth, but she had said nothing to me about it. So, when we were packing her suitcase for school, I asked her whether she was going to tell her friends about her adoption.

'Tell them I'm illegitimate, you mean Auntie Chrissie.'

'Well yes, I suppose if you tell them you're adopted, you're telling them that, too.'

'I've not decided yet.'

'If you keep calling me Auntie Chrissie, I think people will guess, don't you? I know it must be so hard for you, Heather, but it's hard for me, too. I've been a good mammy to you, haven't I?'

'Yes, I can't deny that. You have. But you've deceived me all these years, so I can't trust you anymore.'

Trust. Such a fragile thing. Heather and Fin had trusted me, and I had let them down by not trusting them with the truth.

'Och Heather, I'm so sorry. Is there anything you want to ask me? I promise you I'll answer truthfully.'

She looked at me, and for a moment, I thought she was going to confide in me.

'I'll still call you mammy until I decide whether I'm going to tell people the truth, so you don't need to worry.'

'I'm not worried about that, Heather. I just want you to do whatever you feel is best for you. You're all that matters now.'

She ignored me and continued.

'I plan to write to my mother and ask her if I can visit her when I finish school. I'm hoping we'll get to know each other by writing letters regularly. So, as I'll be busy doing that, I won't be able to send you as many letters as I normally do.'

I took comfort in knowing that she would still write to me, even if not as often as before.

Catriona's mother was dropping her off and after the girls had boarded the ferry, she turned to me.

'I hear your Johnny's back.'

'Yes, that's right.'

I knew what would come next and didn't want to encourage her.

'Poor Janet. It must have been such a shock for her to find out her husband had fathered a child with someone else. Especially when her and Johnny didn't seem able to.'

'Yes. It is a shame. Well, I'll need to go now, Mrs Mackenzie. I've got to get to work.'

When I arrived at the post office, Fin was working away and didn't look up. My heart ached with a deep, lingering pain. How could he go from loving me so much one minute to being so distant the next? I sighed, and that made him look up.

'Did Heather get off okay?'

'Yes. It's always a wrench when she leaves, but it's so much more so today, with things being the way they are between us. Have you been busy?'

'Not too bad. I'll just go through and sort the mail now. Murdo will be back soon to do the deliveries.'

Customers came in and then Murdo arrived, so I was busy. Lots of people asked me about Johnny being back, but they were discrete enough not to mention him fathering a child with Bunty. I wondered what they would say if they knew Heather was Bunty and Johnny's child. That would be a juicy bit of gossip. But then our family were no strangers to gossip, so I could withstand it, so long as Heather forgave me.

Before I knew it, it was finishing time.

'Before you go, Chrissie, I need to tell you something.'

I looked at Fin expectantly.

'The post office has been in touch in answer to my request to be moved.'

I shivered. So, it was really happening. He was leaving me.

'That's good. It means you'll be able to see Daisy and Rosie now and hopefully build those bridges you talked about.'

My lip trembled, and my eyes smarted with tears. His face softened.

'I'm sorry the way things are between us, Chrissie, but perhaps a break from each other is just what we need.'

I nodded.

'Where are they moving you to? Were they able to offer you a place in Glasgow?'

'It's Clydebank, which is just outside Glasgow, so I'll still be able to see the girls often or they might even come and stay with me.'

'I've heard of it. That's where Mr Singer has his sewing machine factory. When will you leave and what will happen here?'

'I'll go at the end of September and have asked if they could put you in charge until they find a replacement. I hope you don't mind. It will mean you working full time, but I thought it would help distract you from all your worries.'

'That was thoughtful. Thank you. I better go now. See you tomorrow.'

Fin would leave at the end of the month and Heather next year. All I could see ahead were endless years of regret and loneliness. I hadn't felt so low since Roderick died.

'Where are you, God?' I whispered. 'Please don't desert me in my time of need.'

I don't know if God answered my prayer, but out of nowhere, a sense of positivity and purpose gradually replaced the feelings of hopelessness and failure that filled me. My relationship with Fin and Heather was a love worth fighting for, and I would not give up. I had to believe that one day, they would come back to me.

CHAPTER THIRTY

Keeping her adoption a secret was easier than Heather expected. After the way Catriona had betrayed her, she had no wish to share her news with her. But it was lonely not having a best friend to confide in anymore. But then it was lonely knowing you were adopted. Knowing your mother and father had given you away. It wasn't a good start for anyone. She often wondered if they had been in love when they made her. It was unlikely, since her father had married another woman. She often wondered what her life would have been like if Mrs Hepworth and Uncle Johnny had married. Would they have lived in North Uist, or would they have moved to Manchester or even Canada? There were so many other lives she might have lived had they been a normal couple who fell in love, married, and had a child. She sighed.

Although Uncle Charles had said she should write to Mrs Hepworth about visiting her, she hadn't done it yet. She was fearful that Mrs Hepworth might not want her to visit, might want nothing to do with her. Her heart would break if that happened. It was all she could think about and walked around feeling miserable all the time. She didn't realise, but she was letting it affect all the other parts of her life. It must have been obvious to everyone else as Mrs MacGregor asked her to stay behind one day.

'Heather, is something bothering you again? You seem distracted. This is your last year at school and it's important to get your leaving certificate if you want to go to the Dough School.'

'I'm okay, Mrs MacGregor. There's nothing bothering me. It's just taking me a wee while to settle into school again. I'll be fine.'

But she wasn't fine. One day, she bumped into Donald John McLeod. It was the weekend, and she had gone for a walk. Walking alone had become her favourite pastime, as she could think about Mrs Hepworth all the time and not have to make stupid conversation.

'What you up to?' he said.

'What's it to you?'

'Don't be like that, Heather. I was only asking. You're a right pain in the neck these days. No-one can say a word to you, but you bite a person's head off. You're not even friends with Catriona anymore.'

'If you knew what it was like to be me, you would understand.'

'What do you mean?'

'I'm not who everybody thinks I am. That's all I'm going to say.'

'Come on, you can't tell me that and then leave me hanging. Come on, have a fag, and tell me.'

She looked at the packet of cigarettes he pulled from his pocket. Mammy would be annoyed if she took one, but what the heck? Why should she bother with what she thinks? She wasn't even her mother.

'Right, I'll take one. But don't expect me to tell you anything.'

He smiled and lit a cigarette with a box of safety matches, took a draw, and then handed it over to her. The smell of it was horrible, but she wouldn't let that put her off. She put it in her mouth and sucked on it. She could feel the heat going down into her chest and then suddenly it all came rushing up again, and she was coughing and spluttering all over the place. It was just like the time she took the fiery ginger wine that Christmas. Donald John was laughing like mad.

'Here, give me that back. I don't want it wasted. Never mind. Wait till the next time, you'll get used to it.'

Next time. There won't be a next time, she said to herself. But of course, there was, and before long, she was giving Donald John a kiss so that he would give her a cigarette. She didn't like that at first either, but she got used to that too and looked forward to meeting up with him. He stopped her thinking about all the other things on her mind.

She wasn't sure what might have happened with Donald John, but Catriona told Mrs MacGregor she had seen her smoking with Donald John McLeod and that was the end of that. The teacher gave her a severe reprimand, wrote to her mother, and confined her to the girls' accommodation for a month. After Auntie Chrissie received the letter from Mrs MacGregor, she paid Heather a visit. It was so embarrassing. Parents never visited their children at the school unless they were ill. But afterwards, she was glad. She took her to a posh tearoom near to where the girls' accommodation was and treated her to a hot chocolate and a sticky bun. Heather wondered why. Wasn't she here to give her into trouble for smoking and going about with Donald John McLeod?

'So Heather, you know why I'm here, don't you?'

'Yes.'

'I know it's silly to ask what's bothering you, but are you able to talk to me about it? You must have so many thoughts going through your head. Have you confided in Donald John? Is that why you've been hanging about with him?'

Honestly, did Chrissie really think she was going to tell the world she was illegitimate? But as soon as she had the thought, she realised something she hadn't before. She was ashamed of being illegitimate and she wanted to go to Canada so that she could get away from that shame. It was time to write that letter to Mrs Hepworth. It was the only way she would find out if her mother wanted her and the only way she could hide who she was. Uncle Charles had said her mother would want her to do well at school, so that was what she would do. No more hanging about with Donald John.

'What is it, Heather? You look as if you've just realised something.'

'I have *Mamaidh*.'

She noticed Chrissie's face lit up when she said *Mamaidh* and felt a pang of guilt.

'I'd like to keep calling you that so that people don't guess the truth, if you don't mind.'

'I don't mind at all, *mo graidh*.'

'But it will only be in front of other people. You're not my mother, and I won't ever forgive you for lying to me. But I promise you I'll stop smoking and will concentrate on my schoolwork from now on. I want my real *Mamaidh* to be proud of me.'

'So long as you do that, I'll be happy, Heather.'

Heather ignored the tears glistening in Chrissie's eyes. She was too busy thinking about what she would put in her letter to Mrs Hepworth.

A reply from Mrs Hepworth in response to Heather's letter arrived in November and it was clear she wanted her daughter in her life.

My Darling Heather

I was delighted to receive your letter and I am more than happy for you to call me mother rather than Mrs Hepworth. It was also a pleasant surprise to hear that you wish to come visit with me when you finish school. I would welcome that very much. When I met you in Helensburgh at Mary's wedding, I loved you straight away. I thought you were a very agreeable girl and could tell you had been well-cared for. You do not know what a relief it was to know that. Although I could not keep you, not a day went by when I didn't regret that. I constantly wondered where you were and if you were happy. So, I will always be grateful to Chrissie for looking after you. I hope you will be kind to Chrissie and to your father. I understand how you must feel betrayed that Chrissie didn't tell you the truth sooner and that Johnny married Janet rather than me. But we all make mistakes, and I made the biggest one by misinterpreting your father's feelings for me. Forgive Chrissie and your father. I think you'll find you will be much happier if you do.

But as you say, it's now our turn to get to know each other. When you are ready to come to Canada, I will come and fetch you. It will give me the opportunity to visit your grandmother and your Uncle Charles. It will be such fun having you here and you'll also meet your nephew, Harry, who is now a boisterous two-year-old.

Work hard and enjoy your final year at school. You will never have such happy days again. And write to me soon with all your news.

With all my love and affection,
Mother xx

Heather cried when she read her mother's letter. It was marvellous. Her mother loved her and wanted her in her life. She wasn't sure about her advice about forgiving Chrissie and Johnny, though. She wasn't ready to do that yet.

'What are you crying for?' asked Catriona, who had just come into their dorm. 'Who's your letter from?'

Heather quickly folded her letter and put it under her pillow, then wiped her nose.

'It's personal.'

'You can tell me.'

'Are you kidding? You told that Donald John McLeod about my Uncle Johnny, so I'll never confide in you again, Catriona. Don't you know that?'

'Okay. Be like that,' she said, grabbing her script and flouncing out of the room.

Heather followed shortly thereafter. As she and Catriona were performing in the end-of-year play, there was no way of avoiding her. But she would never tell her about her birth mother. She was too precious a secret to share.

1939-1943

SECOND CHANCES

CHAPTER THIRTY-ONE

It was June 1939 when Heather left school and we began to prepare for her visit to Canada. Bunty was coming over to England so that she could see Grace and afterwards travel back from Scotland to Canada with Heather. She had booked their passage for the beginning of August, so I had a couple of months with Heather before she would leave me. I planned to make the most of those few months, as I didn't know if she would ever come home. Bunty told me she would travel up to North Uist to collect Heather and hoped to see Johnny so that they could talk and put matters right between them. I immediately wrote back and told her it would be best if Johnny brought Heather to Glasgow. No-one on the island knew Heather was her daughter and so far as I was aware, she still didn't want anyone to know. When I told Johnny, he was uneasy.

'Why does she want to see me? I don't want to see her. She brought so much trouble into my life.'

'Into all our lives, Johnny.'

He looked shamefaced.

'Yes, I'm sorry. You more than anyone.'

'She says she wants to put things right between you. And, for Heather's sake, I think you should see her and make your peace. It helped when she and I talked at Donald and Mary's wedding.'

Johnny had settled back into crofting life and seemed happy. Well, as happy as he could be in the circumstances. Janet had hired a lawyer to get their divorce underway, and Heather still hated him. Sometimes Johnny complained to me about the way Heather had taken Bunty's side.

'I feel like telling her Bunty was no saint and her having a baby wasn't all my fault.'

He had lost his American twang and spoke mostly in the Gaelic again.

'I don't think that's wise, Johnny. She was angry at you for leaving Bunty before she even knew you were her father.'

'But I knew nothing about it. Bunty only told me on the day I was leaving for Canada. What could I have done?'

'I don't know. I suppose she wants to explain how it was for her and ask for your forgiveness, perhaps. And who knows, Bunty might explain everything to Heather in such a way that it will help her realise it wasn't all your fault.'

His face lit up a little when I said this, and he agreed to take Heather to meet Bunty.

I was now the postmistress of the Lochmaddy Post Office. I'd taken over from Fin temporarily after he moved to Clydebank and when they found it difficult to find a replacement, he encouraged me to apply for the job.

'You worked with Roderick in the post office during the war and you've been working with me for ten years now, so it makes sense.'

When I applied, they wrote telling me they would consider me for the job if I could pass an exam. As well as questions on the rules and regulations of the post office, which I knew off by heart, there were questions on English, Arithmetic, Geography and History. Although it was a long time since I'd been to school, I'd been good at English and Arithmetic and, as a mother, had helped my children with their homework in these other subjects. So, I passed with flying colours. I must confess it rather puffed me up when I received my certificate, confirming that I was now a postmistress and needed to sign the Official Secrets Act. But part of me also wished I hadn't needed to apply for the job and that Fin was still postmaster. Our parting had been bittersweet, and I held on to the hope that we might rekindle our love in the future. It started off very businesslike, with Fin officially handing over the running of the post office to me.

'You know what you're doing, Chrissie, so you shouldn't have any trouble. You've been doing it long enough,' he said with a slight laugh. 'Seriously though, if you need help, please telephone me. I will be on the other end of that telephone through there.'

'I hope you get things sorted with Daisy and Rosie.'

'Thank you. How are you feeling about Heather leaving? It must be hard.'

Tears stung my eyes, and I nodded.

'It is hard, Fin. Almost as hard as you leaving.'

He took me in his arms and looked down into my eyes.

'I'm sorry things have turned out the way they have. I love you Chrissie. You know that, don't you?'

'I think so,' I sniffed, brushing my tears away with the back of my hand. 'I'm so sorry. I hope someday you'll forgive me.'

And then his lips were on mine. Tender and affectionate. The kiss you would give someone you cared for. And that was enough.

Johnny and my father worked well together, and I was grateful for that. Johnny's involvement had freed me from the obligations I had felt towards my parents. They were approaching their seventies and eventually would be unable to work the croft as they once had done. I therefore moved into the house attached to the Post Office with an easier heart than I might have done otherwise. At first, memories of the time I shared there with Roderick and our boys haunted me. I felt so lonely. But it wasn't just those memories that made me lonely. Fin was no longer there. Every time I went to bed at night, I thought of him and the passionate moments we had spent together in this room. We still wrote to one another, and he telephoned me once a month. It gave me some hope that one day we might get back together again. Something else that gave me hope for our future was that Daisy and Rosie had moved in with him when he moved to Clydebank, so they were gradually making progress and sorting out their differences. I was so pleased things were working out for him. How I wished they would work out for me and Heather.

We'd heard that the Ministry of Defence had chosen Balivanich on Benbecula as the site of the RAF airfield, which was no surprise as work on a bridge over the causeway between South Uist and Benbecula had begun last year. Murdo, of course, knew all about it.

'I have a cousin over there and he told me people were outraged at the public meeting held in Griminish Hall to tell them the news. They feared the government would take their crofts over for military purposes and it would leave them homeless. It will be an awful thing if the crofters were to lose their land to accommodate it. God, they fought hard enough to get land after the first war,' he said, referring to the land raids that had taken place on South Uist after the Great War. Land was everything to us after the devastation caused by the clearances.

I was more concerned that it signalled war was inevitable. Hitler was becoming increasingly aggressive. If he invaded Poland, then we would be at war as Britain and France had guaranteed their safety. I was relieved that Johnny wouldn't need to fight. The thought of losing another brother in a war was unbearable. But Roddy would, and I was worried sick about that. He was coming home from Spain to say goodbye to Heather before she left for Canada, so I would talk to him about it when I saw him. I was glad Donald wasn't living here anymore. It would have been difficult for him, as I think he would have been a conscientious objector. I still remembered the white feathers and insults thrown at Lachlan when he was returning to the army after going AWOL. The world was on the brink of something terrible, and I dreaded the future. In some ways, I was glad Heather was going to Canada. She would be safe there.

CHAPTER THIRTY-TWO

Heather was both nervous and excited about meeting her mother and going to live in Canada. Her world had changed so much since Chrissie had told her she was adopted. She was still wrestling with the implications and had told no one. Even although she and Catriona had rekindled their friendship, she still couldn't trust her with the truth. Although Catriona knew she was going to Canada, she had told her and everyone else she was going to visit Donald and Mary. No-one knew very much about Bunty or where she lived so they wouldn't put two and two together. Performing in the end of term play was a life-changing experience for her and Catriona. They found they had a shared interest in the performing arts and wanted to pursue that when they left school. Catriona decided she would like to get involved in the backstage side of things, doing hair and makeup rather than just be a hairdresser in a shop in Edinburgh. Heather had other ideas. She found she enjoyed being on the stage in front of a live audience and hadn't once felt nervous. Performing in front of people was less scary than being adopted. They had performed A Midsummer Night's Dream. She played Titania, the Fairy Queen, and Catriona played Bottom. What a laugh they'd had. She wondered if there would be a drama school or something of the sort in Canada she could go to. She knew there was one in London as she'd asked Mrs MacGregor after the play, and she'd told her about RADA, so Heather thought if Canada didn't work out, she could apply there.

When she'd told Chrissie she wanted to be an actress, she was not best pleased.

'But I thought you wanted to go to the Dough School and be a chef or a baker. That's a much more practical thing to do. I think being an actress is quite a hard life unless you become a big star.'

'So, you don't think I could become a big star?'

'I didn't say that.'

'You didn't see me performing in A Midsummer Night's Dream.'

'Well, that wasn't my fault. You told me you didn't want me to come, and I respected your wishes. Didn't people think it strange that I didn't come over for the play?'

'I just said now that you were the Postmistress, you couldn't get the time off.'

Heather was quite proud of Chrissie being the postmistress, but she would never let her know. Although her mother had said she should try to forgive Chrissie and Johnny, she was still finding it hard.

'By the way, Roddy's coming home to see you before you leave, and Bunty's going to meet you in Glasgow after she's spent time with her mother. She's booked passage for you both in August.'

'Oh, I'm glad Roddy's coming. I know he's not my brother, but I'm very fond of him.'

She couldn't resist getting the dig in.

'And he's obviously very fond of you, otherwise he wouldn't have come back from Spain, especially to see you.'

She smiled, then frowned.

'Who'll take me to Glasgow?'

'Your mother wants to meet up with your father while she's in Scotland, so he will take you.'

She was stunned.

'Why does she want to meet him?'

'I think your mother wants to make her peace with him.'

'What has she got to make her peace about? It was him who left her and married another woman. There's no way I'm going to Glasgow with him. I'm away for a ride on Sandy.'

Riding always calmed her down. How she hated these emotions that constantly overwhelmed her, causing her to lash out at the slightest thing. She'd been so looking forward to meeting her mother and going to Canada with her. But it was spoiled now. Why did her mother want to make peace with Uncle Johnny? He didn't deserve her mother's generosity and kindness.

Then she had another thought. What if her mother and father rekindled their relationship, and they all went to live together in Canada? Would that make her legitimate? It surprised her when she felt a pleasurable warmth inside at the thought of this.

CHAPTER THIRTY-THREE

Roddy arrived at the beginning of August. He looked thin, but there was something about him that had changed. Something of the old Roddy has resurfaced. I wondered if he'd met a girl. But it was nothing like that. After he had freshened up, we chatted for a while, and I told him Bunty was coming up to Glasgow to collect Heather and had asked Johnny to bring her down so that she could make her peace with him.

'I suppose that's good, isn't it? If she's going to be looking after Heather, it's better she speaks about Johnny positively. That way, she might forgive you both.'

'How I wish that would happen, Roddy. You don't know how hard the past year has been. I'm dreading her leaving, in case I never see her again.'

'I'm sure she'll come home when she's ready, *Mathair*. What about Donald and Mary? I thought they might have come home with Bunty so that we could meet young Harry.'

'I think they had planned to come, but Donald has just got a job with the Saskatchewan Star and can't get away.'

He looked disappointed, and I wondered if he still had feelings for Mary despite what he had said about her being a way of him getting over Theresa.

'It's a shame they can't come. I must let Rosemary know that her help in getting Donald a job with the Daily Worker has paid off.'

He smiled at me, but then his face became serious.

'I've got something to tell you, *Mathair*.'

My heart sank. What was he going to say? It was clearly something I wouldn't like.

'I've joined the RAF. I'm going at the end of August to start my training.'

'But what about your career? All that training to be a solicitor.'

'It's just something I need to do, *Mathair*. I saw the devastation the Luftwaffe carried out in Guernica, and I know they will do the same to Britain if they get the chance. War is inevitable and I want to be in there now. I don't want to wait to be called up.'

I felt proud as I looked at my boy. My brave boy. But my heart was sore too. It was all too much. Heather was leaving me to go to Canada, Roddy was leaving me to go who knew where, and Fin had left me to move to Clydebank and make peace with his daughters. Would any of them ever come back?

It was tough for all of us on the day they left. My mother and father said goodbye to Roddy and Heather at the croft. They couldn't face going to Lochmaddy to say goodbye. Heather cried when she said goodbye to them and clung to my father for a long time. They had a special bond, but also her grandparents were the only members of her family who were who she had always thought they were. Despite her tears, she looked beautiful with her long black hair, styled by Catriona before she left, and looked every inch a star in the making if she went into show business. I wanted so much for her to be happy, but oh, it was such a wrench losing her like this. I wondered if she was feeling overwhelmed by everything, but then I noticed her brown eyes were sparkling with excitement as we stood waiting for the ferry, and I remembered how resilient and self-sufficient she could be.

When it was time to board, I tried hard to hold back my tears, but they flowed despite my best efforts.

'Write to me as often as you can, Roddy, and let me know you're safe. Perhaps Mr Chamberlain will avert war and you won't need to fight.'

'Don't hold your breath, *Mathair*. War is coming no matter how much I know you'll pray to God that it won't. Take care of yourself. I love you.'

I watched until he had boarded. Then it was time to say goodbye to Heather. As I looked at her, I sensed she was upset, but knew she wouldn't want to let me see, so didn't ask her how she was feeling. I just said what was in my heart.

'Goodbye Heather. You've been a wonderful daughter to me, and I know you will be a wonderful daughter to Bunty. I love you more than life itself and you will always be welcome back home in North Uist.'

When she whispered she would write to me to let me know how she was getting on, I was overjoyed. Maybe this wasn't the end. Maybe she would come back some day.

CHAPTER THIRTY-FOUR

Heather found it wasn't as easy to leave Chrissie as she thought it would be. It was okay when she kissed her goodnight for the last time, as she knew she would see her in the morning. And besides, the thought of seeing her mother the next day was exciting. But it was a different story the next day. It began well enough. A hearty breakfast was waiting for her in the kitchen, and then she and Roddy went for a short walk to pass the time until they had to leave for the ferry. She was glad Roddy would travel with her and her father. She had been dreading going with Johnny by herself to meet her mother. Roddy was easy to talk to. He listened and encouraged her to talk, and before long she told him how angry she was with Chrissie and her father.

'I was angry with him before I even knew he was my father. What kind of man leaves a woman when she's carrying his baby?'

'Not much of a man, I agree. But from what I've been told, Johnny only knew about you on the day he was travelling to Canada with Janet. And I believe Bunty didn't tell Johnny about you until it was too late for him to do anything as a punishment for marrying someone else. She wanted to spoil his chance of happiness with his new wife.'

'Well, I don't blame her.'

'I don't either entirely, but not because she was in the right. I think she did it because she was ill. She wasn't behaving rationally. Have you ever considered what a shock it must have been for your father to hear about you just as he was boarding a ship to another life?'

Heather was silent. She had never considered what it was like for her father. This conversation was unsettling, and she was relieved when they reached the croft and the conversation ended.

When it was time for her, Johnny, and Roddy to leave, Heather felt a panic rising in her. What was wrong with her? She was going to a new life with her birth mother. It was what she wanted, wasn't it? But she had loved her old life. Had loved her granny and granddad, especially her grandad who had been like a father to her. She cried and clung to them when it was time to go to the ferry. When it was time to say goodbye to Chrissie, she felt an overwhelming sense of guilt. She had loved her granny and grandad very much, but more than anything or anyone else, she had loved this woman who she had thought was her mammy. She'd spent her life with this woman. When Chrissie came over to say her goodbyes, she couldn't bear to see the look of anguish in her eyes.

'Goodbye Heather. You've been a wonderful daughter to me, and I know you will be a wonderful daughter to Bunty. I love you more than life itself and you will always be welcome back home in North Uist.'

Although Chrissie was trying to hold it together, her lip was trembling, and her eyes glistened with tears. Heather was finding it hard not to cling to her and ask her not to leave her.

'*Mamaidh*,' she whispered, as Chrissie held her tightly to her. 'I shall write and let you know how I get on.'

'Will you? I would like that very much.'

She smiled and tucked Heather's hair behind her ear the way she used to do when she was a wee girl, and then she went. For the first time in her life, Heather felt completely alone as she looked out from the ferry at the figure of her mammy, which was getting smaller and smaller. Fear gnawed at her belly, but, as her granny would have said, she had made her bed, and she would need to lie in it. She was quiet for the rest of the journey, and it was only when the train pulled into Glasgow Central Station she felt a spark of excitement at the thought of meeting her mother.

'It's her,' she said breathlessly as she gazed out of the window and spotted Bunty standing on the platform. She was about to meet her actual mother. She was unaware of how tense she was until she felt her father's hand on her shoulder.

'This is a big moment for you, Heather. Take a breath. Everything will be fine.'

And it was. Her mother was lovely and gave her a warm cuddle when she got off the train. There was a moment of tension when her father came off the train, but Bunty put her hand out and shook his and the moment passed. Then Roddy joined them and there was a chat about Donald, Mary, and little Harry. It was then Heather remembered she had a sister. A sister was better than a friend like Catriona. She could talk to her about anything. And she was an Auntie. She couldn't wait to get to Canada.

'How are Donald and Mary settling in Canada, Bunty?'

'Oh, they love it there. I don't think they'll ever move back to Britain. But who knows?'

'Did Donald trace any of his grandmother's family?'

'No. He couldn't trace any of Lily's relatives, but I think it's done him good to go back and see where he was born and to visit his mother's grave.'

'I'm called after Donald's mother, you know,' Heather said, wanting to get back into the conversation.

They all laughed and made their way to the hotel where Bunty was staying.

CHAPTER THIRTY-FIVE

A few weeks later, on 3rd September 1939, Mr Chamberlain declared war on Germany. It was a Sunday. Everyone was expecting him to make an announcement at 11.15am as the BBC had been giving regular updates and had told us so. I'd never seen the church as packed as it was that day. There was an aura of excitement mixed with dread as the Reverend Macaulay talked about the possibility of war and the evils of Hitler and the Nazis. The singing in response to the preceptor was full of emotion and I felt tears beginning as we sang the words of Psalm 46: *God is our Refuge and our Strength* and prayed that He would be there for us. There wasn't a lot of chatting after church that day, and we all made our way home without lingering, as we would normally have done. None of us heard Mr Chamberlain's announcement, as listening to the wireless on the Sabbath wasn't allowed. But Fin telephoned me just after 11.30 and repeated the words he had used. *'I have to tell you that no such undertaking has been received and consequently this country is at war with Germany.'*

'God help us Fin. What will become of us if that man tries to invade Britain, and we fall the way all those other countries in Europe have fallen?'

'Have faith in our soldiers, sailors, and airmen. It will be them who save us.'

'What will Rosie and Daisy do now? Do you think they'll want to become involved in the war effort?'

'I don't know. But I can't tell you how relieved I am we've healed the breach in our relationship. The thought of them going to war without us having made up would have been too much to bear.'

I knew exactly how he felt and was grateful Heather was in Canada, away from it all. It pleased me that something good had come from Fin leaving North Uist, but his leaving had been difficult for me. When you think your life is leading you somewhere and then all your plans come to nothing, it's hard to take. I knew I was to blame, and that didn't make it any easier. I should have told him and Heather the truth when I had the chance. But there was no point crying over spilt milk, as my mother would have said.

'We'll probably receive instructions from the Post Office about protecting the mail and their property. Now that you're a postmistress, you'll have an important role to play.'

I hadn't thought about that and wondered what my duties would be.

After Fin hung up, my thoughts turned to Roddy. He had written to say he was going to South Africa to do his initial training, and I shuddered with fear at the thought of him flying a plane, dropping bombs, and shooting down enemy aircraft. Luckily, Heather and Bunty had arrived safely in Canada, so my little girl was safe. Johnny had told me how good Bunty was with Heather when they arrived in Glasgow, and he was sure everything would work out well for them both. He seemed happier after his chat with Bunty.

'She apologised to me for how she'd treated me and told me she didn't blame me for anything and hoped I could forgive her. I told her I could and asked if she would try to get Heather to forgive me. She promised to do that so I'm hopeful all will be well in the end. Funnily enough, I thought Heather was a little disappointed when I left them to come back to Uist. Do you think she was maybe hoping Bunty and I would get back together?'

'Knowing Heather, it wouldn't surprise me. With her vivid imagination, she may have wished for you and Bunty to be like characters in a fairy tale, living happily ever after.'

The very next day, the reality of war kicked in. Many of the men and boys on the islands were Cameron Highlander Territorials or Lovat Scouts and spent every week in the drill halls at Bayhead and other parts of the island having fun and preparing for war. It was a good way to spend their spare time, plus they got to go to camp on the mainland once a year where much fun was to be had. But the night before Mr Chamberlain announced we were at war, they got the call to muster at the drill halls where they trained. The next day they were issued with uniforms and told they would leave on Monday 4th September. It was a terrible day, and I wasn't the only one with a lump in my throat at the sight of the men as they marched in their kilts or rode their horses into Lochmaddy to board the boat that would take them to Kyle of Lochalsh for their onward journey to wherever they were being trained. Many of the islanders had watched their loved ones march off in 1914 in this very same way and knew that some of those going now would never come back. The wail of the pipes echoed the wail in our hearts for these young men who had no idea what was ahead of them.

For those of us who were remaining at home, on 29th September the government carried out a survey of all people living in the United Kingdom so that they could provide identification cards, gas masks and ration books. It was a bit like the National Census, but more complicated. Rationing didn't start until January the following year, but the government issued lots of messages encouraging people to complete the form so that they didn't lose out if food did become rationed. There was also the matter of national security and identity cards needed to be issued to make sure the enemy could not easily infiltrate the country. The government also decreed that children and vulnerable people should be evacuated from cities where bombing was likely to happen. Although the Western Isles wasn't one of the official areas used to house evacuees, an influx of mothers and their children, who were sisters, cousins, or some other relative of the islanders, came to stay. Morag brought her children up to live on the croft with my mother and father, but she didn't stay. Michael and Marion were 8 and 10 now and could help my mother out on the croft with milking and such like. I think it helped her get used to living on the croft without Heather and me.

Johnny had gone over to Benbecula as there were jobs going there building the new airbase. He could make good money working for them and said it would only be for a year and then he would be back on the croft for good. As things turned out, it was the end of 1941 before they completed the work and the RAF Station opened for business. I don't think any of us realised at the time the importance of the airbases that were set up on Benbecula and other Hebridean islands. Without RAF Coastal Command fighting the U-boats that worked in packs to sink our merchant ships, we might have lost the war. Britain relied heavily on these ships to supply food, oil, raw materials, and arms to fight the war with. We were lucky on the islands. Although the government rationed certain foods like sugar, meat, fats, cheese, biscuits, and tinned food, we still had our chickens, sheep, and cattle, which gave us eggs, milk, and meat. Fish were always available to us, too. So, the islanders did as they had always done. They sent parcels of food to their relatives on the mainland. Only now they disguised them as books as it was against government rules. I turned a blind eye and sometimes even sent the odd parcel myself to Katie and Maude or Morag and Michael.

CHAPTER THIRTY-SIX

I thought I would be lonely on my own in the post office house, but as things worked out, I was rarely alone. Many of our young men and women went off to fight in the war or to do other war work like working in the munitions, seeing it all as a big adventure, a way to escape from the island. So, it left us short of workers. Mairi Campbell, who worked as a housekeeper in the post office, was one of them. She had joined the ATS and was now somewhere in England, driving and repairing army vehicles. When I told Murdo, he volunteered his daughter Catriona, who was also Heather's best friend. Poor Catriona. It was the last thing she wanted to do, but Murdo insisted it was too dangerous to go to the big city and follow her dream of becoming a hairdresser and make-up artist. Needless to say, she was morose on her first day at work.

'Good morning Catriona. How are you?'

'Alright,' she said, looking down at her feet. 'Heather's lucky she got to go to Canada before this war started. I wonder if she'll get the chance to go to drama school or something over there.'

'I'm not sure if there will be such a thing where she's staying. It's a small town.'

'Whatever she does, it'll be better than cleaning a post office. Where do you want me to start?'

'Let's start with a cup of tea and a chat.'

By the end of our chat, she was brighter. I'd sort of implied that coming to work with a sour face was not good for her or for us. She should make the best of her position, and it wasn't forever. She would get her chance to do what she really wanted in due course. I also asked her how she would feel about doing a talk at the Rural. Meetings of the Rural continued during the war, where we knitted hats, scarves, gloves, socks, anything that would help keep our soldiers warm.

'The Rural? What would I talk to those old women about?'

'We're not that old, Catriona.'

'I suppose not. You were going to get married to Mr Simpson, weren't you?'

I nodded.

'This war has a lot to answer for.'

There was no way I was going to tell Catriona or anyone else, the real reason Fin and I had split up.

'But what I was thinking was that the women might like to have a demonstration. You could style someone's hair and put make-up on them. What do you think?'

The way her face lit up said it all, and that was how I got a happier housekeeper and a new hairstyle. I was terrified when I sat in the chair and let Catriona cut my hair. My hair had been part of my relationship with Roderick. Brushing it with the beautiful brush he had given me the night we arrived in Canada had become a nightly ritual in the early days of our marriage, and sometimes in the latter days, too. It took me all my time not to cry as I looked at the amount of hair that was gathering on the floor. But it was for a good cause, and when Catriona had finished, I was pleased with how it looked. And so were the other women.

'It takes years off you, Chrissie,' said Morag. 'I think I'll get you to do mine too, Catriona.'

And that was how Catriona partly got to fulfil her ambition to become a hairdresser. The make-up part would have to wait until she went to work at the new Airbase on Benbecula, but that's another story.

I also needed someone to do the job I used to do now that I was postmistress. Shona McIver came to the rescue when I put a card up in the post office window advertising the vacancy.

'My nephew's wife, Dorothy McIver, has come up from Glasgow with her wee boy to stay with us while this terrible war is on, and I know she used to work in the post office. Perhaps she could do it.'

'Get her to fill in this form, Shona, and then she can come for an interview.'

Dorothy was like a breath of fresh air. She was plump in a pretty way and always wore red lipstick and bright dresses.

'Hello, Mrs Macdonald. Thanks for geein' me an interview. Did Shona tell you I used to work in a post office before I had ma wean?'

'Yes, she did, Mrs McIver.'

'Ach, call me Dorothy. Ah must say I wis impressed when Shona told me it wis a woman that ran the post office.'

'Aye, the war has given us women a lot more opportunities, I suppose. Just like it did in the last war. Is your husband in the forces, Dorothy?'

'Aye. Jimmy signed up with the Highland Light Infantry. Wee Jimmy disnae hauf miss him.'

'I'm sure you do as well.'

She nodded and brushed a tear from her eye.

I got her to send a telegram, count out money and sort out mail, and she passed the test with flying colours. So, she joined me in the post office, and I was grateful not only for her help with the work, but with the boost her sunny personality gave me. But a couple of months after she arrived, she seemed down, and I asked her what was wrong.

'Are you alright, Dorothy? You don't seem your usual self. Nothing's happened to Jimmy, has it?'

'No, it's wee Jimmy. He's no made any pals, and he jist hangs aboot Shona's shop all the time. I'm worried about him.'

'Maybe he's just homesick, and it's taking him a bit of time to settle.'

'I know he misses his daddy, but I can't imagine why he would be homesick for the soot and tenements of Glasgow. It's a paradise up here for weans.'

The memory of Bunty and Mary's arrival on the island suddenly resurfaced, bringing with it a rush of emotions. But what stuck in my mind was that neither of them understood the Gaelic, and I recall Bunty complaining about Mary's difficulty in making friends. I thought that was why she encouraged Mary's friendship with Donald, but, of course, she had other motives for that.

'Does he have the Gaelic, Shona?'

'No. Because we live in Glasgow, Jimmy never taught him, or me, for that matter.'

'Well, I think that's the answer. Imagine what it must be like to have your world turned upside down. Here he is living in a strange place away from everything and everyone he knows and can't understand a word anyone is saying to him.'

'I think you're right. It's okay for me. I'm big and ugly enough to talk to anyone, but ma wee boy isn't.'

'How would you feel if I gave you and wee Jimmy some lessons to help you understand our language? It might help him settle in and make pals.'

She looked doubtful.

'I'm no sure. It's bad enough hiving tae leave hame, but now you're wanting us to learn a foreign language into the bargain.'

I laughed at her notion that Gaelic was a foreign language.

'It's nae laughing matter, Chrissie. But ma wean is dead upset, so I'll try it.'

'Gaelic's not a foreign language, you know. It's our native language.'

'Och, I know, but it's foreign tae me.'

So not only did the post office house offer hairdressing services, but it also provided a space for learning the Gaelic language and wee Jimmy never looked back. He made friends with the other children and loved nothing more than running wild with them barefoot in the summer months. I was glad as I remembered how difficult it had been for my boys when their world was turned upside down, albeit for a different reason, and the lasting impact it had on them. I hoped the upheaval of leaving his home and having to learn a new way of life wouldn't have the same lasting effect on wee Jimmy.

When the post office instructed me to hire a telegram boy, luckily, Donald John McLeod, a relative of Janet's family, was too young to go to war yet. So, when his mother asked if there were any jobs going, I hired him to help Murdo with the post and to deliver telegrams. The memories of the terrible job I had during the Great War flooded back. Donald John was too young to carry that burden alone, so I made a point of chatting with him after he had delivered the bad news about someone's loved one. It wasn't until after I'd hired him I realised he was friends with Catriona, and it had been him that Heather had been spotted with smoking the cigarettes when she was at school on Portree. He and Catriona always asked how Heather was doing and I had to make sure I got my story straight. Heather, of course, hadn't told them she was staying with her birth mother, only that she was visiting her brother and his wife. So, I had to tread carefully. The last thing I wanted to do was give away her secret.

The first Christmas of the war, many of our young men came back to visit, including Roddy. He looked handsome in his grey/blue RAF uniform and, like the other young men, wore it whenever he was going out.

'I've learned a lot *Mathair*,' he said. 'But I've not been in active service yet, so I'm not sure what to expect.'

'But you're enjoying it so far?'

'Yes. And I can see you're enjoying being the postmistress. I don't remember seeing so many people when we lived here in the last war. I like your hair, by the way. Catriona has done a good job. Have you written to tell Heather?'

'Yes. She was pleased to hear Catriona was working here, but not so pleased that Donald John was, too. I think she was always jealous of their friendship.'

He laughed.

'Well, Catriona has asked me if I'll take her to the New Year ceilidh, so we'll see whether Donald John gets jealous of that.'

Donald John, like a lot of the young boys, was only biding his time until he was old enough to sign up, so I knew he looked up to Roddy. He was always asking him questions about the RAF, and I wondered if that's what he fancied joining, too.

The New Year ceilidh that year was awash with the swirling kilts of the Cameron Highlanders and the Lovat Scouts. They looked healthy and happy, so it gave us hope that the war would be over soon. But Hitler continued his mission to conquer Europe and when Britain failed to prevent him from taking Norway, Mr Churchill replaced Mr Chamberlain and he set up a coalition government in 1940. Next it was the turn of Belgium, Holland, and France to fall and when we heard about the evacuation of our army from Dunkirk in May, fear struck our hearts. The British weren't supposed to lose wars, that's what the history books had told us. But here was our army, the French and Belgium armies being forced into the sea. I was terrified for Roddy. I knew from the news that the RAF were being deployed to help fight off the Luftwaffe to allow the soldiers to be evacuated and wondered if he was one of them. I prayed fervently along with lots of others during that period, as the Cameron Highlanders were one of the many regiments fighting in France. Then news broke that Churchill had assigned the 51st Highland Division to stay behind and fight with the French Army to allow the soldiers to be evacuated from Dunkirk. It was the worst news when we heard the Germans had captured nearly 10,000 men of the 51st Division at Saint-Valery-en-Caux and they were now prisoners of war. For those on the island who had sons in that division, a bittersweet mix of disappointment and relief washed over them. Among the captured men was Morag Campbell's Archie, and in her own words, it was a terrible blow.

'But at least you won't be sending Donald John with one of yon telegrams for me, Chrissie. I know I'll see my boy again sometime in the future when this is all over.'

I prayed to God she would. At that time, we didn't know how the Germans would treat prisoners of war. People were aware of their brutality towards the Jews and other people they considered inferior, so who knew if they would be the same towards our men, even although the Geneva Convention set out rules to protect them.

CHAPTER THIRTY-SEVEN

Heather and Mrs Hepworth arrived back in Canada before Mr Chamberlain declared war on Germany. She still thought of her birth mother as Mrs Hepworth, even although she called her Mother. But she excused herself, as she had lived not knowing she was her mother for sixteen years. So, it was quite reasonable that it would take some time for her to fully accept Mrs Hepworth as her mother. Their long journey from Scotland to Canada ended in Yorkton, which was the administration centre for that area of Saskatchewan and the place where Donald and Mary had settled. As well as all the usual amenities of a large town, it had a hospital and a newspaper. Mary had worked in the hospital for a short time until she had Harry, but she was now a full-time mother. Donald had got a job as a reporter with the Yorkton Bugle, so it made sense that they would settle in Yorkton rather than Saltcoats. When the train pulled into the station, Heather immediately spotted Donald and Mary with a wee boy, who must be Harry. They were all waving enthusiastically, and she felt a warmth embrace her. Her actual family. She had a sister and a nephew, and they were waiting for *her*. She could hardly wait for the train to stop and, much to Mrs Hepworth's concern, opened the window and hung out to wave to them.

Donald came over and pulled open the carriage door, and Heather practically fell into his arms.

'It's so lovely to see you, Donald, and you, Mary,' she said, giving her sister a hug. She noticed the tears glistening in Mary's eyes and gave her an extra squeeze.

'Come and meet your nephew,' she said, taking Heather's hand and leading her to Harry's pram, where he sat waving his arms about at all the excitement.

'And you must be my nephew, Harry,' she said, hunkering down. He had brown eyes like Donald, but his hair was fair, like Mary's. He was a true mix of them both. She felt a little envious when she thought of the life this wee boy would have with both his natural parents. He would never need to worry that he might be adopted.

'Harry, Harry,' he shouted gleefully.

'I'm your Auntie Heather.'

'Auntie Heather,' he said, holding up his arms for her to lift him.

They all piled into Donald's car and went to their house for tea. It was chaotic, as Harry was at the stage where he just wanted to run around and play chases with his new auntie. Heather obliged, but she had to admit he wore her out after their long journey. So, she was glad when it was time for her and Mrs Hepworth to go home to Saltcoats, where she lived.

Saltcoats was bigger than Lochmaddy, but it was a town rather than a city. There was a hotel, a school, several shops, a post office, a library, a church, and a bank. It was also close enough to be within easy visiting distance of Donald and Mary. Heather wasn't sure what kind of house Mrs Hepworth would live in, but she was pleasantly surprised when Donald pulled up in front of a two-storey house, made of timber, which she was later to learn was called clapboard. It had a cheery red front door and a picket fence surrounding the garden. Pots of pretty red geraniums sat on the porch beside a rocking chair. Heather liked it and wondered what her room would be like. Donald carried their luggage in but didn't linger, and soon it was only Mrs Hepworth and her again.

As her mother bustled about, taking her luggage upstairs, Heather wandered around taking in this place that was to be her new home. A gramophone was sitting atop a cupboard with lots of records inside, and she felt her tummy flutter with excitement. She loved music. When her mother joined her, she couldn't wait to ask her to play something.

'I see you have a gramophone, Mother. Can we play something, please?'

'Yes, of course. We'll just get you settled in and then I'll put on a record that your father and I used to listen to when he visited.'

Heather's stomach fluttered with dismay this time. Her father. Why was she talking about him? And smiling when she was doing so. Did she have fond memories of him? Did she still love him? She remembered the quiver of pleasure when she had imagined that her mother and father might get back together when he took her to Glasgow to meet Bunty. When they hadn't, she had reverted to her previous view of him as a scoundrel.

'Why are you smiling when you talk about him? Don't you hate him?'

Mrs Hepworth looked at her.

'I don't hate him, Heather. Much of what happened was my fault, not Johnny's. I have some nice memories of the time he, Mary and I spent together in the schoolhouse on North Uist. If you would like to hear about them, I'm more than happy to share them with you.'

Heather didn't want to hear about these happy memories. How could her mother have happy memories of a man who had let her down so badly?

'Maybe some other time.'

It was to be a few months before she would listen to her mother's memories and when she did; she was glad. She got some comfort from the fact that, although her father had never been in love with her mother, they had been friends and he had never mistreated her.

'At least, not intentionally. I got the wrong end of the stick and tried to manipulate him into loving me. But he loved Janet, and I couldn't change that. When you fall in love, you'll understand.'

She and her mother spent many pleasant evenings singing and dancing to the gramophone records and '*I love a lassie,*' the one Mrs Hepworth and her father used to dance to, became her favourite. It also led to her going to the Banff School of Drama in the summer of 1940 to do a drama course which set her in good stead to join The Entertainment National Service Association or ENSA for short when she went back to Britain to do her bit for the war. She'd felt guilty about coming to Canada when she heard Mr

Chamberlain had declared war on Germany. It didn't feel right that she would be safe while everyone she knew would need to suffer the horrors of war. Roddy had joined the RAF, and she decided if the war was still on by the time she was eighteen, she would join up too. But she was still only sixteen, so it would be a couple of years before she could go back home.

She got a job in the Golden Sheaf Hotel. Although she knew what had happened to her grandfather there, she couldn't let it put her off as she wanted to work and there were very few options in Saltcoats. It didn't stop her sometimes imagining what it must have been like back in 1896 when the bartender shot her grandfather. It was like something out of the cowboy films that her mother sometimes took her to see in Yorkton. While working in the kitchen, restaurant, and bar, she would sing and hum her way through her day. The Manager heard her singing one day and asked if she would perform at a concert he was organising to raise funds for the war in Europe.

'I would love to, Mr Maxwell.'

When she told her mother, she asked her if she had ever sung publicly before.

'Well, I won the prize for singing at the Mòd in Dundee. I think I won it because when I was singing it I thought of you, and it made me emotional. I've also performed several times at school, so I think I'll be able to do it.'

'I think you will too, if you're singing in here is anything to go by.'

The concert, and particularly Heather, was an enormous success, and she found herself in demand to do similar concerts elsewhere in the area.

One day, when her mother was reading the paper, she pointed out a course being advertised.

'Look at this Heather. Do you think you would like to go?'

Heather looked and saw an advert for a summer drama class at the Banff School of Drama.

'I would love to go, Mother. But where is Banff? Is it near here?'

'No, but you can travel by train to it, and I'll arrange for you to stay in lodgings while you're there.'

She hugged her mother enthusiastically and then became embarrassed. She never knew whether to hug her mother in the same way that she used to hug her mammy.

'Sorry.'

'What are you sorry about? I love when you hug me. Here, give me another one.'

CHAPTER THIRTY-EIGHT

It was March 1941 before I saw Fin again. After he left, we wrote to each other, and occasionally spoke on the telephone. Because we were both in the post office, this was easy enough for us to do. We just shared our news and discussed what was happening in the war. We never talked about our relationship, but I clung to the hope that keeping in touch meant love could blossom again. The reason I got to see him was because Morag phoned to tell me she wanted the children back as there didn't seem to be much danger from the Luftwaffe bombs.

'Michael and I are missing them and there doesn't seem as much danger from the bombing as we thought there would be when we sent them up to Uist.'

'Well, if you're sure. They're missing you and their dad, too. Will you come up and collect them?'

'I was wondering if you fancied a trip to Helensburgh. Michael and I are involved in the Home Guard and they're keeping us busy with training and special ops.'

'Why are they doing that, if there's little chance of you being bombed?'

'It's government policy. Don't you have to do it in Uist?'

'Well yes,' I said, thinking of Johnny, who had joined the Home Guard as he was above the age for conscription, but was required to work the land to help with food supplies, anyway. I also had responsibilities as the postmistress to ensure the post office was protected should there be bombings or an invasion. So, I had a safe to store the mail which was supposed to withstand explosions and sandbags surrounding the post office.

'I'll make arrangements and telephone to let you know when we'll be arriving.'

The day before we were due to leave, Dorothy took a telephone call for me.

'It's that man who phones you every noo and again. Fin, I think he said his name wis.'

'Hello Fin. How are things with you?'

'They're okay. Things are quiet here. Although we've had some early warnings about bombing, it's never happened.'

'Yes, my sister was telling me. It's like we got ourselves all worked up, thinking the Germans were going to go mad and bomb us all right away. That's why they sent their children up here. But because nothing's happened, they've asked me to bring them down to Helensburgh and I'm taking them tomorrow.'

'Helensburgh, you say. Why don't you come and spend a couple of days with me? There's plenty of room now that the girls have moved out.'

Daisy had gone with the evacuees from her school to Sutherland, and Rosie had joined the ATS Fin had told me last year.

'Clydebank isn't all that far from Helensburgh. Perhaps you could get the train.'

My heart fluttered with pleasure, and I readily agreed.

'You're looking awfy happy, Chrissie,' said Dorothy when I came off the telephone. 'Have ye a wee fancy fur that man?'

I felt my face go pink. If she only knew I was head over heels in love with him.

'Maybe.'

'Aw, go on, tell me. You know you can tell me anything.'

'Aye, if I want the entire island to know, Dorothy McIver.'

She just smiled and winked. She'd never lost her Glasgow accent, but her wee boy now spoke the Gaelic and spoke the English with a highland lilt.

We reached Glasgow on 10th March and made our way to Helensburgh by train. The children were excited to see their mum and dad again and chatted the whole way. I found I was as excited about seeing Fin again as the children were about seeing their parents again. I stayed a couple of nights with Morag and Michael and then Michael drove me to Clydebank. He said he needed to pick something up in Glasgow, so it wasn't a problem. I took extra care with my hair, hoping Fin would like my new style and put on some lipstick. When I arrived, it surprised me to see that the place was a hive of industry and had the feel of a town that was doing well. There were shipyards building ships for the government and the Singer Sewing Machine factory, which Michael told me was now a munitions factory. Streets were busy with workers and shoppers and the tramcars that rattled along the main road to Glasgow were full of people.

As I approached the post office, I noticed a large Cooperative store, and wondered whether I would see anything to buy while I was here. The government hadn't rationed clothing yet, although there were rumours it would be. I noticed mounds of sandbags sitting outside of the post office. It must be standard instructions to protect post office property, as I had needed to do the same. I said goodbye to Michael and went inside, feeling a little nervous at seeing Fin again. There was a young woman behind the counter serving customers, so I waited in line.

'Hello, I'm a friend of Mr Simpson. I've come to visit for a few days. Is he in?'

'Hello, you must be Mrs Macdonald. You should've let me know you were here. He's upstairs getting the place ready for you. Let me take you through to the back and I'll point you in the right direction.'

I went upstairs as she directed, knocked on the door and went in. My heart was beating fast, and my voice quivered slightly as I called out to him.

'Hello. Fin. Are you there? It's me, Chrissie.'

I stood in a square hallway with several doors off, dithering over which one to open, when Fin came out of the door immediately in front of me with sheets and towels in his arms. We both stared at one another. I don't know about Fin, but a feeling of joy swept over me as I looked at his handsome face. How I had missed him. Suddenly feeling shy, I didn't know what to do and was relieved when his eyes looked into mine with the old softness and his face broke into a huge, welcoming smile.

'Chrissie, my goodness, it's so good to see you. You look lovely. That hairstyle suits you.'

He put what he was carrying down on a small table, came over, and took me in his arms. The smell and the feel of his body as he hugged me felt so familiar, so comforting after all this time. Then he let me go and picked up my bag.

'I'm just making up your room. It's through here.'

He ushered me through the door he had just come out of, which turned out to be a double bedroom. It had pink floral wallpaper and a rag rug over the wax-cloth flooring. There were two single beds with pink floral bedspreads and pink silk quilts on top. The room also contained a wardrobe, a dressing table, and a nightstand between the beds. It had a small fireplace, which was set with kindling and coal ready to be lit. It also had electric lights. I was thrilled. We still didn't have electricity on the island, although it was commonplace almost everywhere on the mainland. The window was open, and the white net curtain fluttered in the chilly breeze, but I noticed there were heavy blackout curtains hanging ready to be drawn at night.

'Sorry, I'll close this window now. I was just airing the room before you came.'

'What a lovely room Fin.'

'I got it decorated for the girls when we moved in here.'

I smiled. He looked so much happier than the last time I'd seen him.

'I've brought you a chicken and some eggs. How are you coping with rationing?'

'I do okay. There's only me, but it's a treat getting some fresh food like this. Thank you. I hope you don't mind, but I've arranged for us to go to a concert in the Cooperative Hall tonight. I thought you might like it.'

'I would. Thank you.'

It was a lovely clear night, but cold as you would expect in March. The moon was shining bright, so it made it easier to see where we were going as, of course, all the streetlights were dimmed, and the windows blacked out. Men, women, and children packed the hall full of excitement at the prospect of being entertained. I was excited just being with Fin. He had taken my arm as we were walking along and that made me feel like we were a couple. The show was in full swing, when suddenly the music stopped, and the Master of Ceremonies came onto the stage. There were some murmurs of protest while the audience waited for him to speak.

'The air raid sirens have sounded, but it's probably another false alarm. If everyone agrees, we'll continue on with the show.'

There was a roar of approval and the band struck up again. I looked at Fin, not knowing what to do.

CHAPTER THIRTY-NINE

'Sorry, Chrissie,' he said, 'but we're going to have to go. I know it might be a false alarm, but I can't take the chance. I need to be on duty whenever the sirens go. Sadie, who operates the telephone switchboard, isn't allowed to be left on her own during an air raid, and it's my responsibility to protect the post office by keeping watch for fires.'

He must have seen the fear on my face as he continued.

'It's probably nothing to worry about. We've had lots of air raid warnings, but nothing's happened, so I'm not expecting it to be any different tonight.'

He took my hand, and we hurried out of the hall.

In the distance, the sky was the bright pinks and reds of a beautiful summer sunset on Uist. But it wasn't a sunset. It was fire.

'Oh, my God. It's really happening,' Fin cried. 'We must hurry, Chrissie. That's the whisky distillery warehouses at Yoker. They'll be on us any minute.'

The streets were in an uproar. The ominous, ear-piercing shriek of the siren made me shiver with terror. Like Fin and I, people were running, seeking shelter or to get home to their loved ones. And above it all, the drone of the Luftwaffe bombers. Hundreds and hundreds of them. I gripped Fin's hand tightly, and he pulled me along, dodging in and out of people running in the opposite direction. I tripped on something and almost fell, but he grabbed me and kept me upright.

'You're alright. I've got you, my darling.'

At last, we reached the post office and were just about to go inside when the first bomb exploded, then another and another. I froze, staring up at the sky, blind to the devastation their deadly cargo was causing. The drone of the Luftwaffe bombers was relentless as plane after plane after plane flew above us. There was the ack, ack sound of the gunners on the ground firing at them, but it seemed to make no difference. Fin opened the door of the post office and pulled me inside, slamming it behind him.

By this time, I just wanted to cry hysterically. I was terrified. But the look on Fin's face told me this was not a time for weakness. We needed to work together to do whatever was needed. Just then, Sadie came through the door, her face ashen.

'Oh Mr Simpson, the telephone's been ringing constantly and now it's gone silent. I think the lines must have been damaged. What are we going to do?'

'Let's get our protective clothing on in case we need to put out a fire. You know the drill, Sadie.'

'Yes, sir.'

'Chrissie, please go down to the basement. You'll be safer there.'

'Let me help. I wouldn't feel right going down there without you. I would never forgive myself if anything happened to you and I wasn't with you.'

He looked at me for a moment with the old tenderness and my heart soared with hope despite the terrible circumstances.

'Okay. I'll get you a uniform. You are, after all, a post office employee, too.'

We quickly got dressed and were ready to take on whatever came our way. Fin went up to the roof to inspect for fires while Sadie and I put all the precious post office mail, paperwork, and money into the Chubb safe, which was built to withstand fire and building collapse. I prayed we would never find out whether what they promised was true. We made up flasks of tea and made sandwiches just in case the bombing affected the gas and electricity supplies. I got blankets and a torch from the house and took them to the basement in case we had to stay the night there. When there was a lull in the bombing, I went up to the roof to see how Fin was doing. As I looked out over the town, the scene was one of utter devastation. Fires were raging everywhere. The air was thick with black smoke and the sound of fire engines and ambulances filled the eerie peace. The shells of collapsed buildings stood like skeletons against the glow of the fires, and mounds of stone and debris from the collapsed tenements covered the streets, making it impossible to know which was the road and which was the pavement.

'I need to go, Chrissie. I'm an ARP warden and even although my primary duty is to the post office, I think you'll agree this is a unique situation. I can't stand by and do nothing.'

The last thing I wanted him to do was to put himself in danger, but the devastation was so severe that he wouldn't be the man I knew him to be if he didn't want to help.

'I can see that. What do you want me to do while you're gone?'

'I think people are going to need shelter, so please welcome anyone who wants to come in. The basement is the safest place in the post office.'

I wished I could do something too, but didn't know the town and besides, I couldn't leave Sadie on her own to deal with people fleeing the bombs. What if the Luftwaffe came back?

'Okay, I'll do that.'

He got his outdoor clothes and made to go out the door.

'Fin, please come back to me.'

He made a salute and then went out into the night.

CHAPTER FORTY

I stood at the door, taking in all that was happening. I could see ARP volunteers pulling casualties from the debris. Then bedraggled and bewildered men, women and children emerged from the places they had been sheltering, desperate to get home. Thanking God that we were safe, and the post office was still intact, Sadie and I sat down to have a cup of tea, thinking the bombing was at an end. We had no sooner sat down with our tea than the siren began its piercing warning once more. Fin! He would be in terrible danger if this was a second wave of bombing.

The next thing there was an urgent banging on the door. Sadie and I rushed to open it. How I hoped it was Fin coming back. But it wasn't him standing outside. It was a group of adults and children covered in dust, looking terrified. Some children were crying, and some were silently clinging to their mothers' coats. They all spoke at once and it turned out they had been at the same concert as Fin and I had been to in the Cooperative Hall but had stayed on. When the doors blew open, one of them had ventured over to shut it to keep the bombs out and they had sheltered there until the bombing ended.

'We're now trying to get home, but by the looks of things, we might not have one,' said a woman, bursting into tears.

'The bastards are on their way back, so is it alright if we shelter here until it stops?' said a man. 'I know Mr Simpson.'

'Come in. Come in,' I said, at first searching behind them to see if I could see Fin and then searching the sky for the bombers that were on their way for a second round.

'Of course you can stay. Sadie and I have made up some sandwiches and flasks of tea. Come down to the basement. It's safer there.'

'Where is Mr Simpson? I thought he had to stay and look after the post office during a raid?'

'He was here, but when the bombing stopped, he went out to help. He didn't realise the Luftwaffe would be back again. But I work for the post office, so I'm looking after things here in his absence.'

I was trying to speak with some authority to calm people and let them think someone was in charge, although I hadn't a clue what to do if a bomb struck the post office. I guessed we would need to evacuate and leave the Chubb safe to do its job. After having the tea and sandwiches, the group settled down for the duration of the bombing. We covered the children in the blankets and some of them slept. I went up on the roof to keep a lookout for fires, just as Fin had done before, while Sadie stayed with the families. Although I was keeping an eye for fires, I was also scanning to see if there was any sign of Fin. There was none, and he still hadn't arrived back by the time the second bombing raid had finished at 5.30am the next morning.

The bedraggled families left, hoping against hope that their homes would still be there. I prayed to God they would be. However, when I went out to look for Fin, I could see that hardly a house had been left unscathed. Crowds of people were walking around looking lost, and I was one of them. I hadn't a clue where I was going or how I thought I would find Fin in all the confusion. I asked one of the air raid wardens if he had seen Fin.

'He's the postmaster and went out to help when the first air raid finished.'

'I know Mr Simpson, but the last time I saw him he was up at Second Avenue helping get people out of a tenement that had collapsed. But if I were you, Mrs, I would go back and wait in the post office for him. It's dangerous. Buildings are collapsing all the time.'

Just as he said that, there was a creaking noise and then a roar as a building close by collapsed. The man grabbed me and threw me out of harm's way.

'See what I mean.'

I did, but it made no difference. So, I picked myself up and shook as much dust from my coat as I could and moved away toward the post office. I didn't want the man to think I wasn't taking his advice, but as soon as I got round a corner where he couldn't see me, I asked someone where Second Avenue was.

'It's a bit of a walk and there's not much of it left standing, hen. I hope you don't know anyone that lived there.'

I didn't, but that didn't make me less fearful of what I would find when I got there.

CHAPTER FORTY-ONE

My heart thumped in my chest as I stumbled my way through the debris and shrapnel that littered the roads. It must have taken me about half an hour, but I wasn't aware of it. I found Kilbowie Road, where the man had told me I needed to go to find Second Avenue. I could see the Singer Factory with its enormous clock in the distance. A canal ran under the road, and it looked as if the fire brigade had been using it to put out fires, as I could see lots of hoses snaking along the bank. As I passed the Singer factory, I stopped for a moment to catch my breath and thought of Mr Singer and what a wonderful invention the sewing machine had been and how he had made it accessible to people like me. But although the factory still made sewing machines to help with the production of army uniforms, its major production was munitions. It was this that had been a target for the Luftwaffe and the remnants of the huge fire started when they hit Singer's timber yard instead of the factory were still smouldering as I passed. When I saw how close Second Avenue was to Singer's Factory, I understood why it had been so badly affected. I shuddered as I looked at what had once been a street full of homes, full of families all just living their lives, but was now just a mountain of rubble. There would be nothing left of Clydebank if the bombers came back for a third round. As I stared at the destruction in front of me, I feared the worst. Fin might be dead. An overwhelming sense of grief enveloped me, and tears blinded me. This couldn't be happening. I roughly brushed away my tears and moved forward. This was not the time to give up.

And that's when I saw him. I don't know how I recognised him as he was with a group of air raid wardens all wearing the same blue protective boilersuits and tin hats.

'Fin,' I called, but he didn't turn, and I could only watch as he disappeared into a semi-collapsed tenement. I made my way towards the ruins, my heart racing despite the slowness of my progress.

'What's going on?' I asked the man nearest me when I reached the ruin. He turned and looked at me, his face full of fear.

'There's a wean in there. We can hear it greetin,' he answered. 'That man's gone in to see if he can get the wee soul. I told him I think the rest of the building's about to go but it made no difference.'

Our eyes met in terror as we heard the ominous creaking that signalled a further collapse. I screamed as the man pushed me away, and I hit the ground hard. As I lay face down on the ground, the sound of falling bricks and masonry reached my ears and bits of flying debris hit my back. Was I going to die here in Clydebank so far from home? The thought of never getting to say goodbye to my family made me weep. After what felt like an eternity, the noise stopped, and I tried to move. A cloud of dust surrounded me, and I was disoriented and coughing when I sat up. I could see nothing and gasped for breath. Fin, oh Fin, my love. I've lost you forever now.

Then I heard the man shouting again.

'This way, mate. Come on. I've got you.'

My heart swelled with hope. Was it Fin? Was he alive? Had he saved the child? I pushed forward blindly. Then I heard crying. It was Fin.

'She's dead, she's dead. I was too late,' he sobbed.

'You did your best. Come on, give her here and I'll take her over to the ambulance crew. They're dealing with the dead bodies.'

An image of Heather came into my mind, and I sobbed. How would that wee lassie's mother cope with the loss of her little girl? Then it occurred to me she was probably lying dead somewhere under the rubble. Where was God in all this? Why was He letting this happen?

But He gives, and He takes away, and that day he gave Fin back to me. As the dust cleared, I pulled myself up and ran to him despite the pain from my fall and my bloody knee. At first, he looked at me with a confused expression through his red, bloodshot eyes. Dust and rubble clung to his clothes, his hair, and his face. Suddenly, his expression changed as he realised it was me.

'Chrissie,' he whispered.

His fingers stroked my face as if I were the most precious thing in the world. And then I was in his arms, and he clung to me like he never wanted to let go.

CHAPTER FORTY-TWO

When we got back to the post office, Fin sent Sadie home. I prayed her family was still alive, and she had a home to go to. The destruction of the town was unbelievable and yet as we made our way shakily back to the post office, it was amazing to see workers going to the shipyards and factories, ready to do whatever they needed to do to fight the enemy. People were coming from all over to take the homeless families to relatives, friends, or the rest centres that had been set up to take them until they could find housing. Some people never returned to Clydebank. Fin insisted I go back to Helensburgh straight away, just in case the Luftwaffe bombed Clydebank again. I begged him to let me stay. If he let me stay, I could look after the post office while he carried out his ARP duties. But there was no arguing with him, so I did what I was told and telephoned Morag to ask if Michael would pick me up. I was in tears when I spoke to Morag and told her all that had happened the night before.

'We knew something terrible was happening, as we could see the glow from the fires. I'm so glad you're safe, Chrissie. Please, please take Marion and Michael back with you to Uist. I think we're in for it now.'

As I left Fin and Sadie, whose family was safe, thank God, an overwhelming sense of relief washed over me. But guilt too. The people of Clydebank had suffered so much destruction. It didn't feel right that I could go home and escape. It also didn't feel right that I was full of joy. But I couldn't help it. Fin and I had talked and talked after we went back to the post office and had sorted out our difficulties.

'I love you, Chrissie, and nothing else matters. If we survive this bloody war, then I'm marrying you. If you'll have me.'

'I'll have you, my darling. I love you so much.'

He went to his room for a moment and came back holding a small box, which he handed to me. Inside was a beautiful diamond engagement ring.

'I bought this for you when I stayed in Glasgow when you went back to Uist because Johnny had come home. But because of what happened, I never gave it to you. I'm so sorry.'

'Oh Fin, it was all my fault. You've nothing to be sorry for. Please put the ring on my finger. It's so beautiful. Thank you.'

We had one brief hour together before it was time for me to leave.

That night, the bombers came back, and I was frantic with fear. Not just in case they bombed Helensburgh as well as Clydebank and Glasgow, but in case anything happened to Fin. I couldn't bear it if he got hurt or killed. Not now that we were back together, that we were going to be married. He telephoned me the next morning to let me know he was okay, and I sobbed with relief. But from what he said, the Luftwaffe had come back to finish the job they'd started the night before.

'It just felt that they were being vindictive. They weren't targeting the factories so much as the houses. They were after our people, Chrissie. There's hardly anything left undamaged. It's just horrendous. If I believed in God, I would be cursing him right now for allowing this to happen.'

I could understand how he felt, but all I could do was thank God that the post office was still standing and that he was alive.

When he hung up the telephone, I looked at the ring he had given me, sparkling brightly on my finger. I felt so proud wearing it and couldn't wait to get home and let my mother and father know my good news. But in the end I didn't get the chance to tell them. When Marion, Michael, and I got home, my mother and father were waiting for us at the pier when the ferry arrived. I thought the horror of the Clydebank Blitz was in the past, but I could see from their faces that something was wrong, but pretended I didn't.

'Hello, you two. It's so good of you to come and meet me. You must have missed me.'

My mother gave me a fierce hug and then looked at my father.

'Tell her, Angus.'

I thought of Roddy, and Donald, and Heather, and Fin, the people I loved most in the world and wondered which one of them was dead. I felt my legs wobble and my father grabbed me to stop me from collapsing.

'It's your Aunt Katie.'

'Katie?' A brief surge of relief washed over me and then I looked at my father's tear-stained face. He had lost his sister.

'Oh, *Athair*. I'm so sorry. What's happened?'

Katie was too old to be in the forces, but knowing her and Maude, they would have been involved in something that would help people worse off than themselves.

'I don't rightly know.'

He handed me a telegram.

'Young Donald John brought it this morning.'

KATIE IS MISSING-STOP-WILL TELEPHONE THE POST OFFICE-STOP.

Why wasn't I here? I could have telephoned Maude and then broken to the news to my father.

'Let's get up to the post office right away and I'll telephone Maude to find out what's happened.'

It took a while to get through. It wasn't just Clydebank that the Luftwaffe had bombed on those two nights. So many of the telephone lines were down. But eventually I got through to Maude.

'We joined a group of volunteers who were going to Clydebank to help people who had lost their homes. Oh, it was a terrible sight, Chrissie. You wouldn't believe the damage the Luftwaffe caused.'

I could hardly believe that I had been in the same place as my aunt.

'When the sirens sounded, it was chaos, and Katie and I got separated. The bombers weren't interested in the industrial targets. They were deliberately going for the houses. I ended up in an Anderson shelter, but I don't know where Katie went. I searched and searched for her, but I couldn't find her. If she sheltered in a tenement close, it's more than likely she's dead.'

The sound of Maude's sobbing was piteous. She had lost her closest friend. They had shared a house for so long; I was sure Maude felt that a part of her had died, too.

They never found Katie's body. What they found was her handbag lying in a bombed-out tenement where everyone inside had died. Katie's death devastated Maude, but it also had a terrible effect on my father. I think it would have been better if they had found her body, as he kept hoping Katie would turn up, but she never did. And I think that played a part in his own death a couple of years later. When we buried my father, we put Katie's name on his gravestone, too. Katie had played a huge part in how my life had unfolded. It was because of Katie that I married Roderick, and it was because of Roderick that Bunty had come into my life, and it was because of Bunty that Heather had come into my life. Katie was engaged to be married to Roderick but had run away just before the wedding. In doing so, she had tarnished the honour of our family, and my father had offered me in exchange when I grew up. It seems so barbaric now, but it's what happened in the old days. She had married no one else, and I sometimes wondered if her and Maude's relationship was more than a close friendship. But if it was, it was nobody's business but theirs. She died as she had lived, helping people, and I felt immensely proud to be her niece.

CHAPTER FORTY-THREE

The day she left Canada to go back to Britain, Heather hugged Bunty with great affection. She had enjoyed her time getting to know her mother, but she was desperate to go home and help the war effort. Her mother had researched which jobs they were looking for women to do and had discovered ENSA.

'This would be right up your street, Heather. And I think with your experience, they would be happy to take you.'

'I'm not sure. It seems a cushy number.'

'Don't you believe it. You'll be on the front line entertaining all those brave servicemen and women fighting for our freedom. There'll be nothing cushy about it.'

Heather discovered quite quickly that her mother was right. When she contacted ENSA and gave them a resume of what experience she had, they jumped at the chance of having her, so long as she was willing to go to the Middle East to entertain the troops. A band led by a man called Roy Healey was going and he needed three girls to go with them. He already had two and Heather became the third. The first hurdle was getting the vaccinations she needed. Never having had a jag, as the doctor called it, she didn't know what to expect. If she had, she would never have gone. He jabbed her in the arm with a needle and told her it might be a little tender for a while. This was an understatement. Her arm swelled like a balloon, and she could hardly carry her suitcase the following week when she embarked on her first journey as a forces entertainer.

She had hoped to visit Chrissie before she went, but there hadn't been time, so she had spent a few days with Grace and Donald in Manchester. Donald was now a war correspondent and travelled all over Europe, sending back reports to the Saskatchewan Star on the progress of the war. It just so happened he was visiting Grace at the same time she was. Having read some of his articles, she and Bunty had become quite scared sometimes, as it looked like Hitler was getting the upper hand. The worst was reading about all the soldiers who had needed to be evacuated from Dunkirk and the capture of the men of the 51st Highland Division because she knew some of the young men from Uist would have been among them. Although he and others reported on the terrible blitz of London, she knew the Luftwaffe had attacked Scotland too. Chrissie had written to tell her about the terrible night she had spent with Fin in Clydebank in March last year when hundreds of people were killed, and thousands made homeless. Her Great Aunt Katie had been one of them.

Mr Healey had arranged that everyone should meet at the station to get the train to Southampton where they would sail from. It was a troop ship they would sail on, but she wasn't too worried, thinking it would be like the ship she had sailed in from Canada. However, it was anything but. No first-class passage for her this time. She and the other two girls had to share with WAAFS, WRENS, and ATS personnel, and it was a hundred to each cabin. There was no comfy bed to sleep in, only a hammock. It was horrendous. However, as ENSA members were officer class, they dined well. Much better than the other women. During the crossing, there was always the fear that German U-boats would attack the ship, but it landed in Port Said, still intact.

From the port, they boarded a train to Cairo. It was a relief to find out that this time she would only need to share with the two other girls, Shirley and Gloria, who were with the band. Their job was to entertain the troops up and down the line. One place they went was Jerusalem, and she would never forget it. It was like going back in time and made her think of the bible stories taught at school. The scorching sun shone on the white flat-roofed buildings, making them sparkle. The place was buzzing with troops and locals and she and the girls especially enjoyed the markets where they bought souvenirs. She hadn't thought that she was also walking in places where Jesus must have walked until she received a letter from Chrissie in response to a letter she had sent her about where she was. *Oh, how special Heather, to have the chance to walk where Jesus walked. You are such a lucky girl.*

The girls became firm friends during the six-week tour and made a point of trying to get posted together. So, her first year with ENSA was a fun time, and she got to see more of the world than she might have done had she stayed in Canada or gone back to Uist. She also got to meet Harry Lauder that her mother and father had danced to back in 1933 and other actors who were to become famous after the war. Despite the occasional discomfort of their travel and accommodations during tours, they always enjoyed top-notch meals as they were given the same food as officers. But eventually, she, Shirley and Gloria went their separate ways. Heather found this to be the case. You formed intense friendships or relationships for a short time and then moved on. The only exception was when she met Lawrence. In between tours, she based herself in London in digs where other ENSA girls stayed. It was easier to get to Southampton or Calais. So, when Roddy was on leave in London, she met up with him one night and he took her to a club where the RAF boys went. And that's where she met Lawrence and where her fate was sealed.

CHAPTER FORTY-FOUR

It was to be several months before I could tell my mother and father that Fin and I were engaged. I had put the ring in its box for safekeeping when I travelled back from Glasgow and got so caught up in the news about Katie that I forgot about it. It was when I next spoke to Fin that I remembered.

'How did your mother and father take the news of our engagement?'

'Oh Fin, I feel terrible. I haven't told them. They were so upset about Katie, it didn't feel right sharing our good news with them.'

'But didn't you have your ring on? Didn't they notice that?'

'I'd put it away in its box for safekeeping while I was travelling back, so they never got to see it. I've been dithering about how to tell them.'

'Look, why don't I come up to Uist and we can tell them together? I'm desperate to see you.'

'And I'm desperate to see you, too. Yes, please come up as soon as you can.'

I thought I better broach the subject of Fin with my mother and father before he came. It would be a bit much if we turned up unexpectedly and told them we were engaged. Always better to prepare the way. So, the next time I went to the croft, I talked about my visit to Clydebank. I'd never got to tell them the horrors of that night because of the news of Katie, and I wasn't about to tell them now. But somehow I did.

'Fin's coming up for a visit,' I said, as Mother and I were clearing the dishes away.

'Is he now? Why is that? I thought you two weren't so friendly anymore.'

'I visited him in Clydebank when I took the children back to Helensburgh and we kind of made up again.'

'Were you there when all that terrible bombing happened?'

'Only the first night. I went back to Morag's the day after.'

'But you didn't see your Auntie Katie, did you?' said my father, suddenly taking an interest in the conversation.

'No, I didn't *Athair*. I think it was the next day that Katie and Maude went to Clydebank, and I was away back to Helensburgh by then.'

'Was Mr Simpson okay?'

'Yes. The post office wasn't hit.'

I thought back to that terrible night and the image of Fin coming out of the bombed-out building with a little girl in his arms.

'But he was out in the thick of it, trying to save people. You've no idea what it was like. All those buildings destroyed, and all those people trapped or dead.'

As I relived that night, I was oblivious to the impact it was having on my father.

'I wish he could have saved Katie. If he'd found her and taken her into the post office, she would have been safe, wouldn't she? I hate to think of her lying hurt and trapped.'

Tears were running down his cheeks.

'Och, *Dadaidh.* Come on. Don't upset yourself. I don't think she would have felt any pain.'

'How do you know? You weren't there. You were safely in Helensburgh with your sister while my sister was being blown to smithereens.'

I looked at my mother and she shook her head as if to say, '*don't say any more.*'

'Here's a wee cup of tea, Angus. Drink it up and then we'll put the wireless on before we go to bed. Chrissie's just leaving now.'

Fin arrived a fortnight later and I can't tell you how wonderful it was to see him. He looked so much better than the last time I'd seen him after the bombing raid. I met him from the ferry, and we went straight to the post office. Luckily, it was closed for the day, so we had a wonderful reunion. It was almost like old times, but somehow more intense, more passionate. *Absence makes the heart grow fond* is an old saying and, in our case, I think it was true. When I took Fin downstairs to meet Dorothy the next morning, she smiled at us knowingly.

'Well, I see yous two have had a good sleep. You're looking all bright and cheerful.'

I smiled. Not so much a good sleep, but yes, I was certainly feeling all bright and cheerful.

'Hello Mr Simpson,' she continued, putting her hand out towards Fin. 'I'm Dorothy. Pleased to meet you.'

'And you Dorothy.'

The day passed quickly, and before I knew it, it was time to go to the croft. I was a little worried about how my father would react to our news after the way he had been when we talked about Katie. When I told Fin what had happened; he suggested we make out that he'd just brought the ring up and asked me to become engaged. That way, it wouldn't look like we'd been hiding anything. I was grateful for his suggestion and was feeling cheerful as we set off to tell my parents our news. When we arrived, they were sitting waiting for us.

'Hello, Mr Simpson. Nice to see you again. How was your journey?' said my mother.

'It was okay. Not too rough.'

'I hear you were out rescuing people after the bombing,' said my father.

My mother and I looked at each other, wondering what was coming.

'That's right, Mr MacIntosh.'

'You didn't see my sister, did you? They tell me she died in the bombing, but they've never found her body.'

'I'm so sorry to hear that, Mr MacIntosh. I'm afraid I didn't see your sister.'

'Do you think she could still be alive?'

My father looked pathetic and old as he gazed up at Fin with hope in his eyes.

'I don't think so. Not after all these months. I think she would have been found by now.'

Tears began streaming from my father's eyes again. It was awful.

'Right Angus, offer Mr Simpson a glass of whisky. He's come all this way to visit us.'

My father got up and did as he was told. He was almost childlike.

'We've got some news for you,' I said, taking Fin's hand.

My mother looked at us, noticed the ring, and then smiled.

'You're engaged.'

We smiled and nodded.

'Angus, look at this. Your daughter's engaged to be married.'

'Who to?' he asked.

'To Mr Simpson, of course.'

'And when are you going to make an honest woman of my daughter, Mr Simpson? I'll need to get in touch with the minister and make the arrangements.'

This was awkward. Fin and I hadn't talked about when or where we would get married yet.

'Och, we've not set a date yet, Father. But I take it we have your blessing.'

He looked at me and smiled.

'You have my blessing, Chrissie. Good luck to you both.'

I was relieved when we left the croft. My father's moods were becoming unpredictable.

'When would you like to be married, Chrissie?' asked Fin when we got back to the post office.

'I don't know. As you can see, my father's not doing too good just now, so I would probably prefer to wait until he was back to his old self. What do you think?'

'If that will make you happy, then I'm happy.'

He took me in his arms and looked lovingly at me.

'I love you, Chrissie, and I can't wait to make you my wife. But I want it to be at the right time. I want us to start our married life together without any complications.'

So we waited, and it was to be 1943 before we could marry, but even then there were complications.

CHAPTER FORTY-FIVE

It was hard to see in the nightclub where she first met Lawrence because of the haze of cigarette smoke swirling around the room. It was also hard to move as dancing couples swayed wildly to a jazz band belting out all the latest numbers. Roddy seemed to know lots of people and they were buying him drinks and slapping him on the back a lot. Heather thought he must have done something heroic, but he wasn't for talking about it. Heather found she was getting a lot of attention, too. She was now nineteen and knew how to dress in a way that men found attractive, and it was certainly working that night if the number of men who asked her to dance was anything to go by. Apart from entertaining the troops, another duty was to make them feel good. One way of doing that was to dress up and flirt with them. But flirting was as far as it went. They were on strict instructions not to go too far. The army didn't want a load of unwanted babies taking their entertainers away. But sometimes it was hard. Life was so precarious for the boys fighting on the front, and she had been tempted once or twice.

After drinking several gin cocktails, she asked the band leader if she could do a couple of songs. He looked doubtful, but Roddy told him she was in ENSA, so he reluctantly agreed. She never drank before performing, so it was a novel experience for her going on stage half cut. She sang a few of the well-known songs the troops liked to hear, but she knew it could make them sentimental and melancholy, so finished with the St Louis Blues, a slow swing song. The crowd went wild as she moved around the stage, sashaying provocatively. There was a noisy group of men about Roddy's age in the front row shouting suggestive comments at her in plummy accents. Normally, she wouldn't have tolerated such behaviour, but tonight she laughed seductively and playfully let the straps of her dress slide off her shoulders. When she finished her set, she left the stage to go in search of Roddy. She saw him on the other side of the room, talking intensely to a woman with black hair. Before she could reach him, he had taken the woman's hand and was leading her towards the exit. Heather was about to follow, when one of the noisy group asked if he could buy her a drink. He was a tall chap, thin faced with a little ginger moustache. His hair was auburn, but it was his hazel eyes that made her tingle as they locked on hers, waiting for her answer. Roddy was clearly otherwise engaged, so she said yes.

'Why not? A gin fizz please.'

'How about champagne?' he said, taking her hand and escorting her to a table in the corner where a bottle of champagne was chilling. She'd never tasted champagne before.

'My name's Lawrence, by the way.'

'I'm Heather.'

'You must be Scottish with a name like that.'

'I am. I come from North Uist in the Western Isles.'

He moved closer and poured her a glass of champagne. She watched as the bubbles rose and danced on the surface.

'You have the most beautiful accent. I could listen to you all night.'

She smiled, lifted her glass, and moved closer to him.

With a gentle clink, he raised his glass to meet hers, all the while gazing at her as if she were the most beautiful thing in the world.

She heard her laughter tinkle like the sound of their glasses touching and realised she wanted nothing more than to talk to him and tell him her life story. And that's what she did. He was a stranger. What did it matter if he knew she was an illegitimate child whose mother and father had abandoned her? The sounds of laughter and music gradually faded into the background as they sat together, supping their champagne, and talking like they had known each other all their lives.

When tears fell from her eyes, he reached into his jacket and pulled out a crisp white handkerchief. He gently wiped her tears away and planted a tender kiss on her closed eyelids. His eyes welled with tears too when he told her how his father had died when he was just a boy.

'My father was a pilot in the Great War, you know. He died a hero fighting the Bosch.'

'I'm so sorry Lawrence.'

She touched his hand with sympathy.

'I wanted to learn to fly like my father, and I got the chance when my friend Henry's father bought him a plane. We both got our pilot's licence when we were seventeen.'

It shocked Heather that someone would have so much money they could buy their son a plane, and she thought there was something overindulgent about it when so many people could barely scrape a living. But she said nothing. She liked him, despite his obviously privileged background.

'My uncle had the idea of setting up a squad of amateur pilots as reserves in time of peace who could be called upon if war broke out, so Henry and I joined and for our sins are now in 601 Squadron.'

He looked at her and the empty bottle lying on the table.

'Look, this champagne's finished, but my hotel's nearby. If you like, we could order another bottle and talk more privately there.'

She looked round to see if she could see Roddy, but he was nowhere in sight.

'I would love to she smiled, but I'll just powder my nose before we go.'

She was sobering up and wondered why she had been so open with him. But what the hell? She would probably never see him again after tonight. Full of anticipation for the evening ahead, she picked her coat up from the cloakroom. She had never gone all the way with a man and wasn't sure if she was ready. But oh, he was so gorgeous. She decided not to have any more champagne. If what she hoped was going to happen, then she wanted to remember it. They lay on his bed, fully clothed, not touching. Then he turned towards her and drew a finger down the middle of her body. She shivered at his touch. She wanted more and wished he would caress her breasts and kiss her mouth. Then he spoke.

'What age are you, Heather?'

What the hell did it matter what age she was?

'I'm old enough to be here with you,' she whispered and snuggled into him.

He smiled, drew away from her, and lit a cigarette for them both.

'You're so young, so beautiful. Are you aware of the effect you're having on me?' He looked into her eyes and whispered, 'I want to take you now, to make you a woman.'

She thought she might faint and wished he would take her. She was ready.

He took a long drag on his cigarette, then blew the smoke upwards as he let out an enormous sigh.

'But I think my wife might have something to say about that.'

She stared at him. Had she heard him right?

'You have a wife?'

'Yes, Amelia. She's quite beautiful. Would you like to see a photograph of her?'

Tears nipped her eyes as she realised what a fool she'd been. He'd been playing with her. Led her to think he wanted her. Her face flamed red with embarrassment as she thought of all she had told him and how much she had wanted him.

'Why are you being like this?'

'Because I can.'

'You privileged pig. You think because you have money, you can do what you like. I hope the Jerrys get you.'

Grabbing her coat and bag, she slammed out of the room and out of the hotel into the darkened street. It was pouring. Just what I need, a bloody downpour. She screamed like a banshee and not one passerby huddling under their umbrella cast a look in her direction. She was a nobody. Just another stupid girl taken in by an unscrupulous man.

CHAPTER FORTY-SIX

The next morning, around 11 o'clock, there was a knock on her door.

'Heather ducky,' the woman who ran the digs, Mrs Hart, shouted through. 'There's a man at the door asking for you.'

Her heart missed a beat. Was it Lawrence? Then she remembered he didn't know where she lived.

'Says he's your bruvver.'

'Okay, Mrs Hart. I'll be right down.'

She looked at herself in the mirror. What a sight. Hungover and red eyed from crying, she looked in a right state. Quickly washing her face and pulling a brush through her hair, she went down to face Roddy. He would probably give her a hard time for leaving without him. Then she remembered it was him who left without her. Attack is the best form of defence, so she was ready for action when she went downstairs. But when she saw him, looking so bright and cheerful, she didn't have the heart.

'Just came to make sure you got home last night. I'm sorry for leaving you. Mother would have a fit if she knew.'

'I'm a big girl, Roddy. I live in London, you know.'

'I know. Look, grab your coat and I'll take you for a cup of tea and tell you my news.'

'How about breakfast? I've still not eaten.'

As she turned to go back upstairs, he spoke again.

'Are you alright Heather?'

'What do you mean?'

'You look a bit the worse for wear.'

'I'm hungover, that's all. Nothing to worry about. I'll just put some lippy on and I'll be good as new.'

How she wished that was true, but it would take more than a bit of lipstick to help her get over what happened last night.

When they found a greasy spoon café and settled in, they ordered a breakfast and mugs of tea. Heather was famished, and got stuck into the sausages and eggs on her plate. Misery never affected her love of food.

'So, Roddy, tell me your news. It's obviously something good as I haven't seen you looking so cheerful in a long time.'

'I've met someone. Well, re-met them really.'

Heather waited. She could see him thinking about the girl, getting ready to tell her how they had met.

'I met Theresa Dunlop when I was a student and living in Glasgow. We met at the dancing, and I fell for her hard. But she came from a Catholic family and things didn't go well. Her father beat me up and sent Theresa to live in America with her aunt. Mother also threatened to disown me if I had anything to do with her.'

That didn't sound like her mammy, but then she didn't really know Chrissie, did she? She'd lied to her all her life.

'That must have been terrible for you. But she's back in Britain now?'

'Yes. She felt it was wrong to stay in America when we were at war. So, she came home and joined the WAAFs. I couldn't believe it when I saw her in that club last night. She was the last person I ever thought I would see again.'

She could see he was becoming choked up. He must really love the girl.

'Was she the dark-haired girl I saw you with?'

'Oh, you saw me with her? Yes, that's her. That's Theresa.'

'And will you see her again?'

'Yes. Spending last night with her made us both see we had never stopped loving each other.'

His eyes were shining. Heather wished she was feeling like he was now. She'd had such high hopes when Lawrence took her to his hotel, but last night was such a disaster.

'And you won't believe it, but she has a week's leave, the same as me. So, I've booked us a hotel in Brighton. I'm sorry I can't spend more time with you, Heather, but I'll bring Theresa along to meet you before we head off if you're going to be around.'

'Och, it's alright, Roddy. Follow your heart. I'm sure I'll get to meet her at your wedding.'

He laughed out loud, delighted at my remark.

'So, tell me what you got up to last night without me to chaperone you.'

'Nothing much. I had a drink with one of the boys in that noisy crowd when I was singing and then went home.'

'What was his name? I know some of them.'

'Lawrence.'

'Lawrence Moorcroft? Wow! He's in what we call the Millionaire Squadron because they're all wealthy. They're also risk takers and he's bagged lots of German aircraft. There's talk he'll get a DFC.'

'What's that?'

'A Distinguished Flying Cross.'

'I don't know if it was him. He didn't tell me his second name.'

She was trying not to show Roddy how upset she was, but Roddy's face softened, and she could see the sympathy in his eyes.

'I hope you didn't like him too much. He's married, you know.'

'Just as well I thought he was a stuck-up pig then.'

But she knew she wasn't fooling Roddy. He gave her a big hug when he left her back at her digs.

'You'll find the right person someday. Even if, like Theresa and me, it takes eight years.'

Heather didn't believe him. Some people had charmed lives, and some didn't. She was one of the ones who didn't.

CHAPTER FORTY-SEVEN

Life on our island continued as it had always done, following the seasons to eke out a living. Apart from when Donald John was spotted delivering a telegram. Then there was fear. Whose turn was it? Whose father, son, sister, cousin had been lost this time? As expected, Donald John promptly enlisted upon reaching the age of eighteen, and Hector Macdonald replaced him. When the new airbase opened at the end of 1941, Catriona joined the NAAFI. Although the NAAFI employed her, from what Murdo told me, she was also doing hairdressing and makeup for the ENSA personnel who came to help entertain the pilots.

After Katie died, my father grew withdrawn and forlorn. Although she had moved to Glasgow all those years ago, and it was a long time since he had seen her, it was like a part of him died when she did. I had felt something akin to that when Lachlan died in the Great War, but Roderick and my boys had sustained me. However, nothing seemed to help my father. I think losing Katie on top of Heather leaving was too much for him. Johnny was back home from Benbecula now that work on the airbase was finished and my father left him to do increasingly more of the work needed on the croft. Mother was concerned about it.

'I'm worried about your *athair*, Chrissie. He's so listless and disinterested in everything. I wish Johnny wouldn't do so much on the croft. Angus is just sitting back and letting him. But he needs to get up and move about. Keep busy.'

'I've noticed that. What about the children? Don't they cheer him up?'

'No. He's irritable with them, and that's just not like him. They stay out of his road as much as they can.'

'He's grieving, *Mathair*. You might just need to be patient and let him go through it.'

'Grieving is an indulgence, Chrissie. We need to pick ourselves up and get on with things. That's what we've always done.'

What she said was true. Death was part of living for the islanders. But sometimes grief hits you and you can do nothing about it. I'm not saying my father died of a broken heart, he didn't. He died of pneumonia after a bout of pleurisy. But he had lost the will to live and didn't bother fighting it. But that was to be later. I had my own concerns and probably didn't pay as much attention as I should have to what was happening with my father, even although I had agreed to marry Fin when my father was back to his old self.

I knew Heather was back in Britain as she had written to tell me. I thought she might have come up to Uist, if not to see me, to see my mother and father. But she told me she needed to take the first job ENSA offered her, so didn't have the time to come all the way up here. It horrified me when she told me she was going to the middle east. It was so far away and as the year went on, she went to even more faraway places. But at least she was still writing to me, so I still hoped one day she would come back home. I read the news avidly to see what the RAF was doing. They had done so well during the Battle of Britain and now that the Americans were in the war after Japan bombed Pearl Harbour, I knew they were helping the war effort, too. But it didn't lessen my worry, as now Britain was turning the tables on Germany by bombing civilian and strategic military targets. But after seeing the devastation in Clydebank, I was not a supporter of this new offensive. I often wondered how Roddy felt dropping his lethal cargo on ordinary people.

On top of all the worrying I was doing, towards the end of 1942, I received a letter from Roddy, and didn't know what to do about it.

Dear Mother,

I hope this letter finds you well. I was so sorry to hear about Great Aunt Katie and about your horrible experience in Clydebank. Thank goodness you got out safely. I don't know what I would do if anything happened to you. I love you Mamaidh.

I shed a tear when I read that. I mean, I knew he loved me, but it was nice to see it on paper.

I hope Grandad picks up soon. I can tell you're worried about him. I met up with Heather when I was in London, and I took her to a club where all the RAF folk go. She got up and sang a few songs and went down a storm. She really is something. I wish you could get to see her, but she seems to be determined to stay in London before she gets posted abroad again. I think she met someone that night at the club, but from what she says, I don't think it worked out well. Perhaps she'll write and tell you about it.

I felt a little uneasy. Was Heather being reckless and getting involved with men she shouldn't be? Although she still wrote to me occasionally, I doubted she would write to me about the man she had met. I missed her. We had been so close and now it was like I was nothing to her. I knew I was to blame, just as I had been to blame for Fin and me breaking up. But he'd forgiven me, and I prayed daily that Heather would forgive me too.

But I have big news, Mother, and I don't know how you'll feel about it. I wish I could come and tell you face to face. But it's just not possible.

Now I felt really uneasy. Was Roddy being posted somewhere that was highly dangerous? My mind scurried about, trying to remember what I'd read in the newspapers.

On the night I'm talking about, I met Theresa. You remember Theresa?

I remembered Theresa alright and the beating her father had given Roddy. Hadn't she gone to America?

When war broke out, she came back to Scotland and joined the WAAFs. She didn't want to stay in America not doing her bit. And Mother, we still love each other. I know there was all that trouble about her being a Catholic and me being a Protestant, but it doesn't matter anymore. The war has changed everything. Life is just too short to worry about such things. When I get back from my next tour of duty, we're going to be married. It will just be a small registry office affair with a couple of witnesses. No family or

friends. Once the war is over, we can celebrate. I hope you will give us your blessing.
Your loving son,
Roddy.

To say his news shocked me was an understatement. I'd never dreamed that he and Theresa would ever meet up again. I thought of all that had happened when he was a student and how I'd said I would disown him if he married her. But I couldn't say anything like that now. I was engaged to a man who was neither Protestant nor Catholic and would marry him, irrespective of that. So, it would be hypocritical of me to say anything of the sort to Roddy. Besides, after what happened in Clydebank, I too believed life was too short to worry about such things. As I took the news in, I realised I was happy for him. When I thought back over the last few years, he had never been truly happy and if marrying Theresa was going to do that, then I wished him well.

CHAPTER FORTY-EIGHT

My father died in January 1943 and, as it happened, all my children were in the right place to get compassionate leave. Roddy hadn't mentioned if he was bringing Theresa with him, and I wasn't sure how I would feel about meeting the girl for the first time. But they were now man and wife and I had given them my blessing, so I would do my best to make her feel welcome. Donald was in London when my father died, as he was now a war correspondent for the Saskatchewan Star. I was glad he had found a way to be involved in the war effort without compromising his pacifist sympathies. Heather was in France when she got the news about my father, but she asked for compassionate leave, saying her grandfather was like a father to her and they gave her the time off. My father had loved her like his own, and I knew he would be delighted to have her back home. But I wasn't sure she would want to come home.

She hadn't been back to Uist since she'd left to go to Canada with Bunty in 1939. I had hoped she would have come for a visit before now, but she hadn't come and I thought it was because she still couldn't face seeing Johnny and me. But paying her respects to my father was obviously more important to her than her feelings towards us. I wondered how she would be. I wanted so much for us to be reconciled. Fin was also coming up for my father's funeral. Although we hadn't seen a lot of each other since we got engaged, we talked every week on the telephone, and he was always sending me beautiful love notes and sometimes little gifts. I longed to see him, of course, but the situation with Heather was volatile, and I didn't want him getting caught up in anything that might affect our relationship again. I was, therefore, tense as we prepared for my father's funeral.

My thoughts went back to the day of Roderick's funeral in 1933. What an awful day it had been. I had miscarried his child and Bunty Hepworth had ended up in the Long Island Poor House. I wondered if Roddy and Donald would think about Roderick's funeral too. It had been such a hard day for them, and I could still picture them in their wee black suits joining the men as their father was taken to Kilmuir Cemetery. Heather, of course, wasn't even born yet.

The day of my father's funeral, the weather was kind with only a light breeze blowing as my father made his last journey to Clachan Sands Cemetery, where the other members of his family were buried. His funeral was a sombre affair, but people came from all over to pay their respects. Although some of our young folk had died in the war, there hadn't been many funerals, as most of them had fallen on foreign ground or had drowned at sea. I think there was a feeling that by being at my father's funeral; they were also honouring the dead who couldn't be buried here. We all thought of Katie, who couldn't have a funeral as there was not a body to bury. However, my mother had asked the undertaker to put her name on the headstone she had specially chosen for my father's last resting place.

People didn't linger long, although there was plenty of whisky and food for them at the croft. Perhaps they respected that Roddy, Donald, and Heather would only be here for a short time and we would want to spend time together as a family. Theresa hadn't got leave and although I would have welcomed her, I was happy that it would only be us. Morag came up, of course, which delighted Marion and Michael. They were out for a stroll with my mother and Fin went back to the post office, while the rest of us tidied the place up and reminisced about my father. All was going well at first, and then it wasn't.

'I loved Grandad so much. He was the only father I ever had,' said Heather, tears glistening in her eyes.

'And he loved you too, just like you were his daughter,' I said.

Then Johnny spoke. He was trying to be sympathetic, to make Heather feel better, but it was a mistake. It only brought out her resentment.

'I'm here for you now, Heather.'

'Better late than never, I suppose.'

'If you'd only let me in, I would do my best to be a good father to you now.'

'You wouldn't know how to be a good father. You left my mother to fend for herself and even when you knew I was here with Chrissie, you didn't come for me.'

I winced when she called me Chrissie. I didn't know what to do. Should I try to keep the peace or let her have her say? Perhaps it was what she needed. To get everything off her chest. So, I said nothing. Let her and Johnny fight it out.

'Heather, I only found out about you on the day I was leaving for Canada. Bunty wasn't a totally innocent party in all this, you know.'

'Oh, I know. She's told me all about it. But it doesn't excuse your abandonment of me. You chose your marriage to Janet over me.'

She burst into tears.

'You don't know what it's like to be me. Everything I thought was real was just a pack of lies. I thought I was the child of a mother and father who loved each other, but I wasn't. I was the unhappy result of a seedy relationship. Have you any idea how that feels?'

There was silence, and then Donald spoke.

'I do.'

That stopped her in her tracks.

'I know exactly how you feel, Heather. When Chrissie and Roderick told me I wasn't their son, it felt like the end of the world. My father took advantage of my mother, so I too was the result of a seedy relationship.'

Tears streamed from my eyes as I remembered Heather, the first Heather, and how she had placed Donald into my arms and asked Roderick and me to look after him when she was dying. We had let him down by not telling him the truth, and now I had let Heather down by not telling her the truth.

'But your father fought for you,' she whispered. 'Mine didn't.'

Johnny let out a cry of anguish. There was nothing he could say. It was true. But after a few moments, he spoke.

'I knew you would be safe with Chrissie. If I'd come back to claim you, then everyone would have known you were illegitimate. The whole reason Chrissie pretended you were hers was to prevent you from being tainted with that stigma.'

That made her turn on me then.

'Chrissie, you could have told me lots of times that you had adopted me, but you took his side and protected him instead of me.'

'In some ways, what you say is true. I made Johnny the excuse for not telling you, but it wasn't because I was choosing him over you. It was because I was scared I would lose you. And I was right, wasn't I? I have lost you.'

CHAPTER FORTY-NINE

Heather looked at her mother. Was what she said true? Had she lost her? Her mind went back to Grandad and how he had given her into trouble for shouting at Chrissie after she'd told her she was adopted.

'She doesn't deserve it. She's looked after you since you were a two-week-old baby, and you should be grateful.'

What he'd said was true. She had looked after her and there'd never been a moment when Heather hadn't felt her mammy's love. She could feel it now. Her heartache, her longing for them to be reconciled. As she looked round at her family, the hard stone that had been in her heart these last few years dissolved. Every one of them had suffered in their own way. They were just ordinary people trying to do the right thing. Why did she want to cause them any more suffering? This terrible war could cut their lives short at any time, so if they were to be reconciled, this was their chance. They might never get another.

'You haven't lost me, *Mamaidh*.'

Her mammy's face lit up with joy, and when she opened her arms to her, Heather went into them willingly. She was home.

It wasn't as easy to let her father in, but she could see he was a decent man. It would take time, but the difference was she was now willing to get to know him and forgive him.

'I hear tell you're a wonderful singer, Heather,' he said a couple of days before she was due to leave for London.

'So I've been told.'

'Well, I was speaking to Murdo, the postman, and he tells me there's a resident band over at the RAF base on Benbecula and they're looking for a singer. I was wondering if you might apply for it as he tells me your friend Catriona works in the NAAFI over there.'

'I don't know. I quite like my life in London.'

As soon as the words left her mouth, she realised they were no longer true. Though she had enjoyed her time there and the opportunity to go abroad to entertain the troops, she couldn't deny that something had shifted in her. She had only liked it because it provided a distraction from her troubled thoughts. But a sense of peace had come over her the last few days, so she didn't need to block her thoughts out anymore.

'I'll have a think about it ... what should I call you? Uncle Johnny or Daddy?'

'Och Heather, you can call me whatever you like. I would love if you would call me Daddy. But it's up to you how much you want people to know about your birth. I love you so much, you know. I feel like I'm getting a second chance here and I don't want to muck it up. Can I have a hug?'

She smiled and went into his arms. He smelled like Grandad, a mix of pipe smoke, sweat and the fresh outdoor smell of Uist.

She took Uncle Johnny's advice, she'd stuck with that name just now, and applied for the singer's job at the RAF Airbase on Benbecula. She had the experience and when she auditioned, she obviously impressed the bandleader, Sam Carmichael, as he offered her a contract there and then. The facilities were marvellous. It had its own cinema and resident band. They obviously thought the airmen who were there to protect the merchant shipping coming to Britain from the German U-boats were worth it. She briefly wondered if the RAF would ever post Lawrence or Roddy here. She would love it if Roddy came, but would hate it if Lawrence turned up.

Now that she was reconciled with her family, she liked the idea of being closer to home and able to get to the croft more often. She knew how much her granny was missing her grandad and knew it cheered her up when she went over to help milk the cow, collect the eggs, or make the butter. It was easy enough to walk over from Benbecula when the tide was low, and she could call on Angus Fraser to row her over at other times if necessary. What's more, Catriona and Donald John McLeod were both employed in the NAAFI. It was quite like old times, but she wasn't jealous of Catriona's friendship with him anymore. She'd met Donald John on the ferry when she was coming home for her grandfather's funeral, and they'd got talking. He'd been injured in North Africa and was no longer fit for service.

'In some ways it's good, as I can help my granny on the croft. You know my grandad died recently too. But I'll still need to get a job so I might apply to the new airbase on Benbecula. I hear there are lots of jobs there.'

'Yes, my mother wrote to tell me Catriona's left the post office and is working in the NAAFI there now. Maybe she could put in a word for you.'

When they talked about it, she never realised she would end up there, too.

CHAPTER FIFTY

When I got back to the post office, Fin guessed right away that things had gone well with Heather.

'I can see from the happiness shining out of your eyes that something's happened.'

'Heather has forgiven me. Oh Fin, I can't tell you how happy I am. I feel like all my dreams have come true.'

'All your dreams?'

He raised his eyebrows and put his head to one side. I laughed.

'Apart from the one where I become your wife,' I said, going into his arms.

It was an hour or so before we resumed our conversation, and it was bliss. I lay in Fin's arms as we talked about our future together and wondered if I'd ever been this happy before. Although I was sad at my father's passing, I believed he was now at peace. He hadn't been himself for the last couple of years, and it had taken its toll on my mother. She would never admit it, but I think she was relieved when he didn't recover from the pleurisy.

'Where would you like to go on honeymoon, Chrissie?'

I felt a warm glow. Imagine me going on a honeymoon. I had no idea where I would like to go.

'Honeymoon! We need to get married first and we haven't even discussed where we'll get married or what kind of service we'll have.'

Fin frowned. It was difficult. I, of course, would wish us to marry in church here in North Uist, but what about Fin? He wasn't just another religion; he was an unbeliever.

'What kind of service would you like, Fin? I know you're not religious.'

'I suppose I would prefer if we just went to a registry office and had a quiet wedding. But I know your church is important to you, so I'll do whatever you wish.'

I thought about it. I would need to speak to the Reverend Macaulay to find out if he would marry us first. If he refused, we would end up in with a registry office marriage, anyway. And then there was my mother to consider. She might think it was too soon after my father's funeral for me to be thinking about getting married. And what about Heather, Roddy, and Donald? What would they think of us getting married in the middle of a war? My thoughts then went back to the night in Glasgow when we told Fin's family and the frosty reception we'd received. The thought of a quiet wedding began to sound quite attractive.

'Actually, that sounds good. You could post the bans in Glasgow, and I could come down on the pretext of visiting you. Then we wouldn't need to tell anyone until after the wedding and by then it would be too late for any objections.'

'Are you worried about that?'

'A little. Aren't you?'

'A little. I suppose both of us have only recently reconciled with our families, so I don't want to upset the applecart.'

I nodded.

'Me neither.'

'So, we're agreed. We have a secret wedding and tell everyone at a time we think is the most suitable.'

'Oh Fin. This feels like such an adventure. I can't wait.'

We were married in Glasgow three months later. That night we went to the Rogano for drinks and supper, where Maude and Katie had taken me all those years ago. I was as lightheaded as I had been then, but not because of the cocktails I'd drunk. When Fin told me we were spending our wedding night in the honeymoon suite of the Central Hotel, I couldn't believe it. It was sheer luxury. I couldn't help but compare it with my wedding night when Roderick and I had wed. We hadn't even stayed in the same house, let alone shared the same room. I pushed the thought of Roderick aside, but not before saying a silent goodbye and asking him to wish me well.

It was only after we were married that we realised we hadn't discussed where we would live or even if we would live together. We were both employees of the post office, so if we were to live together, one of us would need to give up our job. Fin felt it was safer for me to continue to live in Uist and now that Heather was living in Benbecula, I had no wish to move from there. We knew the war wouldn't go on forever and we would be together then. But still, it was hard leaving him. When Fin put me on the train at Central Station, I was in tears and waved to him until I could no longer see him. But the memory of our wedding and honeymoon kept me going for what was to be a tough year.

1943-1944
A NEW UIST GIRL

CHAPTER FIFTY-ONE

It was several months after Heather had gone to work at the Airbase that Charles Hepworth turned up at the post office unexpectedly. Dorothy and I were both behind the counter when he arrived. So far as I was concerned, everything in the garden was rosy now that Fin and I were married, and Heather and I had made up. But it didn't take long for life to become complicated again.

'Charles,' I said, getting up and going round the counter to greet him. 'What on earth are you doing here?'

He looked at Dorothy.

'Perhaps we could go through to the back, Chrissie.'

She and I raised our eyebrows at each other and then I took him through.

'Would you like some tea?'

'Yes. Thank you.'

'So, what's brought you here, Charles? The way you looked at Dorothy, I thought it must be some kind of official business.'

'Yes, it is,' he slurped his tea. 'And quite serious business, too. A matter of national security.'

'National security?'

'We've recently discovered that letters are being sent from this post office, which we suspect contain coded messages for the enemy.'

I laughed. I couldn't help it. The notion that someone on our island was a German spy was absurd.

'Why do you laugh? It's no laughing matter. The safety of the base at Benbecula and its personnel is at stake here, Chrissie.'

'Yes, I'm sorry Charles. But I just can't believe anyone on the island is a German spy.'

'Perhaps not. But German and Italian prisoners of war are being detained on Benbecula. It's possible that they've paid someone to take their letters and post them in North Uist.'

'I see. But what do you think I can do about it?'

'All the mail on North Uist comes through here, does it not?'

'Yes.'

'Well, I'm going to give you the address where these letters are being sent, and I want you to infiltrate the mail and confiscate them. Then you must send them to an address that I shall give you.'

I almost laughed again at the thought of *infiltrating* and *confiscating* mail. It all sounded so cloak and dagger. Like something out of a spy novel.

'But I don't deal with the mail by myself. Dorothy, that you saw outside, and sometimes Murdo the postman, help me if there's a lot of post. Is it alright if I tell them what to look for too?'

'I'm afraid not. This is top secret. I also want you to find out who's bringing the letters over here from Benbecula.'

'Well, it could be anyone. People don't always bring their letters into the post office, you know. They put them in the post boxes that are dotted around the island.'

'I understand that, Chrissie. But if you're aware of what's going on, then it will make you more vigilant and you may notice something that you wouldn't have before. You've signed The Official Secrets Act, so I don't need to explain what is involved here. You must tell no one what I've told you.'

I was still finding it hard to take what Charles had said seriously, but I would clearly need to do so, as when he left, Dorothy was full of questions.

'Well, who was that?'

'He's a friend of the family.'

'Really? He looked shifty to me. It was clear he didn't want me overhearing what he wanted to talk to you about.'

'He's perfectly nice when you get to know him. You probably thought he looked shifty because he works for the government. I think anyone that works for the government has an air of something about them. I know I always feel uncomfortable when the Post Office Inspectors come here. But it was just a family matter he wanted to talk to me about.'

I wasn't sure she believed me, but she didn't ask me anything more about him. My stomach was in knots. What was I going to tell her and Murdo when they came to help sort out the mail? They would think it odd when I told them I would do it myself. I needed to think up some excuse that wouldn't let them know I was infiltrating the mail. The excuse I used was Catriona's move to Benbecula, even although she had been gone for over a year. I'd never replaced her as my housekeeper and Dorothy, sometimes Murdo, if there wasn't much post, and I kept the post office clean between us.

'I've been thinking. It's not fair getting you two to do the cleaning as well as help me sort the mail, so I'm going to do the mail myself from now on.'

They looked at me, obviously not happy with my announcement.

'I don't think that's fair, Chrissie,' said Dorothy.

'You don't? Why not?'

'I prefer doing the mail to cleaning, don't you Murdo?'

'Och well, I don't mind. I deal with the mail all the time, so I quite like giving the post office a bit of spit and polish. Reminds me of my army days. Besides, Chrissie's the boss and what she says goes.'

Thank goodness for Murdo. Dorothy blushed and said no more.

It only became awkward when the post office was quiet, and they were sitting having a cup of tea while I was sorting the mail. It was a pain in the neck, but I had to do it. Since Charles had told me about the letters, there had been two envelopes with the address Charles had given me. I had forwarded them on as instructed, but I couldn't find out who had sent them. The writing wasn't familiar to me, and I was tempted to ask Murdo as he was good at recognising the handwriting of people on the island. But what if I alerted him to what I was doing? There would be hell to pay. And besides, Charles had implied the letters were coming from Benbecula, not North Uist. I became paranoid and suspected everyone. It was the most awful time and marred the sense of peace I'd been feeling. As it turned out, that wasn't the only thing that marred my sense of peace.

CHAPTER FIFTY-TWO

Heather was singing when she saw Lawrence again. As she recalled their last encounter, her face flushed with embarrassment. She desperately dug her nails into her palms to keep her emotions in check while performing. He wasn't worth it. Although she would have preferred to leave after singing, they expected entertainers to mingle and dance with the men. And that's what she did, and perhaps she was more enthusiastic about it than normal because Lawrence was there and could see her. Although she'd known a new squadron had recently joined the existing Squadron 206, it hadn't occurred to her that Lawrence might be one of them. She wondered if he was going to be based in Benbecula for a while. If he were, then she would just need to get used to him being there and not let him bother her. When the band had finished playing and the dancing was over, all Heather wanted to do was get back to her digs and go to bed. But she noticed Lawrence was sitting at a table on his own, obviously drunk, and not making any move to go. Donald John was talking to him and trying to get him to move, but he wasn't having any success, so she went over.

'Is everything alright here, Donald John?'

'I can't get this silly bugger to move. He's had too much to drink. I'll need to get the MPs.'

'Let me talk to him. I know him.'

He raised his eyebrows and shrugged his shoulders.

'Okay. I'll give you five minutes.'

Lawrence looked up and his face broke into a crooked smile as he recognised her.

'Heather, my lovely Heather. Come and sit with me. Have a drink.'

'The bar's closed, Lawrence, and you need to leave. Donald John's going to call the MPs if you don't get up now.'

'Right. Well, let me put my arm around your shoulder and you can help me up.'

She bent down and put his arm around her and tried to haul him up, but he was too heavy.

'I don't think this is going to work.'

Suddenly, Lawrence began blubbering. It was hard for Heather to make out what he was saying with all the slurring and sobbing he was doing. Then eventually she understood. His best friend, Henry, had been killed in action. She sat beside him and cradled him in her arms, softly humming a lullaby her mammy used to sing to her when she was wee. She heard a light snoring and realised he'd fallen asleep.

Donald John came up and asked what was happening. He didn't seem too pleased.

'He's fallen asleep. Could you help him back to his digs? His best friend has just died on active duty.'

His face softened.

'I'll need to get someone to help me with him in that state. Poor sod. He'll have a right sore head in the morning.'

It was a bit of a struggle to shift him, but Donald John and another NAAFI assistant got him up and half dragged him, half carried him to the officers' quarters. Heather felt embarrassed for him. What a state to get into.

She was sitting in the NAAFI canteen on her own the following lunchtime when Lawrence walked in, looking a lot better than he had done the night before. He came straight over to her.

'May I?' he said, pointing to the empty chair next to her.

She nodded. The chair scraped on the floor as he pulled it out and he made a face.

'Ugh, that noise. My head can't cope.'

'Can I fetch you a cup of tea? It works wonders for a hangover.'

He looked at her with those hazel eyes that had so captivated her the first time they met, and she cursed herself as her stomach fluttered with butterfly wings.

'No. I've had loads, thank you. I just wanted to give you this.'

He took a box of chocolates out of his pocket and placed it on the table in front of her.

'Why?'

'Well, from the little I remember, you took care of me last night.'

'I would have done it for anyone who had just lost a friend. Besides, I think it's Donald John and Malcolm you should give these chocolates to, not me. It was them who got you home. You were in a bit of a state.'

She pushed the box back towards him. He hesitated, then lifted it and put it back in his pocket.

'I don't blame you for not wishing to take anything from me. I treated you pretty badly the last time we met.'

'You did. But it's water under the bridge. I must go. My condolences on the loss of your friend Henry.'

His eyes became bright with unshed tears.

'Please talk to me, Heather. Let me explain about that night. It's not what you think.'

'Isn't it? I can't think of any reason you treated me the way you did other than that you wanted to humiliate me.'

She stood up abruptly, and her chair crashed to the ground, causing everyone to look in their direction.

'And you're doing it again.'

She turned on her heel and hurried towards the exit. Before she could reach it, he had caught up with her and pulled her round.

'What the hell do you think you're doing? Let me go.'

'I did what I did to protect you, Heather.'

'To protect me? From what?'

'From me, from yourself.'

'Are you alright Heather?' asked Donald John, coming over and squaring up to Lawrence. 'Look, this lassie helped you last night when you were in a hell of a state. You shouldn't be bothering her if she doesn't want to talk to you.'

She was grateful to Donald John for trying to protect her, but the situation was becoming embarrassing. She realised she just wanted to escape, and the only way would be to agree to talk to Lawrence.

'Everything's fine Donald John. Lawrence and I are just heading outside to have a little chat.'

She reached over, took his hand, pulled him out the canteen door and into what felt like a force ten gale. It had been sunny and mild when she had gone in for lunch, but island weather was unpredictable.

'My quarters are just over here,' Lawrence shouted above the howling wind. She was still holding his hand, and he pulled her with him towards the Balivanich school, which had been converted into officers' quarters. They were both gasping for breath when they pushed in through the door.

'My room's down here.'

Heather felt uncertain about going to his room, but what else could she do? She was reluctant to go out into that storm again and perhaps if she listened to what he had to say, she could easily make her escape once the storm blew over. He took her coat, and they sat on chairs in front of the fire that was burning merrily.

'I've got some whisky if you would like some.'

'No, thank you. Just say what you've got to say, Lawrence, and then I'll go.'

He didn't speak, and as the silence between them grew, she could stand it no longer and blurted out.

'What did you mean when you said you were protecting me from myself?'

He got up from his chair and stood with his back to the fire, looking down at her.

'I knew you liked me, and I certainly liked you. You looked so beautiful that night. So sensual and alluring, I wanted nothing more than to make love to you, and I knew you wanted me to. But you also looked so young, so innocent, so vulnerable. I couldn't do it.'

'Why? Did you feel you were betraying your wife?'

'I'm afraid I wasn't thinking about Amelia that night. I was only thinking of you. You had absolutely captivated me.'

'Then why?'

Annoyingly, tears started trickling from her eyes and a lump rose in her throat.

'Why were you so cruel? I wanted you so much, Lawrence.'

'You've heard of the saying, *be cruel to be kind.*'

She nodded, wiping her tears with the back of her hand.

'Let me,' he said, taking a handkerchief from his pocket, sitting down again and gently wiping her cheeks.

'Well, you were very open with me that night, if you remember. It was clear to me the shock of finding out you were adopted was making you behave a little recklessly. I think the war has made us all behave that way a little. When I looked at you, I realised this would be a big deal for you. Losing your virginity should be to someone who loved you totally and could commit to you. I think I fell in love with you the moment I set eyes on you, but I couldn't commit to you because I was already married. '

Heather's head was spinning. He loved her. He'd loved her from the moment he'd set eyes on her.

'I was deliberately cruel, as I wanted you to be angry, not lovesick. I wanted you to get over me quickly and get on with your life with no regrets.'

'So why are you telling me this now? You're still married and I'm still a virgin.'

'I don't know. Henry's death has made me realise how fragile life is and I don't want to die without you knowing the truth. I love you, Heather,' he whispered, his voice filled with tenderness.

She moved towards him, not touching him. There was a sudden spatter of rain on the window and the fire flickered as he took her hand and kissed her fingers.

'I think I love you too, Lawrence.'

He smiled and took her in his arms, kissing her gently.

'I know I probably was behaving a little recklessly when I met you last year, but I've now sorted things out with my family and I'm much happier in myself.'

'So, what are you saying?'

'I'm ready. Let's make the most of the time we have together.'

As the storm raged outside, they made love on a blanket in front of the glowing fire and Heather thought she might die of happiness if there was such a condition.

CHAPTER FIFTY-THREE

It was through Heather working over in Benbecula that I discovered who was sending the letters.

'You'll never believe it *Mamaidh,* but there are German and Italian prisoners of war over on Benbecula and they're free to roam about just as they please.'

'I'd heard that. I wonder if Archie Campbell has the same freedoms wherever he is.'

'Has Morag not heard from him?'

'Aye, she has. She says he gets a red cross parcel every week and some cigarettes. Of course, they censor his letters so he can't say all that much. But at least he's alive.'

'I heard from Catriona that the Italian prisoners are women mad. You know how they put little red lights on some crofts to stop the planes from crashing into them?'

I didn't know, but nodded anyway. How awful to have to worry about being hit by an aeroplane every night.

'Well, apparently they went to Mrs Morrison's door one night, thinking because it had a red light, it was a brothel.'

'A brothel! On Benbecula! Oh, my.'

'They got short shrift, as you can imagine.'

'I certainly can. How awful for poor Mrs Morrison.'

'Catriona says you see the Italians all heading to church on a Sunday, but it's the Germans who've been helping people a lot with work on the crofts. Although they're not supposed to socialise with them, some crofters have even invited them in for a cup of tea. Mrs Morrison was one of them.'

My ears pricked up at this. The letters I had confiscated were in German.

'Is Mrs Morrison a young woman?'

'No. She's the same age as you. Why do you ask?'

'Well, people might talk if she has a German visiting her.'

'Don't be daft *Mamaidh*, her husband was there too. Besides, I think he maybe has a soft spot for Catriona. I've seen him chatting with her a few times.'

'Catriona? I think Murdo would be upset if he found out his only daughter was cavorting with a German.'

'Och *Mamaidh*, she's not cavorting. She's only been passing the time of day with him.'

When a letter from Bunty arrived for Heather, I used it as an excuse to do a bit of investigating.

'I'm going to cycle over to Benbecula with this letter for Heather. You'll be okay on your own for a wee while, Dorothy, won't you?'

'Aye, of course. Take your time.'

I had to call Angus out to get his boat over as the tide was in and it was a bit of a struggle to take my bike on, but I managed. Not having been to the airbase before, I was excited but nervous, as it wasn't just a social call. After I handed over the letter from Bunty, Heather gave me a tour of the place and the facilities there amazed me.

'I never thought to ask you over before *Mamaidh*. There'll be a picture on at the weekend, so maybe you could come as my guest. I was going to ask my friend Lawrence, but it would be nice to spend the afternoon with you, *Mamaidh*.'

I felt like someone had given me a million pounds.

'I'd like that Heather. Thank you.'

When I left her, I asked someone where Mrs Morrison lived and cycled over to see her. She looked puzzled when she opened the door.

'Hello. Can I help you?'

'Hello. My name's Chrissie Macdonald. I'm the post mistress over at Lochmaddy.'

'Oh hello. It's your daughter that's the singer, isn't it? Come away in and have a cup of tea.'

We chatted for a wee while about the war and what it was like having an airbase on your doorstep. Then I manoeuvred the conversation round to the prisoners of war.

'And how does it feel having the enemy living amongst you?'

'Och, Mrs Macdonald. They're just young men. Not unlike our own young men who are away at the war. So, I like to make them feel welcome. They can't do any harm while they're here, can they? But you haven't said why you've called on me, Mrs Macdonald.'

'Och, I'm sorry, Mrs Morrison. I've been so enjoying our conversation. The reason I've come is that a letter got damaged in the post and I noticed it was written in German. The envelope is totally unreadable so I can't send it on. And when Heather told me a young German lad helped you on the croft sometimes, I thought I might ask you if he sent letters home and I could give him his letter back.'

She looked puzzled. She wasn't daft.

'But why would he send his letters via your post office? We have a perfectly good post office here on Benbecula.

'Och, I know. I've met Mr Macaulay many times.'

'And besides, I think any letters the prisoners send would need to be scrutinised by the censor before being posted in bulk by the Air Force.'

'Of course, silly me. I hadn't thought of that. It's a puzzle right enough. Well, I better be getting back. I want to get over before the tide comes in. Thanks for your help.'

'Will Deiter get into trouble if it was him who sent the letter?'

'Not from me. I just want to send the letter where it's supposed to go. I would be in breach of post office rules if I didn't.'

I hoped by suggesting I was only worried about making sure I did my job properly might stop her suspecting anything sinister was going on. But her next words told me I hadn't been successful in that.

'I hope you get the matter sorted out, Mrs Macdonald. I wouldn't like to think I was welcoming the enemy into my home if they were working against us.'

'I can understand that, but it's probably nothing to worry about.'

I knew word would get out now, as she was clearly worried. So, I needed to get this matter sorted before the culprit could be alerted. But what was I going to do about it? I didn't want to make a mistake and put whoever was sending the messages on alert. They might stop sending the letters and never get caught.

CHAPTER FIFTY-FOUR

As good fortune would have it, Catriona popped in to see Dorothy and me during our lunch break when she was over visiting Murdo the next day. It wasn't the first time we'd heard how wonderful it was over at the airbase with all its mod cons. It had a generator, so there was electricity and always hot water for a shower. We didn't mind, as it was nice to see her so happy.

'You know I need to wear my hair above my collar when I'm working. So, I use a headband made from the top of an old stocking and roll my hair round the band. Let me show you. Have you got an old stocking handy, Chrissie?'

I found one, and she deftly did a demonstration on Dorothy while I watched. It was quite fetching, I thought, and asked her to do it on me.

'It's called a Victory Roll. But look at this, she went on excitedly.'

She unrolled our hair, and it turned into a beautiful pageboy style.

'Great when you're going to a dance of an evening.'

'So, have you met any eligible pilots over there, Catriona?' asked Dorothy.

'No, I haven't met anyone yet, although I think Heather might have.'

My ears pricked up when she said that, but I was intent on my mission and asked her the question that was uppermost in my mind.

'What about the prisoners of war? Do you have much to do with them?' I asked.

She looked uncomfortable.

'A little. They're free to go about the island, so it's hard not to bump into them.'

'I visited Mrs Morrison the other day, as I heard she had a young German lad, Deiter, helping her on the croft sometimes.'

Her face lit up at the mention of his name, then she frowned.

'But why were you visiting Mrs Morrison?'

'A damaged envelope came through the post and the letter inside was written in German. I thought Mrs Morrison might know who had written the letter and I could return it to them.'

Her face had grown pink at the mention of the letter.

'Do you think Deiter wrote the letter?'

'He might have. He told me he has family back in Germany.'

'Could you arrange for me to meet him? I'm coming over to see Casablanca with Heather at the base at the weekend.'

'I'll see what I can do. I better get going. I'm back on duty tonight.'

'Yes, we'll need to get back to work, too. I think that's someone at the door,' said Dorothy.

I went outside with Catriona.

'Is it you who's been posting his letters for him, Catriona?'

She looked shamefaced and nodded.

'You know all prisoner of war letters should be censored and sent through the proper channels. Why did Deiter ask you to post his letters for him?'

'He said his mother was sick, and it helped her to receive letters from him, but it took too long to go through the proper channels.'

'It's possible he's been sending information about the airbase.'

'He's a spy?'

'I don't know, but it's possible.'

'What should I do?'

'Just arrange for him to meet me at the weekend and I'll do the rest. But don't tell a soul what I've told you. You could be in serious trouble if you do.'

Poor Catriona was on the verge of tears as she mounted her bike. I wondered what Murdo would have to say about it all if he ever found out. He loved the bones of that girl and would hate if anything bad happened to her. I sat and thought about everything that evening after the post office closed. I would need to let Charles know about Deiter, but I didn't want to get Catriona into trouble. She wouldn't deliberately have helped him to send information that would help our enemy. Catriona was just a young lassie attracted to a young man. Why should she be punished? Deiter was the one at fault. So, I took matters into my own hands. I looked out the last letter, which I hadn't yet sent onto the address Charles had given me, and took it with me when I went over to Benbecula to meet Heather. Catriona was on duty in the canteen, and I asked her if she had contacted Deiter to meet her.

'I usually meet him after my shift and share a cigarette with him about 5 o'clock. So, you could talk to him then.'

Casablanca with Humphrey Bogart and Ingrid Bergman was the film I saw, but I remember little about it as my mind was racing. What would Deiter do when I showed him I had his letter?

I was totally unprepared for what happened when I saw him.

'Hello Catriona. Hello Deiter.'

He looked puzzled. Catriona obviously hadn't told him I was coming to speak to him.

'I'm the postmistress over at Lochmaddy. I think this letter might be yours.'

I took the letter out of my pocket and handed it to him. I couldn't believe it when he burst into tears.

'How did you find out? How did you know it was me who sent the letter? Did you tell her Catriona?'

'No Deiter, I promise I didn't. But she says you've been sending information that will help the enemy. Have you?'

'I had no choice. The Gestapo have threatened to hurt my mother and young sister if I don't help them.'

'But how did they find out you were here in the first place?' I asked, suddenly wondering about that.

'I got a letter from my mother. Before I got sent to Africa, I used to work in an office working on codes. I recognised the coded message they had sent. I didn't want to do it. Everyone here has been so kind to me. But I had no choice.'

He and Catriona were looking at me, both in tears now.

'What are you going to do?'

'I'll need to report it. It will be up to the authorities what they'll do, Deiter. I'm sorry for your family, but I can't allow you to keep sending information that could harm our men here.'

As soon as I got back to the post office, I sent a telegram to Charles, and he telephoned me the next day.

'Well done, Chrissie,' he said when I told him who had been sending the letters. 'I'll get on to the PoW commander straight away. Were any of the locals helping him?'

'I'm afraid I haven't been able to find that out, and he wasn't for telling me. He obviously didn't want to get anyone into trouble. What will happen to him?'

'He'll be arrested and tried for treason.'

'You mean they might hang him?'

'It depends how serious they consider his crime to be.'

'But he's so young, Charles. Hardly more than a boy. Couldn't you use him to your advantage? He's clearly sending messages because his family is in danger. Couldn't you get him to send false information or something to the Germans?'

He chuckled down the telephone.

'I should have tried to recruit you for MI5, Chrissie, rather than Donald. I think you would have made an excellent agent.'

I laughed at his joke and wondered what it would be like to work for MI5 and be involved in all that spy stuff. But I knew I wasn't cut out for it. I was too soft. Charles would probably be furious with me if he found out I'd lied to him about saying I had no information about who had helped Deiter.

CHAPTER FIFTY-FIVE

Lawrence had a week off before he was due to go back on ops again, so Heather convinced the band leader, Sam Carmichael, to give her time off, too. So, they had a week together. Lawrence loved the islands as much as she did, and they walked for miles along the machair and the sands of the many beaches on Benbecula and Uist. Being on Benbecula was so different from being on North Uist because of the Airbase. It was much noisier because of the planes taking off and landing constantly, but also the facilities put on for the aircrews and other ancillary airmen were good. So, they ate good food, drank gin, and danced. Lawrence wasn't so good at the ceilidh dancing, but he could waltz like a professional. Lawrence told her the war in the Atlantic had turned a corner, and the government was more confident than they had been a couple of years ago, but it didn't stop her worrying about him.

People had obviously noticed how close she and Lawrence had become, as they didn't hide it. So, when Catriona told her people were gossiping about them, she didn't care. She loved him. Catriona had become all sanctimonious lately and clearly disapproved of what she was doing. But she had seen the way she looked at that prisoner of war, Deiter. Being in love with the enemy was much worse than being in love with a married man, in her opinion. Although, when she thought about it, she hadn't seen Deiter for quite some time. A rumour had gone round that the military police had arrested him, but when she asked Catriona about it, she just went red in the face and told her she knew nothing about it. Perhaps Catriona was just jealous because the boy she'd fancied was no longer on the island.

Although Heather felt bad about Lawrence's wife, she knew Amelia would be the winner in the end. Lawrence would return to his old life when the war was over, and she would just need to accept this precious time for what it was: temporary. They had never spoken about the future, but that night, Lawrence said he wanted to talk to her about what would happen if the Germans got him.

'Don't even think that, Lawrence. They won't get you. You'll get back here safely, just as you've always done.'

'I hope and pray for that, but I still want to talk to you about what will happen to you if I don't come back, and I want to give you this.'

He held out a box, but she wanted to know what he meant.

'What will happen to me? What do you mean?'

'I love you, my sweet girl, but I'm married. If I die, then Amelia will inherit my estate.'

'Well, that's only fair.'

'But I want to look after you, don't you see?'

Her lip trembled. She couldn't bear to think of anything happening to him.

'It's unnecessary Lawrence. I'll always be able to live on the croft and besides, my birth mother comes from a wealthy family, so you don't need to worry about me in that way. Now what's in this box?'

Her face lit up with delight when she saw a gold locket on a chain. She opened it and inside was a picture of Lawrence on one side and a picture of her on the other. She remembered the photo from that time the Band had hired a photographer for some publicity posters. Lawrence must have got a copy from Sam.

'Oh Lawrence, this is beautiful. Thank you. Put it on me, please.'

After he put it on, he kissed her neck, then turned her back towards him.

'Stop changing the subject. What if you have my baby? What will become of it?'

She felt the blood draining from her face. A baby. She had never thought about that, which was foolish, given that they made love whenever they got the chance and making love resulted in making babies.

'I would look after it, of course.'

'Well then, it's only fair that I make provision for you. If I survive, then I will ask Amelia for a divorce, and you and I shall be married.'

When they made love that night, back in his room, in front of the fire, it was different. Still as passionate as it had always been, yes, but there was a closeness between them now they had spoken about their future together. When she waved him off the next day, she had a warm feeling knowing that one day she would be his wife.

CHAPTER FIFTY-SIX

When Heather brought Lawrence to visit us, I knew she was smitten. She had a glow about her that only comes when you make love for the first time. I was happy for her, but I wished she had waited until she had a wedding ring on her finger. He was a few years older than her, but he seemed as much in love with her as she was with him. I just hoped all would go well for them. I would hate Heather to have her heart broken. They had been going out for a few months when I found out he was married.

'Chrissie,' said Murdo one morning when he was picking up the mail for delivery. 'I don't like to gossip, as you know, but I'm hearing rumours that the man who's courting your Heather is already spoken for.'

I felt goosebumps rising on the back of my neck.

'What do you mean? Is he seeing someone else behind her back?'

'Worse than that. He's already married.'

'How do you know?'

'I know because Catriona works in the NAAFI, and she says it's the talk of the place. Heather's well known because she's a singer with the band and if truth be told, some people are jealous of her. They say she's not only got a cushy number, but she's landed a millionaire playboy into the bargain.'

'A millionaire playboy?'

'Aye. Apparently, he's one of the landed gentry and is worth a few bob.'

At first, it annoyed me that Catriona was gossiping about my Heather to her father. She could hardly talk. She'd been fraternising with a German and could have been in serious trouble if it wasn't for me. I wondered what Murdo would say if he knew that. But when I thought about what Murdo had said, I was stunned. Heather had never mentioned Lawrence was wealthy. Maybe she didn't know. But if everyone on the base knew, then she must know. And she must know he's married, too. Oh Heather, what have you done?

I spoke to Johnny and my mother and asked what we should do. Johnny wanted to confront him and ask him what his intentions were towards Heather. He sounded like someone out of a Victorian novel.

'What good will that do, Johnny?' said my mother. 'Heather loves this man and if she's been happy to start an affair with him knowing he's married, then there's nothing you can do about it. You've only just got her back. You don't want to be doing anything to upset the applecart again.'

'I know you're right *Mathair*,' I said. 'But I need to speak to Heather and let her know she can depend on me if anything goes wrong.'

'If she gets pregnant, you mean?'

'Yes, I suppose so.'

'My God. Is this family never going to have any legitimate children?'

I laughed.

'It's no laughing matter, Chrissie. You're not in any position to pretend that any baby she has is yours, as you've done with Heather and Donald. She'll have to decide if she's going to keep it or give it up for adoption.'

'Hold on *Mathair*,' said Johnny. 'We've got her a ruined woman before we've even spoken to her. Let's just calm down and think about how we're going to tackle this.'

In the end, we agreed I should talk to her. I was to approach the matter sensitively, saying what I'd heard and then just see what she had to say for herself. I was not to be judgemental, and I was to say we would all be there for her if she needed us.

I decided to speak to Catriona, as she had so much to say, and find out a bit more about this Lawrence. But it was difficult, as she'd been avoiding me since the Deiter incident. So I roped Murdo into getting her to come and see me.

'Murdo, I've been mulling over what you told me about this Lawrence that Heather is seeing, and wondered if you could ask Catriona to come and pay me a visit. I'd like to find out everything she's heard about him.'

'No problem, Chrissie. I'll let her know you want to have a chat with her.'

When Catriona called on me the following week, she looked nervous.

'My father says you want to have a word with me, Chrissie.'

'Yes, it's about what you told your father about the man Heather is seeing. I'd like to know as much about him as possible.'

She puffed out a sigh and smiled. Murdo had obviously not told her what it was I wanted to speak to her about.

'But before we go on to that, I want to talk about what happened with Deiter.'

The smile froze on her lips.

'You've been avoiding me and I'm not sure why. Dorothy and I miss you coming into the post office.'

Her eyes glistened with unshed tears.

'I miss you and Dorothy too, but I thought after what happened, you wouldn't want to have anything to do with me.'

'Don't be daft, Catriona. You're a young girl who fell for the wrong boy, just like my Heather, by the sounds of it. Did you hear what happened to Deiter?'

'Yes, it was the talk of the island. But also, he wrote to me.'

'He wrote to you. How? Wasn't he sent to prison?'

'No. When they took him into custody, a government representative approached him and saw the potential value of his code-breaking skills.'

I smiled inwardly. Charles must have taken my advice.

'He's now working for the government. He asked them if he could write to let me know he was okay, and they agreed.'

'So, they now know you helped him?'

'No. He just said we had become fond of one another, which

is true. I'm hoping after the war is over, we will meet up again. I don't believe he's a bad person, Chrissie.'

'I'm happy for you, Catriona, and for Deiter. I didn't like that I was the one who had to report him to the authorities, but I couldn't continue to let him send messages to the Gestapo. But it sounds like everything has turned out for the best.'

She nodded, and the smile came back. But I couldn't help wondering what her family and friends would think of her if they knew she was in love with a German boy. Somehow the scandal that Heather was causing by seeing a married man dwindled into insignificance in comparison with Catriona being in love with the enemy, even if he wasn't a bad person.

'Anyway, that's it all over. You can come back and see Dorothy and me whenever you wish. Now tell me everything you know about this Lawrence Moorcroft.'

CHAPTER FIFTY-SEVEN

Every night when she was singing, she waited in anticipation for him to come in to see her. She wasn't unduly worried when a week had passed, and he hadn't turned up. Sometimes that's the way things worked. There was no time for socialising while they were on duty. Storms had affected the number of sorties the pilots could go on and she knew that sometimes during such ferocious weather, they had to land elsewhere as it was impossible to get back to Benbecula. The pilots often complained that fighting the weather around Benbecula was worse than fighting the enemy. But she never dreamed anything serious had happened to him. Not until she was sitting having her breakfast in the canteen one morning. She knew something had happened as there was a lot of toing and froing, and a general air of unease pervaded the canteen.

'What's going on?' she asked Donald John when he passed on his way to the kitchen with dirty dishes.

'I'm not sure, Heather, but something's wrong. The Station Commander has just come in.'

She looked over at the man in his uniform with lots of braids, signifying that he was important, and a sense of dread came upon her.

'May I have everyone's attention?'

A hush fell over the canteen. The clatter of cutlery being put down on the table reverberated around the canteen as everyone stopped eating and looked at the Station Commander expectantly.

'I regret to inform you we've lost several men in a U-Boat attack. We've spent the last few days trying to find if anyone survived, but we have been unsuccessful. Until I have informed their families, their names will remain confidential.'

Heather was sure the Commander looked over at her when he said this, and she took this to be a sign that Lawrence was one of the dead.

'They died fighting for our freedom, and we should all be proud of their unfailing loyalty and courage to King and Country. Please continue with your breakfast.'

He then turned on his heel and left the room. Silence followed, and then the sound of chatting and eating began again. But not for Heather. The unfinished breakfast of now congealed bacon and eggs sat on the table, staring up at her. Lawrence had loved bacon and eggs for breakfast. Now she would never get to have breakfast with him ever again. Would never get to marry him and have his children. Never. What a horrible word. A last word. The end. She didn't know what to do but then decided to follow the Commander and ask him directly. She had a right to know. Lawrence had told her they would marry after the war.

'Commander Jones,' she called.

He turned. He knew her, of course, as he sometimes came in to mix with the men and sample the entertainment.

'Yes, Miss Macdonald. How can I assist?'

'Is Lawrence Moorcroft one of the men who died?'

He looked annoyed.

'I explained that the information was confidential until the deceased men's families had been informed.'

'But I love Lawrence, and he loves me. I have a right to know.'

'You have no rights, Miss Macdonald. Mrs Moorcroft is the woman who has the right to know before anyone else if her husband is dead. I trust I make myself clear.'

As he turned his back on her, for the first time since beginning her relationship with Lawrence, she felt ashamed of that relationship. It didn't matter that Lawrence had loved her and said he would divorce Amelia and marry her. If he were dead, none of that would happen. She would just be some girl who'd had an affair with a pilot, like so many other girls. No-one special. Someone with no rights. But perhaps he wasn't dead. She clung to the fact that the Commander had said 'if' and the flutter of hope it gave her kept her going until the Commander officially released the news. But it was Catriona she heard it from.

'I'm so sorry for your loss, Heather. You know I didn't approve of you going with a married man, but I know how fond of each other you and Lawrence were,' she said, sitting beside her and putting her arm around her.

Fond. What an understatement. She knew she should smile and nod, but she couldn't. He was never coming back. Her love. Her life. There was a kind of buzzing in her head, and while she could see Catriona's lips moving, she couldn't hear what she was saying. She was numb. She rose to go out for some fresh air, and then she heard what Catriona was saying.

'His plane and five others took a direct hit. There were no survivors.'

Her legs gave way, and she collapsed into her chair again.

'Are you alright Heather? Why don't I take you home so that you can tell your mother what's happened? I'll tell Sam Carmichael you've taken the news badly and you need some time off.'

Her mother. Her mother was in Canada. But her mammy was in North Uist, and she realised how much she wanted to hear Chrissie's voice and feel her arms around her. She would know what to do.

CHAPTER FIFTY-EIGHT

I'll never forget the day she came to tell us the Gerrys had shot Lawrence down and he was dead. I was in the back of the post office sorting mail when Dorothy came through to tell me Heather had arrived.

'She looks in a bit of a state. I think she's had bad news.'

I rushed through, my heart racing with fear. Something must have happened to Lawrence. As soon as she saw me, she burst into tears and ran into my arms. Catriona was with her, but she didn't stay. She could obviously see how distressed Heather was, and it was best to leave her with me.

'Oh *Mamaidh*, Lawrence is dead.'

There were customers in the post office, and I noticed some had tears of sympathy and some fear in their eyes, each one of them thinking about their own loved one and whether they would be next.

'Come on through to the back, Heather. We'll have a cup of tea, and you can tell me what you know.'

She came through to the back, blindly grasping my hand as if she were drowning. Which she was. Drowning in sorrow. My stomach was in knots, and my heart was racing. How could I comfort my girl? I remembered how low I'd felt after Roderick died. It was like my world had ended, and I almost walked into the sea that day on Clachan Sands. It was Heather that saved me before she was even born. But how could I save her? When she collapsed sobbing into my arms, I knew all I could do was be there for her; to let her cry, to rant and rave at the injustice of it all, and most of all, to talk about him. Whatever it took to get her through. But, of course, she also had her father and her grandmother and between us we supported her over the first month until she was ready to go back to work. And then it was something else that got her through.

Although Heather was back at work and was still singing with the band, she came to stay either with me or at the croft for at least one night a week. It was one morning after one of those nights that I noticed she was looking peaky and had put weight on round her tummy. I didn't know whether to laugh or cry. She was pregnant. I wondered if she had realised yet. All new life is wonderful, but it felt like history was repeating itself. She was unmarried and her baby would be illegitimate. Would it bother her? She had never gone public with the news of her illegitimacy, and we had never discussed it. So, I wasn't sure if she'd stayed quiet about it because she was ashamed or because she wanted to protect me and Johnny. It was time to find out.

'Heather, you're looking a little peaky. Are you okay?'

'I miss Lawrence every day, *Mamaidh*. I keep expecting to see him coming in when I'm singing, the way he used to do when he returned from ops, but he never does.'

'Maybe you should go see the doctor and see what he has to say.'

'I might. I've been feeling sickly recently, and my periods have stopped too. But it's only natural to feel off when you've lost someone you love, isn't it?'

She looked down at her tummy, rubbed it slowly, then looked at me.

'I'm pregnant, aren't I?'

'I think so.'

'What an idiot I am, not to have put two and two together.'

She sat on the kitchen chair, gazing down at her tummy.

'Lawrence said this might happen, but I never thought it would. I don't know why. Oh, *Mamaidh,* why couldn't he have lived?'

Her sobbing was pitiful to listen to and all I could do was put her on my knee the way I did when she was a girl and rock her in my arms until it subsided. When she calmed down, she went to wash her face, and I made a pot of tea. I told Dorothy that I was not to be disturbed.

'I can't believe I didn't know. How could I not recognise the symptoms of having a baby? Everyone knows you feel sick and stop having periods.'

Through her red-rimmed eyes, I could see her eyes were sparkling. She was happy.

'Och, you've had so much to cope with. I'm not surprised you didn't know.'

'I can't help it, *Mamaidh*, but I feel so happy. Lawrence will live on through this child. If God didn't mean for me to have him, he's given me the next best thing. And I can't tell you how grateful I am.'

'What about Lawrence's family? Will you let them know your news?'

I knew I'd said the wrong thing as I watched her face transform into a stormy cloud of anger. She stood up, and I braced myself for what was to come.

'Why did you have to mention them? You've spoiled everything. The next thing you'll be asking me if I'm keeping my baby or having it adopted, so it doesn't have to suffer the stigma of illegitimacy.'

'Heather, I'm sorry. That isn't what I meant. I just thought that Lawrence's family would feel the same as you. The thought of him continuing to exist through your child would bring them comfort.

But she wasn't listening and stormed out of the room. I had made a real hash of it yet again.

CHAPTER FIFTY-NINE

Heather grabbed her coat and walked back towards the causeway. Why did Mammy have to mention Lawrence's family? Why couldn't she let her have some time just to be happy that she was having his baby? A momentary surge of joy flooded through her before the thought of Lawrence's family came back into her mind. She didn't want to think about them because it meant she had to think about his wife, and she didn't want to think about her. She didn't want to think what it would be like for her to find out about Lawrence's betrayal. It didn't matter how much she and Lawrence had loved each other; he had betrayed Amelia. It also meant she had to think about all the stuff that Chrissie must have thought about when the first Heather got pregnant and when her mother got pregnant. But she didn't know how she felt about her child being illegitimate because she still hadn't figured out how she felt about being illegitimate herself. Although she had given Chrissie a hard time for not telling her the truth, she had told no one else the truth about her birth. Apart from Lawrence. She had told him everything.

The sky grew dark, but she didn't notice until large drops of rain began falling on her. She realised she wouldn't make it to the causeway and turned back. Her face flamed with embarrassment at how she had yelled at Chrissie. But Heather knew she would forgive her. Her mammy loved her unconditionally, just as she would love this wee one she was carrying unconditionally. The wind rose and before long, a gale was blowing. She huddled into her coat and put her head down. The wind was blowing so fiercely it was almost like being pushed along by a steam train and the next thing she found herself on the ground. She lay for a moment trying to gather herself, with the wind raging and shrieking around her, when a figure appeared through the storm.

'Well Heather Macdonald, what the hell are you doing out in this weather?'

It was Donald John.

'I could say the same to you, man.'

'I saw you from my granny's window. I didn't know it was you, of course, or I might not have come out to help you.'

'My hero.'

'Come on. Let's get you up and you can come into the house until this blows over.'

She felt his powerful arms gripping her, pulling her up. He put an arm around her, and they pushed together against the wind until they reached Mrs McLeod's house.

'Och Heather, *mo graidh*. What are you doing out in this weather?' said Catherine McLeod. 'Come in and get your wet coat off.'

Mr McLeod had died not long before her grandfather, so Donald John had moved in to help with the work on the croft when the army discharged him.

She took her coat off and Catherine hung it in front of the peat fire that was glowing in the hearth.

'It was fine when I left the post office, but this storm started up so quickly I didn't even notice until it was too late.'

'I expect you have things on your mind.'

Heather knew she was referring to Lawrence, and tears slipped from her eyes. She wiped them away with the back of her hand and sniffed.

'Here, sit down and I'll make us all a nice cup of tea. Just as well, Donald John had time off from his job in the NAAFI and was here. I'd never have been able to go out in this storm to get you.'

'Thanks Donald John. I'm very grateful?'

The tears rolled down her cheeks again, and it surprised her when Donald John took a hanky from his pocket and gently wiped them away. Then he thought better of it and handed it to her.

'Here, blow your nose. Would you like a fag?'

'I certainly would not. Those woodbines are horrible.'

She laughed, glad that they were back to their usual banter.

When the storm subsided, he walked her back to the post office.

'You've not said why you were out.'

'I was visiting my mother, but I got annoyed with her and left. It was selfish of me.'

'Selfish?'

'Yes. She's so good to me, but I can't help flying off the handle at her sometimes.'

'From memory, I don't think it's just your mother you can fly off the handle with. Remember that day I asked you and Catriona to come to Bayhead with me? You went in a mood and cycled home on your own.'

Heather laughed, remembering how annoyed she'd been that Catriona wanted to spend time with Donald John rather than her.

'I've just found out I'm going to have a baby.'

He raised his eyebrows at her.

'Should I congratulate you? Are you happy about it?'

'Yes. I'm delighted that Lawrence will live on through his child.'

'So why did you get annoyed with your mother?'

'She asked if I was going to tell Lawrence's family, as she was sure they would feel the same happiness as me. And she's right, of course, but I got annoyed at her. I just wanted to savour this time on my own without thinking of consequences or of anyone else.'

'It's a lot to take in. I'm sure your mother will understand.'

When they reached the post office, she put out her hand to shake his.

'Thanks for rescuing me from the storm, Donald John.'

'Any time, Heather,' he said, taking her hand. 'It was my pleasure.'

CHAPTER SIXTY

It was four months after Heather realised she was pregnant that a letter arrived in the mail for her. I looked at the envelope. It was an expensive one with Heather's name and address at the airbase on Benbecula written in a flowery script. It must have come to us by mistake as we only normally received the mail for North Uist. There was a crest on the envelope, which usually meant it was from somebody important. I wanted to hold on to the envelope until I could give it to Heather personally, but that would mean interfering with the mail, a jailing offence. I wasn't sure what to do. Asking Murdo to deliver it would mean he'd have to go over to Benbecula, which wasn't part of his delivery route. So, I decided I would deliver it myself. That way I wouldn't be interfering with the mail, just carrying out my duty as postmistress. Murdo gave me a lift in his van, and I then got Angus' boat over to Benbecula.

It was cold but bright and crisp, a perfect winter day. I would normally have enjoyed the walk to Balivanich on such a day, but the noise from the aero

planes flying in and out disturbed the peace. I wondered how the locals had taken to having their quiet lives interrupted like this. However, I soon forgot about the aeroplanes when my mind went back to the day Heather had realised she was pregnant, and how worried I'd been when the storm broke. But she had arrived back unharmed and was full of apologies for getting angry with me.

'It was lucky Donald John was at Catherine's, *Mamaidh.* I don't know what would have happened to me and this wee one if he hadn't rescued us.'

'How is he getting on at the NAAFI? It must be hard for him working on his granny's croft and doing a job too.'

'He's doing okay. I see him sometimes when he's in the canteen during the day when I go in for lunch or sometimes at night when I'm singing.'

'Wasn't he your boyfriend at one time?'

'Not my boyfriend, *Mamaidh*. Just someone to help get me through finding out you weren't my birth mother.'

My heart sank. Was she going to have a go at me again?

'Don't worry *Mamaidh.* I'm not going to shout at you again. I think we need to talk about me being illegitimate. I've only ever told Lawrence and I realise it's because I'm ashamed and I don't understand why.'

We talked and talked, and I can't tell you how happy I was that we did. When we went to bed that night, both exhausted but happy, we agreed she didn't need to decide about telling Lawrence's family until she was ready. She would just take time to become used to being a mother.

With the arrival of the letter, it now looked like her time might be up. As I drew nearer to where Heather lived, I recognised by the butterflies fluttering inside that I was anxious about the letter and what news it was bringing. I suspected it was from Lawrence's family and wondered if Heather was ready to tell them about the baby yet. She was nearly five months pregnant and showing, so it was no longer a secret that she was pregnant. But it didn't seem to bother her she might be the subject of gossip. Gossip that might have reached the Moorcroft family.

When I arrived and asked if I could see Heather, the man in charge told me she was rehearsing over in the NAAFI. I could hear '*We'll Meet Again,*' being sung, and wondered if Vera Lynn was visiting. Then I realised it was Heather. I'd never seen her performing before. Although I knew she had a sweet voice because I'd seen her winning a prize at the Mòd, she sounded so different. She had only been a girl then, of course. Not letting her know I was there, I stood at the back of the hall so that I could watch her performing. I'd never realised the hard work that went into rehearsing. I suppose if you're not a performer yourself, then you don't. But it looked hard work, all that stopping and starting just to get things right with the band.

When it was over, she turned round and saw me. Her face clouded over.

'What's wrong *Mamaidh*? Is something wrong with Granny?'

'No, no. Nothing like that. I have a letter for you. I think it must have ended up in our post bag by mistake, so I thought I should bring it over. You were just wonderful there, Heather. I never realised you were so talented.'

'Thanks,' she said, barely looking at me as she scrutinised the letter I'd handed her.

When she looked at me, I could see the fear in her eyes.

'It's from Lawrence's family, isn't it?'

'I think so. That's why I brought it straight over. It's addressed to you here, but it ended up with the post for North Uist by mistake by the looks of it. I thought you would want to see it straight away.'

CHAPTER SIXTY-ONE

When Heather saw Chrissie, her first thought was that something was wrong with her granny, but it was worse than that. She had a letter, and it looked like it was from Lawrence's family. After staring at it for a couple of minutes, she tore it open. She bit her bottom lip as she read it.

Dear Miss Macdonald

You don't know me, nor I you. But I believe you knew my husband well. I won't beat about the bush. One of Lawrence's friends has informed me that you and he were having an affair while he was stationed in Benbecula. I'm heartbroken to hear this. Lawrence and I were inseparable before he went to war, so I'm finding it hard to believe he would have been unfaithful to me. I can only assume the daily trauma of fighting for his country made him reckless in the face of such an uncertain future and that you took advantage of this. I know what you girls are like. You have affairs with any man who is desperate enough. I know very little of your background except that you are a singer paid by the government to help keep up the morale of our troops, and you appear to have done your job well where Lawrence was concerned. I expect, though, that Lawrence's wealth was a factor in you luring him into having an affair with you.

I believe you are now pregnant and are telling everyone that the child is Lawrence's. But I've been told you have had several men friends over the last year and that the child could belong to any of them. I am therefore writing to let you know that if you attempt to make any claim on Lawrence's estate for the upkeep of your child after it is born, I will challenge it. I have taken legal advice and can tell you that your bastard child will have no claim on Lawrence's estate. You cannot prove that the child is his and you cannot put his name on the birth certificate in his absence. I hope this makes my position clear.

Yours faithfully
Amelia Moorcroft (Mrs)

Chrissie was looking at her expectantly, so she passed the letter to her to read.

'Oh my, Heather. She's not beating about the bush right enough. What a horrible letter.'

She couldn't speak. Amelia's letter was horrible, but no wonder. To find out your husband was unfaithful was bad enough, but to find out his mistress was having a child was even worse. Mistress. That's all she was. Not a fiancé, not a wife. A mistress, a woman with no morals. An illegitimate child having her own illegitimate child.

'What does she mean you've had other men friends?'

'I don't know. The only man I've ever been with is Lawrence. My child is his.'

'How dare she try to slander you like that? You should write back and tell her so. And what a cheek making out you only went with Lawrence because of his money. What does she take you for?'

'Oh *Mamaidh,* you're not helping. Stop going on and on. I need to think about all this. Thanks for bringing the letter, but I'd like to be on my own for a while.'

She could see the hurt in Chrissie's eyes, but this wasn't about her. It was about her and Lawrence's baby. Until the letter arrived, she had never thought about making a claim on Lawrence's estate. In fact, a part of her didn't even want his family to know about the baby. But what would he have wanted her to do? He had told her he wanted to marry her so that would have meant her becoming part of his life, part of a wealthy family and all that goes with it. They had never discussed it, and she hadn't even considered what marrying Lawrence would mean. Love had blinded her. But she had to think about it now. Did she want to make a claim on his estate for the child? Did she want that kind of life for him or her? Everyone already knew she was having a child out of marriage. There was no hiding that. But she wanted her child to know who his or her father was and that she and Lawrence made them with love. There was no way she could let this woman imply there was any doubt about who the father of her child was. But how? Some people at the base had changed towards her when the baby began to show, and Catriona had told her they were saying a lot of unkind things about her. If she was a source of gossip, her reputation was in ruins, so it would be difficult for her to defend herself against Amelia's claim. She didn't know what to do.

CHAPTER SIXTY-TWO

Although it hurt that Heather wanted me to leave her on her own, I understood. Sometimes you just had to sort things out yourself. I wished Roddy could come home on leave so that he could advise Heather on what her rights were and what the rights of Lawrence's family were. But he was goodness knew where. I hadn't heard from him in ages. When I got back to the post office, it was busy with customers.

'I'll just hang my coat up, Dorothy, and then I'll be through.'

'Take your time. You've got a visitor.'

My heart thumped with joy. Had Roddy got some leave? I had a huge smile on my face when I went through to the back, but it wasn't Roddy who stood up to greet me. It was a dark-haired woman I hadn't met before, but I knew immediately who she must be, and the smile left my face.

'Hello, Mrs Macdonald,' she said nervously in a kind of Glaswegian/American twang. 'I'm Theresa. Roddy's wife.'

I didn't know quite what to do. Should I hug her or shake her hand? What was she doing here, anyway?

'I'm sorry to just turn up like this, but I needed to tell you the news face to face.'

It was then I noticed there was a bump under her coat. She was pregnant. I was going to be a granny. My heart swelled with joy. My boy was going to be a father.

'I can see why,' I said, smiling widely and pointing to her tummy. 'Welcome to North Uist. Let me take your coat and you can tell me everything. I haven't heard from Roddy for ages. Does he know?'

She burst into tears.

'That's not why I'm here, Mrs Macdonald,' she said, holding out a telegram.

I froze. No. Not my Roddy, please God. No.

'What's that?'

Stupid. I knew what it was.

She put the telegram down and held my hands. I could feel them trembling as she looked into my eyes. Her voice was soft as she spoke the words I didn't want to hear.

'The telegram says Roddy is missing and as they have no further information, they must presume he is dead.'

Her voice broke as she said the last words. Then she shuddered as anguished sobs gripped her body. At last, I knew how to greet my new daughter-in-law. I encircled her in my arms, and we clung to each other like lost souls in a dark, unfathomable ocean.

The next few months were some of the most difficult I've ever experienced. I thought losing a husband was the worst thing that could happen to a woman, but losing a child is unbearable. It's not the natural order of things that your children die before you. How I wished God had taken me instead of him. I kept waiting for him to appear. Not having a body to bury meant I clung to the hope that he was still alive. I took to walking down to meet the ferry every time it came in at Lochmaddy. And every time my heart broke all over again when he didn't come off it.

I asked Theresa to stay with me if her parents would allow it and they agreed, as they thought it would be safer on Uist than in Glasgow for her and the child when it was born.

'How did your father take it when you told him you and Roddy were getting married?'

'I didn't tell him and my ma until after we had been to the Registry Office. I didn't want to give him a chance to stop us. But, as it turned out, he didn't raise any objections. I think the war has affected him, made him more mellow.'

I smiled.

'Yes, like us all, this war has made us realise life is precious and all the things we got hot and bothered about hardly matter in the scheme of things.'

'How did you feel, Chrissie? When Roddy told you? I know you were against us marrying, too.'

I'd told her to call me Chrissie. It sounded too formal, being called Mrs Macdonald all the time.

'I think, like your father, I've mellowed.'

As I thought back to the time when Roddy had told me he'd met a Catholic girl and I had said his father would turn in his grave and I would disown him if he went ahead with the marriage, tears suddenly overwhelmed me.

'Oh Theresa, I was terrible back then. I told him I would disown him. As if I could ever have done that. But I feel so guilty now. I hope when that plane was going down he knew how much I loved him.'

I could see her swallowing, trying hard to hold back her tears.

'Of course he did.'

'Did he ever tell you that when I was carrying him, I got caught in a blizzard and almost got attacked by a wolf?'

I remember, when we found out he was bullying Donald and Roderick had to give him a slippering, wondering if that had affected him in some way. Made him hot-headed and temperamental sometimes.

'No, I don't think he did. We haven't really known each other that long when you think about it. So, I would love to hear all the stories about Roddy and about your family. Then I can pass them on to this little one that I'm carrying. Tell him or her all about their daddy and his family.'

I wondered how Theresa would react when she found out that Roderick had buried a man and took his Cree wife to live with him. That Donald was a quarter Cree, and Heather was the illegitimate daughter of my brother. She might find our family secrets scandalous and decide to keep her child away from us. I changed the subject.

'What about the child? Will you bring it up as a Catholic or a Protestant?'

She looked at me with a glint in her green eyes, and I wondered if she thought I was challenging her.

'It will be a Catholic. Roddy and I wrote to each other when we found out I was expecting, and he said he didn't mind. I can show you the letter if you need proof.'

'No, no, of course I don't need proof. It's your decision, Theresa. Please don't think I'm trying to interfere. I promise I'm not.'

'In some ways, I feel it's even more important now that Roddy won't be with me and our baby, as I wouldn't know the first thing about bringing a child up as a Protestant.'

'We could help with that, of course. But I think if there were more mixed marriages, perhaps there would be less intolerance between all the different religions.'

'I think we're still a long way away from that, Chrissie.'

CHAPTER SIXTY-THREE

Heather was full of rage when she found out Roddy was dead. It just compounded how she felt about Lawrence. Why was this happening to her? What had she done that was so wrong except love a man who was already married? Was that so bad that she needed to be punished? What kind of God did this to people? What kind of God allowed war? Her head was full of all this when Donald John sat down beside her in the canteen one day, not long after she'd heard about Roddy.

'Sorry to hear about your brother, Heather. This effing war.'

'It's alright you can swear if you want to. I want to curse like a trooper I can tell you. I mean, how do they know he's even dead? They've not found a body. He could still be alive for all they know.'

'Well, maybe he is, and the Germans have taken him prisoner.'

She hadn't thought of that and wondered how the Germans treated their prisoners of war.

'Well, if he gets as well treated over there as these German and Italian prisoners of war get treated here, he'll be okay. I think it's ridiculous they get to roam about the island as free as birds, living off the fat of our land while my Lawrence is dead, and my brother might be dead, too. I hate their guts.'

'Come on now Heather. Try to calm yourself. That wee baby of yours will wonder what's got into you.'

'Och Donald John. It's just not fair. I hate that Lawrence will never get to see his baby. And now his wife is saying I only had an affair with him because he was wealthy. But worse than that, she's accusing me of seeing other men while I was seeing Lawrence and that the baby isn't even his. I can't bear it.'

She let out a screech and put her head in her hands. Everyone was looking, but she didn't care.

'I wish I could die too, and then me and the baby could be with Lawrence.'

Someone ran to get Sam Carmichael, and he rushed into the hall.

'Heather, Heather. Come on, calm yourself, love. I think you should stop working now. You're nearly six months gone anyway, and you're clearly distressed.'

'Are you sacking me, Sam? Well, don't bother I'm going.'

With that, she jumped up and made towards the door of the canteen. She could hear Donald John talking to Sam.

'I'll go after her,' he said.

'Yes. Take her home, son. She obviously needs to rest up. Hearing of her brother's death on top of Lawrence's has been too much for her. Borrow my car.'

Donald John helped her pack her case and then put it in Mr Carmichael's car. Luckily, the tide was out, and they got over the causeway with no trouble. She didn't utter a word the entire way home, and Donald John let her be. Not until they reached the outskirts of Lochmaddy did she speak.

'Can we sit at the pier for a wee while, please Donald John? I'm sorry I was behaving like a madwoman back then. But there again, it's in my genes.'

He drove down past the post office and parked up on the pier. All was quiet, with only the sound of the water lapping against the walls of the pier.

'What did you mean when you said it was in your genes?'

'I'm not who you think I am.'

'I remember you said that to me when we were at school. What do you mean?'

'Chrissie isn't my birth mother. She adopted me.'

'And your mother was a madwoman?'

'At that time, yes, she was.'

'So, Chrissie did you a favour, taking you in.'

'Yes, I suppose so. Who knows where I'd have ended up if she hadn't? But, of course, she had another motive. My father is her brother, Johnny.'

'Wow! My granny would love to hear all this. But I won't tell her. You can trust me.'

'Can I Donald John? I remember when I told Catriona about Johnny, and she told you. It was you who told your mother, and everything went wrong.'

'Aye well, I didn't know you so well back then. And you didn't like me much, so I'd nothing to lose.'

'You've nothing to lose now, either.'

'I know. But I've got to know you and I care about you. You've had a hard time lately. I wouldn't want to cause you any more bother.'

'I don't even know if I care who knows I'm illegitimate. In the scheme of things, it's nothing.'

'What about the accusations his wife's making that you were seeing other men? What are you going to do about that?'

'I don't know. She's only saying it because she thinks I want his money. But I don't. I want to do what's right for my child and for Lawrence. He told me he would get a divorce and marry me when the war was over. So, if he was still alive, his child would have lived the same life that Lawrence lived.'

'And is that what you want?'

'I don't know what I want. I need to get legal advice. I was hoping my brother could help me, but he can't. He's lying at the bottom of the sea somewhere or in some prisoner of war camp.'

She cried for a while, leaning her head on Donald John's shoulder. When she was ready, he took her to the post office and the loving arms of her mammy.

CHAPTER SIXTY-FOUR

Heather came to stay with me when she left Benbecula, so the post office house was a busy one again. It got me through the dark days wondering what had happened to Roddy and if he was still alive. When Fin asked me how things were going and did I think we were any closer to moving in together, I had to tell him no.

'I'm sorry Fin. But I've now got two pregnant girls living here with me. Where would they go if I gave up my job and had to leave the post office? I don't think it's a good time.'

'No, I think you're right. Let's wait until the babies are born. Although, knowing you, if you have two new grandchildren, I can't see you wanting to leave North Uist any time soon.'

I wondered if he was right. But I was his wife. I should be with him.

'Let's wait and see what happens. Who knows where the girls and their babies will end up moving to?'

Luckily, Heather and Theresa got on well and seemed to draw comfort from each other. Although I was grieving the loss of Roddy, having the two girls there and knowing I was going to become a granny made all the difference. The three of us discussed what Heather should do about the letter she'd received from Lawrence's wife. I said little for fear Heather wouldn't want to hear what I had to say. I realised I was still treading on eggshells a little with her. But Theresa said just what I was thinking.

'I think that woman has a cheek, saying those things about you, Heather.'

'She's every right to be upset, Theresa. It must have come as a terrible shock to find out her husband had been unfaithful to her and that I'm having his child. Imagine how you would feel if it turned out Roddy had met someone.'

Theresa's face crumpled, and huge tears tumbled from her eyes.

'Well, he won't be meeting anyone ever again now, will he?'

Heather put her arms around her. 'Sorry Theresa.'

They sat like that for a while until Theresa was calm again.

'The thing is, it's not about Amelia or about me. It's about Lawrence's child and what's best for him or her. I think I need to challenge Amelia for my child's sake.'

'Why don't you contact Maude and see if she can give you any advice? She's been really helpful to our family in the past.'

'Do you think she'll be okay with me doing that? It's a while since Aunt Katie died.'

'I think she'll be happy to be of use to Katie's family again. Why don't I telephone her tonight?'

As I rose to go through to the telephone exchange, there were several loud bangs on the door of the post office house. We looked at each other with a mixture of hope and dread. Could it be Roddy, or was it more bad news coming to our door? Heather rose first to answer the door. Donald John was standing there, his coat and cap dripping with rain.

'Donald John. You gave me a fright. What're you doing here? You better come in.'

'I need to speak to you, Heather.'

'Alright. What's so urgent? Come in out of that rain.'

'Oh hello,' he nodded at Theresa and me. 'Hope I'm not interrupting anything.'

'We were just discussing what I should do about the letter from Mrs Moorcroft,' said Heather. 'sit down and I'll get you a cup of tea.'

It surprised me she was talking to Donald John so openly about the letter, but his next words told me he already knew quite a lot about it.

'That's what I've come to see you about. There are private detectives over at the base. They're trying to get evidence about your *friendships* with other men. Word is Amelia Moorcroft has hired them.'

'Well, they'll not get anywhere with that. You and Sam are the only men I'm friendly with, and you'll be able to tell the detectives that our relationship is purely platonic.'

'I've already told them that, but they offered me money to say that we were, you know, intimate.'

Donald John was wringing his hands as he spoke.

'I hope you didn't take their dirty money,' said Theresa, as forthright as usual.

Donald John looked annoyed.

'Don't be daft. I would never do that. But there are others that might. There's not a lot of sympathy for Heather on that base. Many people see her as a woman of loose morals.'

'What a bitch that woman is,' continued Theresa. 'It looks like she'll go to any lengths to stop you from making a claim on Lawrence's estate.'

'I'm definitely going to contact Maude now. She can't get away with this. Will you ring her Mammy?'

'Yes, of course. I'll do it now. In some ways, this helps us. If it ever goes as far as the courts, Donald John here can tell them what Amelia's been up to. I think she would be the one to look bad and not you.'

'Well, I better get going then. I just thought you should know what was going on, Heather.'

'Thanks Donald John. I appreciate you taking the time to come over.'

After he left, I telephoned Maude. We chatted about Katie for a while, and then I told her about Heather's situation.

'So let me get this straight. Amelia Moorcroft has been told by a family friend about Heather and Lawrence's affair and that Heather is having a child. She's insinuating that Heather manipulated him into having the affair and engaged in relationships with other men at the same time as she was involved with Lawrence. Consequently, she argues that Lawrence is not the father of Heather's child and has no claim on the Moorcroft Estate. Desperate to discredit Heather, she has resorted to hiring private detectives who, when they could not get the evidence they needed, offered bribes for false information about Heather. Is that right so far?'

'That's right Maude.'

It was horrible hearing it put so plainly.

'But Heather doesn't care about making a claim on the estate. She only wants Lawrence's name to be on her child's birth certificate.'

'I'm afraid she won't be able to do that. When an unmarried mother wants to register the father on her child's birth certificate, the father needs to go along with her. But as Lawrence is dead, this won't be possible.'

'Oh, I see. I think it's best if you speak to Heather yourself and tell her what you've told me. It all sounds rather complicated.'

'Okay. I'll hang on here.'

'Thanks Maude. I don't know what our family would have done without your help in the past, and it means so much to us to know you're helping us again. Katie was fortunate to have such a kind and loving friend.'

'I miss her so much, Chrissie. She was my life.'

Her voice broke as she said the words. It must be so hard for her. This damned war.

'I'll just go get Heather. Hold on.'

I left Heather to her telephone call and went to wash up the cups. When I went back through to see how it was going, I caught the tail end of her conversation with Maude.

'I want to put Lawrence's name on my child's birth certificate because I know how it feels to be told lies about your natural parents, and I don't want that for my child. I want him or her to know we wanted them and that they're not just the offspring of some sordid affair. Lawrence and I loved each other, and I know he would have married me if he had lived.'

I felt sad hearing Heather telling Maude about being lied to about her natural parents. If only I'd told her the truth earlier, perhaps things would have been different. I hoped she wasn't making the wrong decision about this because of her own experience.

When she came off the telephone, she looked relieved, and passed the telephone back to me so that Maude could tell me what she was going to do.

'Heather has instructed me to write to Amelia Moorcroft on her behalf. I am firstly to refute the allegations she's made about Heather's reputation and state unequivocally that Lawrence is her child's father, and I am to confirm that she has no interest in making a claim on Lawrence's estate. If all Mrs Moorcroft is worried about is money, then I think we shall hear no more from her. The only other issue is getting Lawrence's name put on the child's birth certificate. I think we would need to go to court but I can't see how we can prove Lawrence is the child's father unless we go the way of Mrs Moorcroft and hire private detectives to get statements from people on the base who knew they were having an affair. I'll send a copy of the letter in the post for Heather once I've prepared it.'

'Thanks again Maude. We all very much appreciate your help. Goodbye for now.'

I prayed Maude was right and we wouldn't hear from Amelia Moorcroft again. And we didn't. The person we heard from was Lawrence's mother.

CHAPTER SIXTY-FIVE

After Maude wrote to Amelia, another letter arrived in the post. This time from Lawrence's mother. Heather and Theresa were sitting in the kitchen with their feet up, both looking uncomfortably large because of their babies. They were due in July, so it wasn't long to go for them both. I was sorting through the mail when I noticed a similar envelope to the first one with the same crest on it. Surely Amelia wasn't writing to Heather again. I thought all correspondence was to be between the solicitors now. Taking the letter through, I couldn't help smiling at the two of them. They were like the plump seals that we sometimes spotted sitting on the rocks up at Berneray and as ungraceful in their movements.

'Can I get you a cup of tea, Chrissie?' said Theresa, pushing herself off the chair and waddling over to the range.

'No, thanks dear. I've just brought this letter through for Heather. It looks like it might be from Lawrence's wife again.'

Heather looked up at me and sighed.

'Will you read it to me, Mammy? It will probably just be more of the same.'

I sliced open the letter and scanned it.

'It's not from Amelia, it's from Lawrence's mother, and I think you will want to read what she's saying.'

Heather looked at me and put her hand out for the letter. She too scanned it and then read it out to us.

Dear Miss Macdonald

I understand that you have already received a letter from my daughter-in-law. Please accept my apologies. While I realise it has come as a shock to her to find out about your relationship with Lawrence and that you are carrying his child, she had no right to contact you without telling me. While I cannot condone Lawrence's behaviour, I do not want his child to suffer because his wife is jealous. To have something of Lawrence in our lives through his child will be a wonderful blessing.

I have therefore instructed the family solicitor to liaise with your solicitor to discuss what an agreeable way forward would be for our family and for yourself. I don't wish my son's name and his indiscretions to be dragged through the courts or the papers, which is what would happen if you tried to get a court order proving Lawrence's paternity of your child. And if you loved him, then I'm sure you will feel as I do.

Lawrence was the sole heir to the Moorcroft estate, and as he and Amelia have no children, there is no-one to inherit the estate apart from a distant cousin who lives somewhere in India. I am, therefore, proposing that Amelia adopt Lawrence's child and that he can then inherit what a legitimate heir would have inherited. The child would, of course, know you were his mother, and you would have visiting rights, but his upbringing would be here with Amelia and me at Moorcroft Castle, and he would go to Eton like his father before him.

I know you have no interest in money, but as a mother, surely you would want the best life for your child. Had Lawrence lived and you and he had married, then this is the life your child would have lived. I humbly request that you take this plea into consideration, understanding its sincere intention.

Yours faithfully

Madeline Moorcroft (Mrs)

I expected Heather to be outraged at the contents of the letter, but she wasn't. She took it from me and scanned it again. It was Theresa who spoke up.

'What a bloody cheek. All she wants is an heir. I wonder if she'll be so interested if you have a girl. And that Amelia sounds a right cow. I wouldn't want her to adopt any baby of mine. Sorry Chrissie, excuse my language.'

When Heather didn't answer her, she spoke again.

'You're awfy quiet Heather. What are you thinking?'

'I don't know what to think, Theresa. What she says is true. Had Lawrence lived, he and I would have married, and we would have lived at Moorcroft Castle and so would any children we had.'

'So, you might consider it?' I asked.

She shrugged her shoulders.

'I suppose it would mean your baby wouldn't need to live with the stigma of being illegitimate. It's a huge burden being a bastard,' said Theresa.

Heather's face grew red.

'I think I know more than you do what it's like being a bastard, Theresa, so don't tell me what a burden it is.'

Theresa looked at me and then at Heather.

'Sorry, Heather. I just open my mouth and let my belly rumble. Just ignore me.'

'I'm going for a walk.'

'Is that wise? Your baby's due anytime.'

'I just need to get out into the fresh air and think *Mamaidh*. This is a huge decision I need to make.'

It certainly was, and she would need the wisdom of Solomon to make it.

CHAPTER SIXTY-SIX

Heather left the room, still feeling annoyed at what Theresa had said. She was far too opinionated sometimes. What did she know what it was like to be adopted and not know who you truly were? Well, her child would know. As things turned out, Heather didn't get out for her walk. Just as she reached her bedroom, she felt a warm sensation running down her leg. Surely I've not peed myself. Then she laughed. It was time. She was going to have her baby.

'*Mamaidh*, *Mamaidh*, get the nurse. The baby's coming,' she shouted down the hall, which was now covered in a pool of water.

At once, the door of the kitchen opened, and Chrissie was there. They knew what they had to do. They'd talked about it. Unless there were complications, the nurse delivered all the babies on the island.

'Have your waters broken?' she asked, running through to the telephone exchange.

Heather nodded. She could see Theresa in the background. Would she want to come and help or was it too near her own time to find out exactly what went on at a birth? Suddenly, Heather felt scared. Having a baby was painful. Everyone she knew who'd had a baby had taken delight in telling her just how painful. But Chrissie had told her it was a pain you forgot easily, so it couldn't be that bad, could it? She walked into the bedroom and grabbed the neatly folded sheets and towels they had prepared for the delivery from the sideboard and put them on the bed. She must still have a while to go, as she didn't feel any discomfort yet, so began getting the bed ready and was in the middle of doing it when Chrissie and Theresa joined her.

'The nurse will get here as soon as she can. She's got another delivery over at Paible. Fiona Morrison, you know, Catriona's cousin.'

'But she was due after me. Has she gone early?'

'It sounds like it,' said Theresa. 'She and I were due about the same time, and I'm not due for another couple of weeks. How are you feeling, Heather? Any pains yet.'

'I'll just mop this water up,' said Chrissie, 'while you two chat. I won't be long.'

'No pains yet, Theresa. Sorry for shouting at you.'

'Och, I deserved it. Anyway, don't think about any of that now. Just you concentrate on getting that kid out of there safe and well.'

'I'm scared.' Heather's lips trembled. 'I wish Lawrence was here with me.'

'You're kidding me, aren't you? I wouldn't want a man anywhere near me when I'm giving birth. And realistically, no man would want to be near you in that condition. Lawrence would probably have fainted or run a mile at the first sight of blood.'

Heather laughed. She liked Theresa. She could see why Roddy loved her.

'Anyway, don't you worry. Me and your mammy are going to be with you every step of the way. Now let's get you sorted, ready for the nurse when she arrives.'

Theresa was true to her word. She and Chrissie mopped Heather's brow, squeezed her hand when she screamed, told her to swear like a trooper when the pain got too bad and, generally, made Heather feel she was not alone. When her daughter finally emerged into the world, it was Chrissie who handed over Lawrie Chrissie Bunty, wrapped in a clean towel and screaming her head off. Heather thought she had never seen such a beautiful thing in her whole life and burst into tears. So did Theresa and so did Chrissie. Then they crowded round her, and they all giggled like excited schoolgirls. A new Uist girl had joined the family.

She put everything on hold while she got used to being a mother and found out more about her little girl. Lawrie looked like Lawrence. She had his auburn hair and those hazel eyes that had so attracted her the first time she met him. Anyone would know he was her father from looking at her. A couple of weeks after Lawrie was born, Maude telephoned Heather to let her know Mrs Moorcroft had contacted her again. Now that the baby had been born, she thought it would be best if she and the child came to

Moorcroft Castle as soon as she could travel while the adoption paperwork was being sorted out with the solicitors.

'She's talking as if you've already agreed to the adoption, Heather. It's a bit of an assumption, don't you think?'

'And a bit of a cheek. But I'm still undecided, Maude. I've not given it a thought for the last couple of weeks.'

'Well, you've been busy with your new little girl, Heather. Take your time. Don't let her bully you into making a quick decision.'

'I won't.'

'I'll write to her and make it clear you are still considering her proposal and that you have agreed to nothing yet.'

'Thanks Maude.'

She suddenly needed to get out of the house on her own.

'Mamaidh, I need to go out and get some fresh air and think about the adoption. Would you mind looking after Lawrie?'

'I can't *mo graidh.* A post office inspector is coming today, and I don't think he would be too pleased if his Postmistress was in charge of a baby while dealing with the mail. Why don't you ask Theresa? I mean, I'll only be in the post office if she needs help.'

So that's what she did.

As she rode her bike out of Lochmaddy, she didn't know what to think. What Mrs Moorcroft had said was right. If she and Lawrence had married, then Lawrie would have had the same life as Mrs Moorcroft was now offering. She just didn't know what to do for the best. Hadn't she talked about this very thing to Donald John? Perhaps she should talk to him. He was a good listener and would just let her talk and think things through. She wasn't sure if he would be at the airbase or at his granny Catherine's house. She went to Catherine's house first and was glad to see him just arriving with a creel of peat on his back. When he saw her approaching, he put the creel down.

'Hello, Heather. To what do I owe this pleasure? I hope you've not abandoned that wee girl of yours just to visit me.'

'As if I would, silly.'

'Are you here to see my granny, then? She's not in if you are. She's away to a meeting of the Rural.'

'No, it's you I want to see Donald John.'

'You're looking awfy serious. Come in and I'll make us a cup of tea.'

She watched as he put the kettle on the range and put the tea in the pot before speaking.

'I've had a letter from Lawrence's mother.'

'The mother. What does she want?'

'She wants me to let Amelia adopt Lawrie.'

'What? You've said no, I take it.'

'I've not said anything yet. I've only just got her letter. Do you remember that day you brought me back from the airbase?'

'Yes, I do. You said a lot of things that day. Are you regretting telling me now? Is that why you're here?'

'No, it's nothing to do with that. I know you won't betray any of my secrets.'

'Go on, then. Tell me.'

'Do you remember I told you that if Lawrence had lived, he would have divorced Amelia and married me?'

'Yes.'

'And that would have meant that my child would have been raised with the same values and beliefs as him.'

'Yes.'

'Well, that's basically what Mrs Moorcroft is offering. She's offering my daughter the same life she would have had if Lawrence had lived. And I don't know what to do.'

'And you thought I might help you think it through?'

'I guess so. You're a good listener. What do you think?'

He thought for a moment, then smiled at her.

'Do you love your daughter?'

'Yes, of course I do.'

'Do you want to be involved in her life?'

'Yes, of course I do.'

'How much involvement in her life will you have if this Amelia Moorcroft adopts her?'

'Well, Lawrence's mother says I'll have visiting rights and that she'll tell her about me.'

'Then she won't be having the same life she would have had if Lawrence had lived. Because in that life, you would have been her mother and would have lived with her all the time. In this life, you will be in the shadows, only seeing your daughter once or twice a year if you're lucky.'

Heather found her hackles rising, and fiery blood flooded her face.

'Do you think I'm daft enough to let that woman adopt my daughter without having guarantees about my rights concerning her and her life?'

'Don't fly off the handle, Heather. You asked me what I thought, and I've told you. I can't help it if you don't like my answer.'

'Oh well, excuse me. I won't ask you again. Anyway, I better go. Lawrie will be due a feed.'

She jumped on her bike without a backward glance and almost fell off as she peddled furiously back to the post office. By the time she reached it, she was in floods of tears. Was Donald John right? Would she just be some shadowy figure in her daughter's life if she let Amelia adopt her? And Theresa had been right when she said Amelia was a cow. Did she want that woman to have responsibility for her child?

As she opened the door, Heather could hear Lawrie crying and Theresa trying to comfort her. She wiped away her tears and went through.

'Thank the lord, you're back,' she said, laughing. 'This girl's ready for her next feed, I think.'

'I'll just take off my coat and then you can pass her over. Thanks for looking after her.'

'What's wrong Heather? I can see you've been crying.'

'I'll feed Lawrie and settle her down and then I'll tell you all about it.'

As she sat with Lawrie at her breast, she thought of all that Donald John had said. Did she want to be a shadowy figure in her daughter's life? She knew she didn't. But this wasn't about her, was it? It was about what was best for Lawrie. Maybe it was better for Lawrie to experience the life she would have had if Lawrence had lived. It would be a completely different one from the life she was offering her on the island. She would have wealth and power that she could never have if she lived with Heather. And yet, there was something so special about life here on Uist. It wasn't an easy life working a croft, but the satisfaction of working the land and making use of all the fruits of that land made it all worthwhile. And island people looked out for one another. They were a community. Although everyone would know Lawrie was illegitimate, she believed eventually it wouldn't matter. They would accept her as one of their own.

Theresa set a tray down with tea and scones.

'Right, my lady. Tell me what's going on.'

'As you know, Lawrence's mother wants me to let Amelia adopt Lawrie, and I was actually considering the notion. But then I spoke to Donald John, and he made me see I couldn't. I was angry at him for pointing out the obvious. But while I've been feeding this wee one, I've made my mind up and now know what I'm doing.'

'You're keeping her.'

'Yes. But I don't mind if Madeline has a part to play in Lawrie's life. She's her grandmother, after all. But she'll be the one in the shadows, not me.'

'Good for you Heather.'

As Theresa stood up, she let out a cry of dismay as a pool of water formed on the floor.

'Oh, oh. Here we go.'

'I'll run and get Mammy. The post office inspector will just have to get on with it without her.'

CHAPTER SIXTY-SEVEN

Heather felt a rush of happiness when Theresa's little boy was born. Knowing that Lawrie had a cousin so close in age made her glad. She'd never had cousins and had always felt slightly envious of Catriona, who seemed to have loads. Theresa called him Roddy Patrick Macdonald, a tribute to both Roddy and her father. Chrissie was proud as punch and kept smiling whenever she looked at her two grandchildren. It was hard for her and Theresa, knowing their children's fathers would never see them.

'I think he looks like Roddy,' she said after he was born. Her eyes shone with love as she looked at her son, then they clouded with tears. 'I wish Roddy was here to see him.'

They had all paused for a moment, remembering this wee boy's daddy, wondering if he was dead or captured by the enemy somewhere.

'I've sent a telegram to your mother and father, telling them they now have a grandson. I've also invited them to come up if they can manage.'

'That's kind of you, Chrissie. I doubt they will, but who knows? I want them to see their new grandson, but I'm not up for travelling just now. Besides, I've got used to being here with you and Heather. We're like a wee women's cooperative.'

'Aunt Katie would have loved to hear you say that, Theresa,' said Chrissie and they all paused again, thinking of another one of their family who had become a victim of this war.

After all the excitement of Theresa's delivery, Heather got on to Maude and told her what she had decided.

'I've decided not to agree to the adoption, Maude. I'm going to keep Lawrie with me. But if they want to get to know Lawrie and play a part in her life, then I'm happy to let them do that.'

'What you've decided sounds reasonable to me,' said Maude, 'and if they're wise, they should accept your offer.'

'Will you also tell them I shall bring Lawrie down to Moorcroft Castle as soon as I feel she can travel if they agree to what I'm suggesting?'

Maude did as Heather asked her, but it turned out they decided not to be wise and threatened to have Lawrie made a ward of court on the grounds that Heather was an unfit mother. This scared her a bit. Part of her job had been to entertain the troops, not just by singing, and she'd been good at it. She remembered the young men she'd met on tour who had become infatuated with her and pursued her. Despite feeling sorry for them, she'd resisted the temptation to go further and now felt relieved that she hadn't given in. The memory of the first time she met Lawrence also flooded into her mind, and her cheeks grew pink with embarrassment. Before going on stage that night, she had over-indulged on the gin fizz and had behaved provocatively on stage. What if someone had told Amelia about that?

As was becoming a habit, she spoke to Donald John about the latest development. She had apologised to him for her outburst, so they were friends again. He was reassuring and told her she shouldn't worry about it.

'You were only doing your job, Heather. Singing and flirting with the troops doesn't make you an unfit mother and remember, you still have the evidence that Lawrence's wife tried to bribe people to tell lies about you.'

'How could I have forgotten that? I'll get on to Maude straight away.'

A few days after their conversation, Donald John turned up, asking if she was up for a walk.

'That would be lovely. I'll just get Lawrie ready.'

They hadn't been walking for long when Donald John told her he wanted to ask her something.

'What about? Not this blasted threat Lawrence's family has made. I'm sick of thinking and talking about it.'

He stopped and gazed at her and then at little Lawrie in the pram. Her stomach fluttered. What could he want to ask her?

'You look anxious, Donald John. What is it you want to ask me?'

'Will you marry me, Heather?'

Heather stared at him, dumbfounded. She would never in a million years have guessed this was what he wanted to ask her.

'Marry you? Why would I want to do that? We're friends. I've never thought of you in that way.'

He blushed, and she felt rotten for him. She was being too blunt, as usual.

'Don't get all big-headed thinking I'm in love with you. I know you don't think of me like that.'

'Well, why are you asking me to marry you, you eejit?'

'I've been thinking about all this carry on with Lawrence's family. If you and I got married, and we put me as the father on Lawrie's birth certificate, then it would mean Lawrie wouldn't be illegitimate and Lawrence's family would have no grounds for claiming her.'

She looked at him. It made sense and it could make all this trouble go away. But...

'But why would you do that, Donald John? Men like you are in short supply on this island, so you could have your pick of girls to marry. Why marry someone you don't even love?'

His eyes took on a soft look.

'Maybe in time I could grow to love you and you me. All I know is that I want to look after you. I want to make things okay for you.'

She didn't know what to say. She'd only ever thought of him as her friend.

'Can I think about it, Donald John? I'm so grateful for your offer. It's the kindest thing I think anyone has ever done for me.'

'You take your time, Heather, and do whatever you think is right for you and Lawrie. I'll still be your friend, no matter what you decide.'

When she told Chrissie and Theresa about Donald John's proposal, they were as flabbergasted as she had been.

'Och, it's like something out of a fairytale, Heather. What a lovely man.'

'I know. But I'm not some pauper in a fairytale waiting for her prince. I already found my prince and I have his daughter.'

'But perhaps you could just put Donald John's name on Laurie's birth certificate. That would achieve the same thing, wouldn't it? You wouldn't need to marry him.'

'You're a genius, Chrissie,' said Theresa. 'I wonder why Donald John didn't think of that?'

She winked.

'Perhaps that man's in love with you, after all.'

'But the whole point of me starting all this was to get Lawrence's name put on Lawrie's birth certificate because I wanted her to know who her father was.'

'But will you be able to do that? Maude seems to think it'll be hard to prove Lawrence is her father. If you put Donald John on as Lawrie's father, it makes the Moorcroft family go away and you can tell Lawrie the truth later when she can understand.'

Theresa and Chrissie looked at Heather, wondering what decision she would make. But she had no idea what she was going to do.

CHAPTER SIXTY-EIGHT

Heather didn't marry Donald John. She decided she would be a hypocrite if she did. But they are such good friends, I wonder if one day they might become man and wife. She got her wish and put Lawrence's name on Lawrie's birth certificate, ironically because of what the Moorcroft family had tried to do. In the end, they decided not to pursue her through the courts for Lawrie. When Mrs Moorcroft senior found out that her daughter-in-law had used private detectives and bribery to discredit Heather, she gave up. But she drew up a trust deed for Lawrie to ensure her future welfare and this was enough to get a court order certifying Lawrence as Lawrie's father. Heather took Lawrie down to Moorcroft Castle to meet her grandmother as she had promised she would if they agreed to her proposal. She told me it was a difficult meeting.

'It was awful at first, Mammy, especially with Amelia. She could hardly bear to look at me, and who could blame her? But by the end of the week, this wee girl had worked her magic, and they were eating out of her hand.'

'I'm pleased for you, Heather. It will be good for Lawrie to get to know her father's side of the family and that will be much easier if they're not bearing any grudges.'

'All I ever wanted was for Lawrie to know the truth about her birth and who her father was. I'll always be grateful that you took me in and cared for me. You've been a wonderful mother. But finding out you had adopted me was such a shock. I never wanted that for my wee girl.'

When I saw how most people in our community rallied round Heather, I wondered why I had worried so much about hiding the truth about what I'd done. There are still some who think her behaviour is a disgrace, but there's nothing we can do about it.

Fin contacted me and told me the post office was sending him to London in October.

'How do you feel about coming with me? Is it time to tell our families we're married, do you think?'

I hesitated. The war in Europe was progressing well. The allies had landed in Normandy in June, and the Free French Army had supported American troops to liberate Paris in August. It was too soon to celebrate as the war in the Pacific was still raging and soldiers were still being killed. But it felt like the worst was over and there was a feeling of optimism that our loved ones would return home soon. I prayed fervently every night that Roddy would be one of them, although I feared the worst. If the Germans had taken him a prisoner of war, Theresa or I would have heard from the RAF by now and would surely have received a letter from him. Archie Campbell was a prisoner of war and Morag received the occasional letter from him. But we had heard nothing. But hope is the only thing that keeps us going in times such as these and hope still fluttered in my heart. Not knowing for certain was torture, but I wondered if having no hope was worse. But what if Roddy came home, and I wasn't here? What if I was in London with Fin? What ifs? Were they a reason to put off going to London with Fin? He had been so patient for so long, I couldn't put him off again.

'Chrissie, are you still there?'

'I'm still here, Fin and yes, I think it's time to tell our families and yes, I would love to come with you.'

'I can't wait to be with you all the time, Chrissie. I love you so much.'

'I love you too, Fin. Thank you for being so patient. You are a wonderful man, you know.'

He laughed down the telephone.

'Thank you, kind lady.'

'Heather is having Lawrie baptised in September, so I'll give the post office a month's notice and we can go to London together.'

'Perfect. There's only one thing we must decide now.'

'What's that?'

'How will we tell our families?'

That took the wind out of my sails. I remembered the reaction of Rosie and Daisy back when we told them we were engaged. Would they still feel the same? I thought my family would be okay. Heather and Lawrie could move into the croft with Johnny and my mother, and Theresa was talking about going back to live with her parents until she could get a place of her own. But what if Heather felt I was deserting her by leaving so soon after she'd had Lawrie?

'You've gone quiet, Chrissie. What are you thinking?'

'I'm thinking I'm nervous. What if Rosie and Daisy are still unhappy about us getting married and what if Heather feels I'm letting her down?'

'They're all adults. We've done all we can for them, Chrissie. It's our time now.'

I knew he was right, but I still felt uncomfortable. It didn't feel right putting myself before my family, but why wasn't it right? It was the order of things that you do your best for your children and then you set them free to find their own way. I had to do this, or I would lose Fin again.

'Could you come up for the baptism and we can tell them together?'

'Yes, of course. I'll also invite Daisy and Rosie and they can all find out at the same time.'

There was only one thing that still didn't feel right. It was the way Fin and I had married. What we had done was legal, but I wanted God's blessing for our marriage.

'How would you feel if I asked the Reverend Macaulay to bless our marriage after he's baptised Lawrie?'

'Whatever you want, sweetheart. So long as he doesn't try to convert me, I'll be happy.'

Fortunately, when I spoke to the Reverend Macaulay, he was understanding of the situation I'd found myself in and said he would be happy to give our marriage a blessing.

It was the day before Lawrie's baptism when we made our announcement to the family. We had invited everyone for lunch to the Lochmaddy Hotel. Our family had never done anything like that before, and my mother was all hot and bothered at going out to lunch. There were fifteen of us, including the babies. There were Fin and me, Rosie and Daisy, who'd arrived the day before, Theresa who was delaying going back to Glasgow until after the baptism, baby Roddy, Theresa's mother and father who had unexpectedly turned up to meet their new grandson, and my mother, Johnny, Morag, who'd come up to take her children home, Marion, Michael, Heather, and Lawrie. Only Roddy and Donald were missing and how I wished they could be here, too. There was an air of expectation as we sat down to lunch. We had agreed that Fin would do the talking, with me chipping in if needed. The lunch was a lovely lamb roast, and everyone was relaxed. Fin stood up.

'Thank you, everyone, for coming to lunch with Chrissie and me today. We have something to tell you and as most of the people we love are here to celebrate the baptism of Lawrie, we thought this was an ideal time to tell you our news.'

Everyone looked at him expectantly. I looked round their faces, trying to work out whether they had guessed our news, but I don't think anyone had.

'Chrissie and I are married, and we're moving to London together next month.'

There was a stunned silence, and then everyone talked at once. Much laughter and tears followed, but what struck me was the goodwill of everyone. Even Rosie and Daisy hugged me enthusiastically. When it was time to go, those of us not staying at the hotel moved outside to make our way home. Theresa's mother and father were staying at the croft, and Fin arranged for my mother, Johnny and Mr and Mrs Dunlop, to go home in the hotel taxi. We were waiting for the driver to bring it round when we saw two motorbikes approaching, their horns blaring. We all turned to look, wondering who it could be making such a racket. But as I watched the motorbikes heading towards us, their wheels spitting up the gravel on the road; I knew who it was. It was my Roddy and if I wasn't mistaken, my Donald was with him. I would know them anywhere. Theresa knew it was Roddy, too. She thrust baby Roddy into my arms and dashed towards the motorbikes. Roddy almost skidded as he braked, jumped off the motorbike and pulled her into his arms. I had a lump in my throat as I watched them. God knows what he had been through these last couple of years, but he was safe; he was home, and his wife and child were waiting for him. God had given me the greatest gift a mother could wish for. Soon everyone was crowding round him, hugging him, and slapping him on the back, even Patrick Dunlop. And as usual on the island, the word had got out that Roddy Macdonald was alive and was home and before we knew it, a crowd of well-wishers arrived outside of the Lochmaddy Hotel all wanting to talk to this man who they thought was dead but had come home. His arrival gave them hope. Maybe their loved ones would come home safely, too.

I just stood, waiting to get the chance to speak to him. I had so many questions. Where had he been? Why hadn't he contacted us? How did he get here? Heather came over, took baby Roddy from me, placed him in his pram, put her arm around me and gave me an enthusiastic squeeze. Then Donald parked up and was hugging me. I clung to him, treasuring the feeling of my son in my arms.

'Oh Donald, it's so lovely to see you and you've brought Roddy home. Thank you, thank you. Tell me how you found him.'

'I found him in France. When I went over to report on the D-day landings, I found him in a village with some French freedom fighters I was interviewing. It was pure luck that he was there with them.'

Luck or God's grace.

'But how did you get him home?'

'He came back as part of the press group I was with. No-one looks at us too closely, so it was easy for me to sneak him through. When we got to London, we reported to the RAF, and after checking Roddy was well, they gave us travel permits to Lochboisdale. The airbase gave us the motorbikes to get over here. Donald John told us you were all meeting up in the Lochmaddy Hotel today.'

'Thank God you're both safe and well. Oh, come here my boy.'

I was clinging to Donald when Heather spoke, trying to lighten the mood, I think.

'I didn't know you could ride a motorbike, Donald.'

He turned to her then, and I let him go.

'I've had to learn Heather to get about when I've been on war news missions. I can't wait to get back to Canada and watch Mary's reaction when she sees me ride up on a motorbike. She loved the couple of times she rode on the back of Roddy's bike.'

'Is someone talking about me?' said a voice I knew and loved so well. And there he was. As he put his arms around me and held me to him, it was too much. I just broke down and sobbed with utter joy.

CHAPTER SIXTY-NINE
North Uist, October 1944

As I look at my family, I know I'm doing the right thing. Fin and I are on our way to London to start a new life, and I wonder where it will take us. We had married in secret at the beginning of last year and somehow, every time we decided we would tell our families and move in together, a new obstacle arose. I look at my husband and my heart fills with love for him. I am so grateful for his patience and loyalty despite my failure to be honest about Heather when I should have been. We had partly married in secret because of religious differences, so it had been wonderful to stand in the church after Lawrie's baptism and receive a blessing from the Reverend Macaulay. As we had stood in church in front of our family, and our friends, the sacredness of the occasion helped me to feel I was now married not only in the eyes of the law but in the eyes of God.

The ferry comes into view and again, I think of Roderick. I'd stood on this same spot when he and I left North Uist for our new life as husband and wife in Canada. It all seems so long ago now and so much has happened since, much of it a result of Roderick's life in Canada before he met me. I think back to the first time I met him. Colin Donaldson was drunk and manhandling me at the market, and it was Roderick who saved me from him. I can still picture him riding up in his buggy, wearing a long coat and a wide-brimmed hat, quite different clothing from the islanders wore. He had jumped down from the buggy and told Colin to leave me alone. When Colin turned his attention to Roderick and tried to punch him, he easily got him in an armlock and stopped him. Like all the best heroines in the books I've read, I almost swooned, and he caught me and held me in his arms. I smile at the memory.

'What are you smiling at, Mammy?' asks Heather.

'I'm just remembering the first time I met Roderick and the last time I left North Uist to start a new life. And do you know something, Heather? The way things have turned out, I don't regret a single thing because I would never have had you in my life.'

She hugs me, and we share a moment. Now that Heather and Lawrie can no longer live at the post office house, they're moving back to the croft to live with my mother and Johnny. Heather always loved her life on the croft, so I'm glad for her and for myself. Knowing she has my mother and Johnny to rely on makes me feel less worried about leaving her.

'Do you think you'll ever come back?'

'I hope so. This is my home, and my heart will always be here. But I love Fin and I want to be with him. Thank goodness he still wants to be with me. It's been a bit of a journey.'

'It certainly has,' says Theresa. 'You deserve some happiness. I'll never be able to thank you for taking care of me and this wee one.'

'It was all my pleasure, Theresa. I'm so grateful you spent the time here with me and I got to be at my grandson's birth.'

Theresa is moving back to Glasgow with her parents until she and Roddy can find a suitable house. Now that Roddy is home safe and well, I don't need to worry about her or my grandson. He is back on active duty, but given his experience of being shot down over France and spending the last year with the French Resistance, the RAF agreed he could stand down from fighter pilot duties. It's a relief to know he won't need to fly again.

Donald has already left to cover some other news story, and I reflect on how much he has changed from that quiet, worried boy he used to be to this confident, intrepid news reporter. Fin and I have promised to visit him and Mary in Canada after the war is over. It will be lovely to meet my other grandson, Harry.

I turn to my mother and Johnny.

'Thanks so much for everything, Chrissie,' says Johnny. 'Especially for looking after my daughter. You've done a grand job. I couldn't be prouder of my girl.'

I hug him and turn to my mother. The woman who brought me up and has stood by me through thick and thin.

'*Mamaidh*, thanks for everything. I shall miss you so much.'

'Och away with you,' she says, embarrassed. But she still hugs me fiercely, and we cling to each other for a long time. I'm glad she has Johnny to look after her now that my father has passed.

When all my goodbyes are over, I notice Murdo, Dorothy, Shona and Morag are there to say their goodbyes too and I hug them all warmly. They have been part of my story, and I am so grateful to them for their friendship and support. At last, it's time to go and Fin takes my hand and squeezes it, knowing how hard it is for me to leave. But as I wave to my family from the ferry, I marvel at how my life has changed. I'm not worrying about them any longer. There are no more lies, no more secrets to carry, and the prospect of a new life with my new husband beckons. I plan to seize it with both hands.

The End

If you would like to hear about new releases and other news, sign up for my Reader Newsletter at
www.marionmacdonaldwriter.com

ACKNOWLEDGEMENTS

This is the last book in The Uist Girl Series and I've shed a few tears while writing it. Partly because I've become attached to my characters and felt emotional when writing about the things they were going through, and partly because of researching and writing about the Second World War. I read a lot of first-hand accounts on the BBC website - WW2peopleswar/stories. It's an amazing site and well worth having a look at if you're interested in the Second World War. I was also lucky enough to chat to some people who remember the war or had memories they had heard from people who lived during the war. For example, what happened to Katie is based on a story I heard from Jean, a woman in my ukulele group. I set the book mostly in North Uist and Benbecula, but I wanted to show the effect of the war in other parts of the country, so I moved Fin to Clydebank.

The scenes set there come mostly from the BBC site mentioned above. I don't live far from Clydebank, so on Remembrance Day I went to see where the post office and the Cooperative Hall used to be and took a walk along the route Chrissie would have followed to reach Second Avenue when she was searching for Fin. It was quite an emotional journey.

I found out about the Millionaire Squadron online too and have used creative license by setting Lawrence on Benbecula. So far as I know, 601 Squadron was never based there.

I feel it's the right time to end the series and hope you won't be too disappointed. I've really enjoyed writing it and have learned so much from the research I carried out. This last book, I hope, ties together all the strands from the previous books and provides a satisfying ending.

As usual, I carried out most of my research on-line, but I found the following books helpful to get an understanding of what life was like during the war for the islanders and about what it was like to work for ENSA. Heather's experience of going to the middle east is based on the book by Mary Lee.

The Hebrides at War by Mike Hughes, published in 1998 by Birlinn Limited, West Newington House, 10 Newington Road, Edinburgh. EH9 1 QS.

Forever Francie, My Life with Jack Milroy, by Mary Lee, published in 2005 by Black & White Publishing Ltd, 99 Giles Street, Edinburgh.

The Finlay J Macdonald Omnibus by Finlay J Macdonald, first published in three volumes between 1982 and 1985 by Futura Publications a division of Macdonald & Co (Publishers) Ltd, Orbit House, 1 New Fetter Lane, London EC4A 1 AR

The Silent Weaver by Roger Hutchinson, published in 2011 By Birlinn Limited, West Newington House, 10 Newington Road, Edinburgh. EH9 1 QS.

I've been lucky to receive help and information from several sources and I would like to thank those people who took the time to help me. You were all so generous.

I visited North Uist, Benbecula and South Uist in May 2023. So first I would like to thank Joan, Eilidh, and Caitriona, the staff of Lionacleit Library on Benbecula. When I turned up out of the blue asking for their help with my research, they went the extra mile. Caitriona even transcribed a Gaelic text for me by a man who lived on Benbecula during the war. How I wished I could understand Gaelic, as I was sure the personal reflections of local people about the effect of the RAF Station on Benbecula would have been invaluable. Catriona Muir from the Benbecula Historical Society also took the time to meet me and talk to me about the RAF

Station. It was through Catriona that I found out there was a big band at the airbase.

Clydebank Local History Society was also very helpful when I contacted them trying to find out where the post office in Clydebank used to be situated. That was how I found out it used to be on Chalmers Street and they even sent me a photograph to let me see what it looked like then and what it was now. It wasn't hit during the bombing.

I would also like to thank two friends from my ukulele group, Susan and Lindsay, who got me a ticket to the Mòd in Paisley in October 2023. As I had Heather performing at the Mòd, I thought it would be good to see what being at a Mòd was like as I'd never been before. I loved it. I'd also like to thank Jean from my Ukulele group and Cathy from my church, who shared their stories about the war.

The following are special people in my life, without whom I couldn't do what I do. Thank you so much for your help and support.

My readers, Liz, Margaret, Elizabeth, and Kenny. Thank you for reading and making comments. I appreciate the time you give to this and for your constructive and helpful comments.

My sister, Catherine, for her enthusiastic encouragement and commentary on my manuscripts.

My husband, Charlie, for reading and commenting on my manuscript. I loved it when he told me how emotional he'd felt when reading this book. I couldn't do what I do without his support, which has been unfailing since I began writing. He's a superstar.

Finally, thank you for buying my book. It would really help other readers to decide whether to buy it if you left a review on Amazon or Goodreads. Thank you.

ABOUT THE AUTHOR

Marion Macdonald is a Scottish novelist who lives in Glasgow with her husband, Charlie. She developed an interest in creative writing when she retired from her job as Director of a Housing Association and enrolled on a course with the Open University in 2015.

She wrote and self-published her first novel, One Year, in 2017. It was runner-up in the Scottish Association of Writers' Competition for a self-published novel in 2020. Since then, she has written and self-published a further five novels. Her next novel, Act of Love, is due out in October 2024,.

Marion was born and educated in Scotland and has an Honours Degree in English Literature and History from the University of Glasgow

Scan the QR Code if you wish to join her reader newsletter group.

OTHER BOOKS BY THIS AUTHOR

THE EWAN AND SUZIE SERIES

THE UIST GIRL SERIES

The QR Code will take you to my Amazon Author Page where you can buy my books.

Printed in Great Britain
by Amazon